$\mathcal{V}$OICES OF THE $\mathcal{S}$OUTH

Do, Lord, Remember Me

Do, Lord, Remember Me

GEORGE GARRETT

George Garrett (signature)

The full soul loatheth an honey-
comb; but to the hungry soul
every bitter thing is sweet.

PROVERBS XXVII, 7

LOUISIANA STATE UNIVERSITY PRESS

BATON ROUGE AND LONDON

This book is gratefully dedicated to a few good friends whose friendship, interest, and concern never flagged during the long and difficult times which have dogged this book from inception to publication, whose love and goodwill made the work of doing it seem light after all: Babette Deutsch, James and Marian Jeter, R. H. W. Dillard, Martin and Ruthe Battestin, James B. Meriwether, William Peden, and Calhoun and Elizabeth Winton

Now preye I to hem alle that herkne this litel tretys or rede, that if ther be any thyng in it that liketh hem, that therof they thanken oure Lord Jhesu Crist, of whom procedeth al wit and al goodnesse. And if ther be any thyng that displese hem, I preye hem also that they arrette it to the defaute of myn unkonnynge, and nat to my wyl, that wolde full fayn have seyd bettre if I hadde had konnynge.

Chaucer—*The Canterbury Tales*

I

And they were all amazed and were in doubt, saying one to another, What meaneth this? Others, mocking said, These men are full of new wine. ACTS XII, 31

Here they come, walking right in the store just after we open up, two of them. There's the tall skinny one all dressed up for a day in the big city with two-tone pointed shoes, with a bow tie of the clip on kind and the point of his adam's apple peeping over the top of the bow, up and down like a man trying to hide. Also sporting a dandy straw hat on top of his head. Tall, skinny fellow with a snaggle-tooth grin. Put me in mind the way he moves, insinuates hiself you might say, of some kind of a bug. Maybe a worm you would stick on the end of a fishing hook or step on. The other one's a tub of butter, short and fat. Dark complected with a long nose and big, wet-looking eyes like a dog's or a woman's, and almost bald headed. Has little bitty legs and feet as small as a girl's. That big belly all puffed out in front like he maybe took a tube in the morning and blew it up as far as it would go, just for the hell of it.

That's what I'm thinking, watching them come in the store, how if a fella could get hold of a bicycle pump maybe he could pump him all up the same way, equal all over. And then I guess he would rise up real slow and easy and float off in the sky and then the breeze would catch him and carry him along right up, up and over the top of the mountains with all the kids and stray dogs in the County running after him, barking and ahollering, and everybody else pointing and watching him go. Or take it another way. Say you happen to have a pin or a needle or a lit cigarette. Just reach out quick and poke him in the middle of that gut. *Phitt-t-t-t*! He'll sail backwards all around the store, with the look of pure surprise on his face getting smaller and smaller, until finally he'd fall out and gasp his last on the floor.

And all that would be left would be a little bit of elastic, nothing else.

Don't pay any attention to me. I have a habit of speculation to kill the time. To kill the afternoon time of my life, because I passed the high noon too long ago to remember.

Anyway here we are in the morning and we have just opened up. The salesgirls is all busy arranging their counters, chittering and chattering about who is banging whom or giving birth or wasting away and drying up. All of them pretty good girls who no doubt will have their share of banging and giving birth and wasting away. I like to look at them and listen to them talk trash. But don't get me wrong. Women! They got more sense and understanding than we give them credit for. A fair subject for speculation. Some people claim to understand them, too. I can't.

Mr Percy is standing near the door, all dressed up for the day with a flower in his buttonhole, just a peek of clean handkerchief in his pocket and a nice silk tie I'll bet the price of he just picked off the rack and ain't studying about paying for. Pacing up and down, squeezing his hands behind his back. Hoping for the first customer to walk in and break up the memory of breakfast with his Mother. One of the times she no doubt daily reminds him that here he is going on forty and he ain't brought home a wife yet, and all she wants – which isn't too much to ask is it? – is a fat baby grandchild to bounce on her knee.

That's when the bell on the door tinkles. Percy's hands let loose of each other and he advances toward them with a smile and a little tip of the head that might be called a greeting.

"Gentlemen? Can I be of assistance to you all?"

The worm whips off his straw hat and opens his mouth to say something, but the fat one has already beat him to it.

"We're looking for the owner."

So they cut around Percy on either side and leave him standing there like a bent lampost. The fat one already seen me, leaning against the wall back here in my shirtsleeves. He's the brains of the two, don't you think? The other one is too busy fooling with his hat, putting it back on his head and squaring it just so, so he can whip it off quick again, to be thinking. I bet some girl called him goodlooking one time. Drunk in the pitch dark and he was probably paying for it too. Well, it don't take more than a suggestion to inflate a man's natural vanity. Take Mr Percy. Sure he's the best-dressed man in the store and he walks around in front like he owns it. And he'll act like he owns it lock, stock, and barrel, if somebody gives him half of a chance. How come, then? How come nobody, not once, even a stranger to town passing through, ever has thought or ever will that Mr Fancy Pants Percy owns my store? Where has Justice fled to? Does it dwell now only in caves and hollow places, crawling around naked like a madman and howling? No, sir, Percy. Whoever told you there was any Justice in this world? I'll tell you something, boy. No matter what kind of clothes you got on your back – hell you could get yourself a new face or a Halloween mask and it wouldn't make no difference – people are going to take one look at you and see a clown. Two tone suit and a cap with jingle bells on it. Which may be sad, boy, but is a damn sight better than naked. But just remember this: there is no kingdom, no territory, even one shrunk down to the size of this here secondrate department store, which has ever been ruled by a man in a cap and bells. You may end up owning this store. I may even leave it to you in my will to prove my point. Because even then, when I'm dead and gone and you got the deed and the title in the bank deposit box and you can sit at the desk in the back room behind a frosted glass door with your name etched on it, even when the bills come in to you and you sign the checks one at a time, nobody is ever going to believe you own my store.

"Howdo," I say. "You two boys looking for a job?"

The skinny one has his mouth open to make a sound but he swallows it. His adam's apple peeps out over the tie and then ducks out of sight. It's a wonder that the clip don't come loose from the collar sometime and let that tie fly away like a polka-dot butterfly.

The other one hands me a card. Up close he's got a dark complexion that obviously comes with the model. Must be some kind of a foreigner. Maybe he's an Armenian but how would I know? I never seen one.

"My name is Moses," he says.

I laugh. What else can I do? Laugh or cry, that's what it all boils down to. Except for those mixed up states of high feeling when you have to do a little of both at the same time. I've had a taste of high feeling and it can be good, but I'm old enough now to get along without it.

"We're here on behalf of Big Red Smalley."

"Never heard of him."

"Why don't you read the card?" the worm says.

I can't do it justice without my spectacles which just happen to be sitting on my desk unless I forgot again and left them home, but, doing the best I can to be sociable, I pull the card up to the end of my nose and read some blurred words to the effect that there's going to be AN OLD TIMEY TENT REVIVAL MEETING – TONIGHT AND ONE NIGHT ONLY at which there will singing, praying, preaching of the Gospel, and healing of the sick by WORLD FAMOUS BIG RED SMALLEY who seems to have travelled the length and breadth of the LAND in his unceasing CRUSADE to bring the GOODNEWS to EVERYBODY etc.

14

"We're giving out a few tickets and we'd be honoured if you and your wife. . . ."

"She's dead. Been dead as a doornail for years. You can have her in the state she's in."

That reaches the Worm. He lets go with a donkey laugh. The fat one just blinks like a bullfrog and goes right on.

"We'd be happy if you'd accept a complimentary ticket."

"What's in it for me."

"Ten percent of the gross, tickets and offering. Cash money."

"What do I do?" I say. "I used to could play on the harmonica."

"You are a card, Mr Loomis," the Worm says. "Ain't he about a bird and a half?"

"We've found," the fat one says, "that when we come into a town it usually works out best if we have a friend among the leading citizens of the community. It is merely a matter of being able to mention your name in case that should be necessary."

"Where you parked at?"

"The Old Fairgrounds."

"Okey dokey," I say. "I'll fix it where don't nobody bother you unless you commit a felony or something. I'll even send you somebody to help you put up your tent. Do you need folding chairs?"

"Yes, sir, we usually borrow them."

"Done," I say. " If anything comes up, just call on me. On one condition."

"What's that?"

"Boys, I was born and baptized a Christian, but I ain't been inside of a Church in many years. I only want to go in Church one more time and that will be in a pine box, heels down and face up, with a smile on my face and plenty of hothouse flowers and the biggest godamn choir this town has ever seen."

"You don't have to be there," the Worm says.

"That's nice," I say. "Tell you what though. I'd like to send my assistant manager and some of the girls. They might get a lot out of it."

"A pleasure," the fat one says. And he hands me a stack of tickets.

"Hey! Don't be giving those things away like that," I say. "This is a small town and I only got ten per cent."

The Worm grins and winks. Somebody ought to keep that boy on a leash.

We shake hands all around and they turn and start to leave the store. I'm still wondering what the fat one really is. A Greek? A Cuban? A A-rab? The bell tinkles again and out they go. The Worm has that hat on again and he's strutting now. The fat one that calls himself Moses, he is hunched over, hands in his pockets, looking down. I guess he must be about the saddest, tiredest looking man I've ever seen outside of the privacy of my own mirror. I don't know what it would be that would put a smile on his face, except maybe the end of the world.

Then I have to smile at myself. If I send Mr Percy out there with a carload of the girls, if everybody gets to singing and shouting and feeling the Spirit, old Percy may wind up in the bushes with somebody. Going to change that boy's luck yet.

MOSES

Even today, with a little luck and some advance work, Red can draw a good crowd. Not in the cities, of course. Not often or much in the big, growing, ambitious towns, intoxicated with the idea of becoming a city. But take an ordinary middlesize place like this one – and there are still God's plenty of them scattered across the map of the Land like carelessly dropped pennies – the kind of place that maybe used to be something and has long since lost all dreams of being somewhere, and where now there are only quiet streets and the old people, the aging, the fearful and the losers, and always the children just waiting to grow up and go away. And do not forget all the others too, too poor in fact or in spirit to move on. There will be always the churches and the dusty court-houses and the school-houses too, places with broken window panes and faded brick assigned to house Wisdom, and their swings and jungle gyms and seesaws set lonely on the wide, dusty playground.

Playgrounds where maybe sometimes they gather ghosts of all the children gone   just at twilight oh lovely sigh and wink of time between sunset and nightfall like the moment of falling asleep and just before a dream begins

they gather in rings and groups there and call out their names to the first evening star   names we have forgotten   playing games we have forgotten   we see but cannot hear them   shrill bells of everlasting laughter and birdsong voices here and there and near but unheard like dog whistles too high for human ears   we see and do not hear and pass on sad and wistful for all our lost companions going into the flat light of front porches and into the smell of dinner cooking and maybe if we are lucky the odour of one good woman in the house   the furniture sofa and coffee table and old armchairs and sometimes a piano nobody plays anymore and nobody ever played well though once upon a time who cared and what cared we when we joined together our voices in the old songs baying at the far bright coin the moon   stand still now a perfect stranger among these things these known worn things   the furniture has not moved since morning nor the pictures on the wall yet suddenly now a stranger having had a vision of something anyway

something of lost children and their sweet imagined voices and old forgotten games   a vista of the fringes of far Paradise

Oh towns places of old squat buildings and offices and store fronts
walls for the weary and the loafers to lean against
  while always and ever the idle lazy careless prayerwheels of gossip
and speculation and history creak and groan and turn

Take any one of the whole burnt out fading galaxy of dying
towns. Let us arrive, easing into town at dawn. Park the truck
and the trailer in some field. Then wake Red briefly and Miami
helps him into the trailer and to bed. We will shave and clean
up by the rearview mirrors of the truck and Miami's car. Then
take her car and drive into town, maybe stopping for coffee if
there's some place open, but driving on, moving along the
quiet streets, looking the place over. If it looks right we will put
up a rash of the posters and then vanish, going somewhere for
breakfast this time, while the people awake and up now, hurrying to work or school see the posters with amazement almost
as if they had popped up simultaneously and mysteriously as
if by magic, and thus have something new to talk about all
morning.

Up goes the tent in the early afternoon. We tug and pull and
strain, cursing each other, until at last somehow it is smoothly
in place, squatting in the field like a huge khaki toadstool. By
evening, the sun still flaring, the first of them will be there,
waiting for the sun to burn up and leave the sky free at last for
the first, tentative, glittering entrance of the evening stars. By
midnight it will be all over, all the cacophony and gibberish, all
the singing and praying and soaring. They will go home then,
worn out, wrung dry of tears, empty as a broken bowl of
everything but air. And we will have chased the Devil across
the County line. By dawn we'll be following, hot on the trail
again. What if we ever *did* catch him? Caught him and put him
in a cage? We couldn't even sell tickets, Red says. They all

know the Devil too well. So we chase and he runs and I suppose the chase itself is the only thing that matters.

CARTWRIGHT

That freaking Jew bastard! I mean, here we are fine as wine, done got everything set and ready and it ain't even the middle of the morning yet. Got it made! No sweat and nothing to worry about at all. And old Moses is going around moping with a sad face like the doctor just told him to give up cigarettes and whiskey and even thinking about women.

That would tend to give a fella a sad look, don't you reckon? We'll get to fighting tonight when it comes time to count up the money. That's the way it is all the time. The way I look at it, it just don't pay to have two business managers. Specially ones as different as me and Moses. Not that I grudge him anything. I don't pay him that much mind. The whole thing is, Moses is a big, fat New York City Jew and I'm a plain old country boy even though I was actually born in a suburb of the city of Memphis, Tennessee.

I don't know why or how come we all worry about the money so much. Red, he can smell a missing penny and Moses was born pinching them. I mean, it ain't like a travelling gospel show is Big Business or something. It is nothing like it used to be in the good old days. Nowadays every little old tumble down nigger shack by the side of the road has got a big T.V. antenna sticking out of the roof and if sitting on their ass and watching the T.V. don't suit them, why then they can all just run outside and pile in that big shiny new car parked in the yard [cause everybody's got a set of wheels even if they don't eat regular] and scratch out in a cloud of dust and squawks and chicken feathers and roll, go somewhere, do something! Even so, though, Red can still get them up off their deadass and pack them in, all mixed up like a pocketful of marbles, black and white alike. And it don't take long before he's got them all ahollering *Glory!* and *Amen!* and *Joy to the World!*

I have quit on him more than one time. I'll be long gone, and loose and shed of him. Maybe I'll be somewhere sitting on top of a barstool having myself a tall cool one and waiting for some action [by action what I mean is the kind that come walking *clickety-clack* on a set of high heels] to come along. And then all of a sudden there he is, standing right by me. Done tracked me down as easy as J. Edgar Hoover and his whole F.B.I.

"Hey there, Hookworm!"

Which happens to be the dirty nickname he put on me.

"Hey, you, Hookworm! You better put down that glass of beer and get up off of your bony ass and come with me. Cause we are fixing to roll. Where are we going? We are going clean over top of the Great Smoky Mountains and way on down to the edge of the Gulf of Mexico. We may end up as far west as Wichita Falls and then come back east all the way to Fernandina. You listen here! We're going to pack up the truck and the trailer and roll this time. Going to roll across the whole South singing and shouting and bringing the Goodnews to poor folks and the crippled, to the halt and the lame and the downtrodden and the downhearted. We're fixing to stand up tall and preach the everlasting, everliving, never-changing Word of Almighty God! And everywhere we go, wherever we wander, all the little souls will shine again. Shine, man, shine! Just like gold and silver and precious stones. Brighter than the brightest star in the sky. Then God Himself will look down upon us. He will smile upon our labour. And then, man, *then*, with the last drops of our sweat and tears poured out in prayer and sacrifice and finally standing empty and shining in the light of the eternal smile of God, we'll be so high, so light-headed and light-hearted we'll want to run and jump and leap high, wide and handsome, as frisky and graceful as young lambs at play . . . . !"

Wherever I am I guess I will get up and go with him. And it's the same with the people. Rich or poor, fat and sassy or as skinny and mangey as a woreout wetmop, they'll come too to hear him preach.

I don't know why. Maybe you're like me, just born to doubt everything except the value of a dollar and the pleasures of a woman, and you don't have the least notion of believing any of that yourself. But, believe me, you're bound to believe without a doubt that Red believes. Sometimes when he tosses his head high and then bows it to pray you can almost swear and testify that you can see that white dove of the Holy Ghost he talks about, see it fly down and sit on his shoulder. At a time like that the breath comes out of you like it was yanked out by the roots. And then the breath of life dances in front of your eyes like a young girl dancing alone in front of her mirror.

Nothing like that. Nothing more beautiful. A young girl, probably a virgin, one with little rosebud nipples and sweet little fur at the crotch and a ass as white as a Easter lily. Oh, lead me to it!

"Hey!" Moses says, giving me a shove. "Here's the car."

"I can see as good as you can," I say. "So you don't have to shove a fella."

"Ungh."

That's all he answers, climbing in on the near side and leaving it for me to drive.

"I don't like you pushing and shoving and all."

"Ungh."

"What's wrong with you, anyhow, Moses?"

"I've got a feeling," he says. "I've got a feeling we're due for a session of bad luck."

Moses is a born pessimist and he would put the bad mouth on it if a sack of gold was to fall out of the sky and land at his feet.

"You wanna know something?" I say. "You full of shit like a Christmas turkey."

"Ungh. . . ."

That's all he says.

MOSES

We drove all night coming across the mountains. Miami drove her car with Red asleep in the back seat, and I drove the truck with that lazy bum, Cartwright, snoring beside me. I didn't mind, though. I wouldn't trust him driving at night in the mountains. It was just dawn when we came down to the town in the valley, a quiet place, a hollow with the mountains, blue and green and cloudy all around us.

Things have been going well for us this year. We have been going almost eight weeks without a break. Not one slow night, rain or shine. I can remember many times when we had plenty of time on our hands, but this trip has been pack up after midnight and go, unpack and do the show, pack up and go again. We are all tired, but I think Red is worn out. He has dark circles under his eyes and the skin is stretched tight over the bones of his face. Usually he sleeps during the day, but he can't seem to sleep much any more. The only way we can keep him going is with plenty of good whiskey and the dangling promise that once we have finished this swing we will go somewhere and stay in a hotel or a fancy motel. Red likes motels with their swimming pools and air-conditioning, the wall-to-wall carpeting and free stationery. Last year it was Virginia Beach. All this year he has been talking about Galveston. Well, we'll see about that.

Meanwhile there's Cartwright to worry about. It isn't just that he's lazy and worthless. I can tolerate that. You can always make allowances if you have to. One of these days, though, now that we've had a good season, he's going to get sticky fingers. It's bound to happen and when it does it will be the one time I take my eyes off him for a minute. And then Red will blame me because that's what you have to expect from Cartwright.

Miami is another problem. I don't worry about her in the same way. Of course, she's always teasing Cartwright about how they ought to take off together for far places. It keeps him as nervous and excited as a man with a nickel in front of a ten cent toilet. Only a game she plays, yet I think she may half mean it. She'll go one day all right. Not with Cartwright, even though she may plan to use him as a means, to keep him for insurance until she's ready to dump him. It wouldn't take a reason. Something would have to happen so that she can feel *right* about it. When it does, we'll wake up in the morning somewhere and find she's gone.

I don't blame her either. But it's one thing to anticipate the actions of a man like Cartwright and another to keep one step ahead of a real woman. You can keep a slight edge on even a shrewd man. All you have to do is to keep multiplying yourself, raising yourself to one more power higher than he is. Just as long as you can see yourself as he sees you, know what he knows, you are one full step ahead of him no matter if the two of you shatter yourselves all the way to infinity – like being trapped between two sets of mirrors in a barber shop. But a woman lives on *feelings* the way a light-bulb burns. And feelings, your own or anyone else's, are the one thing you can never be sure

23

of. You lose the edge, the one step that can save your life. You are at the mercy of your own feelings, so why not a victim to a creature of feelings?

"Look ayonder!" Cartwright is shouting as we turn off the highway and under the arch. "Look at that!"

"Pull over," I say. "Pull over and stop before we get killed."

CARTWRIGHT

Here it comes across the field, bouncing, coming right for us, wide open and lickety split, tearing out, man!, like a huge blue bug on wheels. A tiny thing to make such a racket and go so fast, coming at us low to the ground, bucking, not even looking for the ruts but just cutting across the open field from the trailer.

But wait! Look who's driving the thing!

I pull over all right, not because I'm scared like Oldmaid Moses, but mainly to be polite and also to get a good look when she zooms by. She's a little thing with red hair blowing in the breeze, going up and down off the seat every time the car bounces, hanging onto the steering wheel like for dear life. Like maybe if she did let go she would sail right off into outer space and become the first little redheaded bitch in orbit.

Now she sees us and turns and here she comes straight for us. I'm all set to bail out of here. I'm not ready to meet my Maker just yet. . . .

E-E-E-E!

She stops on a dime right beside us. Good looking girl in a black Navy raincoat. Wild-looking, but good.

"Hello there," she says.

"Howdo."

24

I tip my hat and give her a friendly smile.

"I wonder if you can help me. . . ."

"I'll try," I say. "Whatever it is, I'll damn sure try."

"Is Big Red Smalley going to preach here tonight?"

"You better believe it, honey."

Now I am smiling into dust and empty space cause she has gone already like somebody goosed her. Jet-propelled! Me and Moses choking and drowning in dust and she is nothing but gone. And by the time the dust clears up enough so you can see which way she went the road is empty as far as you can see both ways. Just a big blank. I'd be willing to believe she wasn't here in the first place or else just vanished in a puff of smoke except I still hear the sound of that engine like a bumblebee or a gnat in your ear.

"What kind of a car is that?" I say. "What's the name of that car she's driving?"

Moses looks at me kind of disgusted the way he usually does. Like spitting on me would be a waste of good saliva.

"That was a broomstick," he says. "She rides around on a broomstick."

Smartass!

"You know something?" he says. "I've seen that girl before somewhere."

"The world is full of girls," I say. "Praise the Lord, the world is always full up to the brim and overflowing with flat-bellied, cute-titied, smooth-assed, quimmy bitches and right now I feel like I could take 'em all on, one at a time, red ones and yellow ones, black and white . . . !"

"Your appetite exceeds your ability."

"Look who's talking!" I say. "When's the last time you got a little?"

"That girl is following us for some reason," he says trying to ignore the question and change the subject. "I'd swear I saw her night before last."

"I would have seen her if she was hanging around," I say. "I would have seen her first."

"Why? Why would she be following us?"

"Maybe she's a secret agent that works for the Russians," I say.

Moses puckers up his lips and gives me the look again. I believe he would spit on me if he thought he could get away with it.

MIAMI

Well, here they come finally. Taking their sweet time as usual.

Oh, I saw the girl all right, the kook in the black raincoat, the little bitch in the blue car. She came up and walked all around the truck and the trailer just looking. She's going to be trouble I guess. But she's only a woman. I'll take my chances even with a crazy one. It's that car I can't compete with. The car may just raise his eyebrows and put a smile on his face. How can you compete with a freaking car? Put on four wheels and start farting?

Well, I will worry about that when the time comes. Worry about the car and even about the girl if I have to. One trouble at a time. The next one always comes along quick enough. If there's one thing plentiful it's trouble.

Now they pull up near the trailer and I walk over to them, tightening the sash on the bathrobe for Cartwright's benefit. He just grins and winks. He don't even know when he's doing it. It's just a bad habit. Maybe he can't help winking, but if I was stuck with a set of teeth like that I'd try my best to remember to keep my big mouth shut.

"You're looking good," Cartwright says.

"I got news for you," I say.

"What? What's that?" Cartwright says, starting to get nervous right away.

"Take it easy," I say. "You might just as well relax and enjoy it. Because the shit has finally hit the fan."

CARTWRIGHT

"I knew it! I knew it!" Moses is saying.

I am the only one who can always keep calm, cool and collected. Let them piss and moan. I light myself a cigarette and lean back and take a few leisurely puffs while they carry on like some kind of a duet. When they get through the last chorus of generalized groaning, I have the good sense to ask Miami what the hell she thinks she is talking about.

"He's tired. He's wore out," she says. "He ain't going to preach here tonight."

"We better go back to town and call the whole thing off," Moses says.

"Wait a minute! Wait just a big minute!" I holler. "We got ourselves a nice set up here. We can't quit now."

"What do you propose to do about it!" Moses says.

Just like him. Pass the buck to me every time.

"Me?"

"Do you have some profound solution to our problem?"

That's how he gets every time. Talks fancy trying to prove how smart he is. We'll see who's the smart one around here.

"Maybe we could kind of persuade him," I say.

Miami just looks at me and laughs in my face. When the two of them gang up against you, what are you supposed to do?

"Do you want to try?" she says.

"I was thinking you might be able to."

"He says he was *thinking*, Moses. Do you believe that?"

That's the trouble with women. When they get to feeling nasty and bitchy there's nothing you can do to please them. Except maybe you could just close your eyes and lay back and let them clip off your pecker with a pair of garden shears. And I'll tell you one thing for sure, there ain't nobody been born I want to please that much.

"I guess if anybody could persuade him I could," she says.

"That's what I say. That's all I'm trying to tell you."

"But I'm not going to."

"How come?"

"I don't feel like it," she says.

"Oh, that's just fine," I say. "Just fine and dandy."

"I don't care," she says. "One way or the other it's no skin off of my ass."

I ought to kick Moses in the teeth. Whenever you really need him he ain't one damn bit of help.

"Now you just looka here," I say.

"You don't have to yell at me," she says.

We look at each other and I decide right now that I'm not too proud to try another way.

"Miss Miami, I think you know how much I admire and respect you. . . ."

Busts out laughing again. Won't hardly give a fella a fair chance.

"What's so funny about that?"

"Don't stop," she says. "You're killing me."

I am going to really try one more time to be nice. I mean it. I mean, there is a whole lot riding on this little conversation whether these two morons know it or not. And, like they say, a truly big man can afford to swallow his pride over something that matters.

"Talk to him, Miami," I say. "You can do it. I'll make it up to you. I'll make it worth your while, I promise."

"How?"

"You just name it."

"You sure do sound eager."

"Jesus, I *am* eager."

"Anything?" she asks.

"Anything within reason."

"He's already starting to welsh on it, Moses."

"You just name it," I say, looking her dead in the eye.

She puts her finger to the side of her head and rolls her eyes. "I'm thinking," she says.

"You think all you want to. The offer stands."

"I imagine, if I was to put my mind to it, I might be able to think of something interesting."

"Please, Miss Miami."

How low does a guy have to stoop? What does a fella have to do?

"Say 'pretty please'," she says.

"Pretty please . . ."

Now they are both laughing. The two of them laughing on both sides of me. I think I will turn around and bust Moses right in the big middle of his fat Jew face. . . .

Only I'm not even going to get a chance to do that. Cause here comes Red.

"Damn you!" he hollers. "Damn you straight to hell! How do you expect me to get any sleep around here?"

He's barefooted, ain't got on nothing but his jockey under-shorts and he's got a whiskey bottle in his hand, shaking it like a club.

So now we wait. Miami stands by the car. I sit and sweat. The sun is getting high now, bright and hot, and I'm one of those people who sweats. Cartwright just sits. He licks his lips and blinks. I know that we must not ever, ever, ever hold a human being responsible for his height and weight, the conformation of his eyes and the tilt and shape of his jaw. And I know that nobody, not even an actor, can be sure that the expression on his face equals exactly the feeling he intends to express. Maybe a woman, a really beautiful woman. Maybe almost any woman, because, even though they like to be flattered and can be flattered too, they know exactly what they are and look like. They are supreme realists, living easily with illusions, but able to live without them and seldom duped or victimized by them, not haunted by illusions the way we are. For the longest time, a grey waste of time it is shameful even to think of, I woke each morning and faced my mirror with a very real and burning hope that looking back at me would be a young, handsome stranger, someone with the shine of health, whose blood was money, whose energy was boundless and depthless and on whom Lady Luck looked with benevolent bright eyes. And never once was that stranger there. Instead a familiar friend I loved and hated. Oh, what a time it was, what a bitter time it was before I learned (making a virtue of necessity, a bookish man would say) to live with that friend. Since he was there, always to be cared for and comforted, fed sugar sometimes and spanked at others. An ugly, shambling pet whose hungers were infinite and whose language was a fugue of howls, since he was there and would never leave me and would finally (the last and best laugh) die, dragging me into the dark with him, I had better accept him first and then try to master him and use him. And I have done the best that I can (with of course, occasional deplorable but inevitable lapses into such offensive folly as self-pity). So now, in the game of multiplying and dividing that is our only union with another soul, the one step edge in the terrible footrace of survival, I know anyway what the thing another looks at, the thing called Moses looks like. And I wear my face like a mask, knowing, triumphant, if knowing a simple fact can be called a triumph, that what I am will never really be read by any man (and I will only read a little like a man newly blind and learning braille). Nor will I ever read into the heart of any other human being. I am stuck with the ticking and tremors of my own. For better and worse, for richer and poorer, in sickness and in health, till death us do marvellously part.

I am a wedding, a continual copulation of spirit and flesh, of monster and man, beauty and the beast.

I should have been a woman. I should have been heavy-breasted, broad-hipped with a brood in shrill circles around my feet.

I will not blame Cartwright for any of it, even now as, without knowing it, he vigorously picks his nose.

CARTWRIGHT

There isn't nothing a fella can say when Red is like this. You just sit there and wait.

Red takes a long slurping drink out of that bottle, like he was drinking a Pepsi or something. He can drink whiskey all right, but nobody can drink like that without some kind of trouble. And here it comes now. He wipes the back of his hand across his mouth and laughs.

"What are you all so busy talking about?"

Nobody else has the guts to answer so I guess I will have to.

"Nothing, nothing at all. We was just having a little conversation with Miss Miami."

"Must've been interesting."

"Yes, sir, it was," I say.

"Miami can't talk worth a damn."

"Thanks a bunch," Miami says.

"Think nothing of it," Red says.

"Don't worry, I won't."

"Now, honey," he says. "You wouldn't want me to stand out here in broad daylight in the sight of God and man and tell a lie would you?"

I can't help laughing a little bit. I mean, you can fight it but sometimes even then it gets away from you.

He turns on me.

"What was the topic of your conversation?"

"Nothing. I done told you, nothing at all."

"Well, then, don't mind me. Don't pay any attention to me. I'll just stand here and you all keep right on with the conversation, huh?" You couldn't cut the silence with a meat cleaver.

"Talk!" he says. "Talk, godamn you!"

I swallow and say to myself what's the use? But here goes.

"Going to be a hot one, Miss Miami, don't you think?"

"Yes," Moses says, "I'd say it was warm even for this time of the year."

"Is that what you want me to talk to him about?" Miami says, "The weather?"

I could kill her. I could stake her out like the Apaches do in the movies. Get me a razor blade and slice her up an inch at a time.

"Hey! That's a good idea," Red says.

"What is?"

"Talking about the weather. It's always interesting. The main thing is that there is always some. Can you imagine, can you just picture no weather at all?"

"No, sir, I can't."

"Tell me all about weather, Cartwright. Tell me about the seasons of the year."

"Aw, Red, quit kidding around."

"Tell me about it!"

"What do you want me to tell?"

"You come from Tennessee, don't you?" he says. "So tell me about the weather in Tennessee. I'll tell you what, make it easy for you. All you have to do is tell me about one season. Tell me about springtime."

"It's a mighty pretty time of the year."

"Pretty? Is that the only word you can come up with? Tell how it is up there in the mountains after a long, long, hard winter, a winter of grey sky and iron cold. Tell how the air all of a sudden one morning turns all sweet and fresh like milk. How the little wild flowers drip with sweet like honey itself and drive the bees drunk and crazy. And the birds. The birds coming back from the south, all sizes and shapes and colours, a living testament to the Imagination of Almighty God. How the new leaves are full of them. They sing and sing like a whole choir of silver bells. Tell how the dogwood comes into bloom. And the redbud all glittering like fresh, new blood. . . ."

He stops there to take a swallow. His eyes are all bright like new coins and his big hands are trembly. So he has to take the bottle in both hands to drink.

"You son-of-bitches are planning something!" he yells at us. "Cooking up mischief. That's what you're doing."

"No, sir," I say. "You know us better than that."

"Maybe," he says. "Just maybe you're planning to sneak off with all the money and leave me asleep in the trailer. Just snoring and dreaming. Leave me here all alone, not a dime to my name or a friend in the world. Just leave me to rot and die for all you care, stranded in . . . stranded in . . . Where the hell are we?"

"High Pines, Red," Moses says, coming in just in time to get some credit as usual.

Red grunts and looks across the big empty field at the archway.

"It's a nice town, Red," I say, "a real nice place."

"Parked out in the middle of an empty field near a place called High Pines," Red says, almost to himself, like he couldn't quite believe it and wanted to convince hiself.

"This here's the Fairgrounds," I say. "See that big old arch over yonder? This is the place where everything happens."

"Don't look like they had a fair around here for a long time," he says, looking at the scrubby grass and weeds, spitting in the dust by his feet.

"That's the whole thing," I say. "They'll all be here. Everybody and his brother's coming to hear you preach."

"We oughta be in Galveston," he says.

"We'll be there pretty soon," Moses says.

"Yeah, Red," I say. "Time we get through with this place we'll have enough to run on down to Galveston and really live it up."

"How come we're not already on the road, rolling on down to Galveston?"

"You speaking to me, Red?"

"What the hell do you think, you anaemic hookworm? You think I'm speaking to you? I'm looking right at you."

"I already done told you. As soon as we get the money."

34

"Money!" he says, "Seems like we always got money troubles. Never quite got enough. I wonder where it all goes to?"

"Well," I say, trying to stay calm and not lose my temper, "you know how it goes. We got a lot of different expenses and things."

He looks at me and laughs. Laughing, he tilts the bottle up high and drains the last of it and then throws the bottle high away in the field. He stands looking at it sail and fall like he is kind of proud how far he can chunk a empty whiskey bottle.

"Miami," he says, "bestir your ass and get me another bottle."

She don't change the look on her face. She don't hesitate. She's already gone, gone to the trailer to get it for him.

"Look at you!" he says to me and Moses. "A fine couple of managers I got, a fine pair! A fat Jew and a ignorant ridge-runner that ain't got sense enough to come in out of the rain. Here I am all worn out, worn down to a nub, dead on my feet, weary, man, weary! Down to the marrow of my bones and the roots of my soul. And you two want me to get up and preach tonight. You want to make me, the way I am and the way I feel to stand up one more time and preach! What do you know? Parasites! Leeches! Cockroaches! Blood suckers, living off my blood and my sweat. . . ."

Hold tight, everybody. Here we go! Round and round and nobody wins.

We got a breather anyway because here's Miami now with a new bottle of bourbon and it's going to take him a minute to rip off the wrapping and pull the cork.

That's a blessing!

35

He finally gets the bottle open and takes a sip. I could have opened it myself or anyway offered to, but damn if I would and damn if he will ever ask me to.

"Moses," he says. "You're a Jew, ain't you? Don't be shy. You can't fool me. I can *smell* Jew. You smell just like a Jew to me."

Fat Moses don't say a word. He only shrugs and squints his eyes. Moses is a big baby. Times like this, when he just won't fight back and won't do anything except squint his eyes a little, he makes you feel like you want to hit him square in the middle of that huge, soft belly of his, drive your arm in up to the elbow in that tub of lard. It's an ugly feeling – an ugly thing that you know would make you feel good and clean again and then guilty again for feeling that good and clean about it etc.

Oh I have known and hated that a thousand times before now   the ones who induce ugliness in you and make you like it too and lap it up like a dog lapping vomit   I recall an Episcopal minister fat pudgy fishbelly-coloured man with skin like a baby's and pudgy baby-face and thick glasses he would oh so carefully remove and put on the dresser fastidious off came the clerical collar and you never get used to that funny as it is and the shirt and the pants and the coat so neatly hung and the shoes side by side so shiny

wore high socks and garters a fat soft white man with soft hairy legs and the pink spoiled place where the garters had pinched the skin and left a mark and last the undershorts all clean and ironed and fresh

fresh put on for his visit and a woman you just couldn't help wondering what woman it was who kept his clothes so clean and so careful ironed those undershorts he'd fold them neatly too and turn to face me with a little smile his soft pudgy dingdong softly slowly rising so little and small you wanted to laugh not at him or it because you have already seen them all shapes and all sizes and it don't make no difference in spite of what men think because there's always a way a position for each one and all nature is neutral but fair enough he'd nod at me smiling gently to reassure me it was all right

fatherly almost and sweet and considerate had charity truly if that means he knew you had a soul too and your own mystery and God's eye was on you too whore or murderer or pickpocket or pimp he had that much but not enough to love himself or believe that God could love him too

poor man he must have dreamed himself the chief of all sinners because he knew the terror and wonder of God's love and forgiveness

glimpsed that much of the mystery and maybe nearly fainted for joy like a window-peeper but then felt guilty because of knowledge and lacked faith to believe God's mercy extended to such as himself must do God's work for Him must be punished and defiled   you wanted to take him in your arms and hold him like a child to find the right way and fake the squeals and moans   oh papa don't stop don't leave me oh papa don't stop don't stop don't ever no never oh papa papa papa   til he rose from the bed snorting   manhood like a stallion a porpoise sleek with the shine of himself

he was having none of that old cure   who didn't want to be cured but always to remain in debt in terror in dirt to God   who came to me for that

no love lost no love except for the moment of that little smile that cheered me like a rose to work open his little black bag like a doctor's and take out the riding crop   I mount him and ride him ignoring his howls and soon they turn to the grunt of a pig satisfied lax and lazy as a sow he cleans himself dresses himself so careful and correct wipes his glasses with a tissue leaves the money on the bureau and then a look more shameful ugly than scabs a running sore making me feel a scaly

37

creature of scabs a running sore not love now but pity which was not
and never will be his or anyone's to offer and I feel the hate inside and
nothing will please me nothing will cleanse me but fury and madness
uproot his manhood make wine of his grapes scratch out eyes and
rip out tongue by the roots feed flesh to mongrel dogs carve bones into
flutes ashtrays piano keys by the time he was gone I was all bathed
in a cold sweat to know to learn and then know I had such a store of
fury and hate in my soul

But Red will not raise his hand against Moses.

"You fat, old, ugly Jew," he says. "Let me tell you something. I guess I've got everything running in my veins. Jew blood, nigger blood, Indian blood. Hell, I probably got Chinese. And when I cut my finger it bleeds the same colour as yours."

He turns. He's saving it all for Cartwright who knows it and can only wait.

"Hey, Hookworm, where was you at when I found you?"

"I was working in a carnival."

"In the freak show?"

"I was a talker. You know. They call it a barker. I talked people to come inside of the tent and see the show."

"You carried a cane in those days," Red says, just like it really was a long time ago. "As I recall you stood on a platform and sold tickets to a nekkid dancing show. What else did you do for a living?"

"I used to be a Bible salesman before that."

"I'm not talking about selling Bibles."

"I guess I don't know what you mean," Cartwright says.

"Didn't you do anything else, Hookworm?"

"My name ain't exactly Hookworm."

38

"Would you just look at him!" Red says. "Even a no-account creature like that has got his pride. Poor old Hookworm, he's got a little fig leaf of pride."

"Lay off of me, Red."

"What else? Tell us what else."

Now Red is narrow-eyed and mean looking. Looks mean enough to take a knife and clean Cartwright from stem to stern like a catfish.

"Well," Cartwright says softly. "I guess some people would say I was, you know, what they call a kind of a . . . pimp."

"But you was married. You were a married man, weren't you?"

"You know that."

"I'm asking."

"I was. I mean, I happened to be married at the time."

"Aren't you still married, Hookworm?"

"If you was going to be strictly legal and all, going by the letter of the law, you might say so. I mean, I ain't had no divorce papers served on me or nothing."

"Correct me if I'm wrong," Red says, "but didn't you get married to one of the dancers?"

Cartwright nods sadly. He can sure look pitiful sometimes.

"What was her name?"

"Cartwright. Same as mine."

"What was her first name?"

"Aw, you already know that, Red."

"What was it she called herself?"

"You mean her stage name?"

"What else?"

"She was known as Dreama," Cartwright says. "Dreama, the Denver Bombshell."

I have to laugh. Cartwright glares at me and pouts. Moses,

39

who must be a million miles away, looks straight ahead, mopping at the beads of sweat on his forehead with a handkerchief. My laughter accomplishes nothing. It doesn't help Cartwright or keep Red from finishing. He goes on now like a dentist drilling, grinding away at the nerve of a rotten tooth.

"Did you used to pimp for her?"

Cartwright swallows and nods his head, a dry swallow and a tight nod. There is nothing else he can do.

"How could a man fall so low as to become a pimp for his own wife?"

"I didn't have no choice."

"Somebody forced you to do it?"

Cartwright has only a whining whisper left now. "We had to have the money," he says. "We was both of us on the stuff. You know – dope, narcotics."

"Do you mean to tell me you were *dope fiends?*"

"They call it being 'hooked'," Cartwright says. "It ain't like really being a *fiend*. Nobody says 'dope fiend' anymore."

"I do."

"Well, I guess you might say we were a couple of dope fiends."

CARTWRIGHT

we was hooked all right but it wasn't all my fault honest Dreama was already hooked before I ever knew her long before and if I had've only known but how could I I mean you take a guy right out of the country so to speak even a smart guy with plenty of ambition and drive like me and all the guts in the world but don't know nothing much yet except what they teach in the public school and that ain't much and you still green enough to believe what you don't know can't hurt you say and that fella's got a weakness everybody's got some kind of a weakness

The Lord deals them out along with all kinds of misery and trouble like a poker hand from a cold deck   The Lord give me the weakness for Women   a burning a hunger a thirst   so how could I know and how can they hold me to blame   all dressed up in my best coat and tie and only nineteen I go to the travelling carnival show not alone I never would go nowhere alone except to a cathouse or the men's room

I had a date with Evelyn Snead   Miss Snead the new school teacher not pretty but plain as pig tracks homely as a picket fence a dog a pig a total loss all skinny and bony less tits than a sow with hair like a mouse's with hands the size of mine and chewed finger nails from nerves if you touched her she'd tremble like a leaf in the wind and feet bigger than mine for God's sake and whatever she put on no matter what colour looked like a sack   took Evelyn Snead exactly and because she was like she was

because nineteen I already knew the one gospel truth it ain't none of it bad   already knew it takes work time energy effort goodlooks good job money a future and always saying the right thing at the right time which I wasn't and ain't exactly what you would call Famous for it's one of the few faults I've got if you only want those beautiful ones then you got to be ready to spend a whole lots of time at it and when the time comes you gotta be ready to pay the price   nineteen years old and a Bible salesman making out pretty good and going to make out real good soon as I get enough experience the Boss hiself said so but nineteen years old and just barely able to meet the payments on my new Ford anyway what happens because I know now and have had more than my share and more than the average guy but you never get enough and probably die with a hard on   if there's a heaven do the angels do it

that would be Heaven world without end amen   what happens when finally you shuck off the skivvies of a beautiful woman you done made the effort you done paid the price said all the right things right up to the time she says now baby now baby now hurry now   more

likely than not don't Nothing happen nothing special that ain't
happened before she values herself so high she thinks you're getting a
Gift a Blessing and Milk and Honey and Manna from Heaven   give
me a dog a dog who knows she's a dog and then You are giving Her a
Blessing she appreciates it

but you gotta be ready to move on quick because she all of a sudden
is talking license preacher wedding bells which is why I guess I'll
always be a travelling man

Me and Snead went to the picture show saw cowboys and Indians
I prefer them best held her hand it trembled at first but soon got still I
smiled in the dark to myself she took to giving me a squeeze put my
arm on the back of her seat and keep on chomping popcorn and watching the picture not her   pretty soon she let go and nestles

her perfume smells sweet as any other who cares   we go for a ride
in the country taking a nip from a pint I got that loosens her up to
where she's talking about how lonesome she is a schoolteacher in a
strange town don't know nobody   I tell her me I'm lonesome too   but
not going to be any more glad I know her we don't have to never be
lonesome no more anyway then she give me a kiss with her tongue like
a lizard's as good a kiss as any except for the tickle of her little
moustache that's all peroxide so you won't notice right away but what
the hell a kiss is better than no kiss and a guy can't have everything not
at least all at one time   I'm getting hot and ready to bet so is she   But
it takes more than one kiss then we run into that Carnival lights
winking like stars from the big wheel and the merry-go-round and all
those rides   music playing voices laughing and squealing and good
strange smells canvas sawdust candy hot dogs and hamburgers cooking
cotton candy candy apples sweat perfume

what the hell she's so happy like a little girl why not blow a little
cash on the bitch and make it a sure thing and maybe for more than one
time   it's always good to have Something besides that to talk about
later nice to have something in common you know

42

we done everything there was to do including the freaks except the tent where they had the girls dancing   come with me I say   you go she says   Aw come on it might be fun you go I'll wait for you haven't you ever seen one before they really ain't Bad thinking that maybe it'll be just the thing to get her ready no thanks she says but you go you go and I'll just walk around and see everything just look and see I am so happy but you go you go and get haha an eyeful then hurry back to me hurry back giving my hand a hard squeeze thinking to myself she can't go nowhere cause I got the keys to the car   she probably wants to be alone to make up her mind for sure and she's already made up her mind and knows it or else she wouldn't send me off to get haha an eyeful excited because she's a dog and no dog in her right mind can afford to be a Tease you know   you go she says winking and I'll just walk around and be waiting for you   don't you run off with no handsome strangers I say to make her feel good like somebody might be drunk enough crazy enough to do that she laughs I'll follow wherever you go I'll pursue you and kill you you cannot escape old eagle-eyes I say

she laughs because I say looking sad and mournful as a undertaker I only just found you I'll die if I lose you I'll lay down and die

she takes off her glasses to wipe them tears in her eyes I give her a peck on the cheek and leave her to buy my ticket to the dancing girls

Maybe she's still waiting for me somewhere wiping her glasses tears in her eyes waiting

and I wish to God I had never left you Elaine Snead   You dog of a schoolteacher

you could have saved me from buying a one-way ticket for a trip straight to Hell

MOSES

Maybe after he's worked off all of his pent up anger and frustration on us he can get some sleep. Anyway he'll be calm again and then maybe we can find out what's going to happen this time. I'd just as soon be in Galveston as here. You carry your problems with you from place to place like a Santa Claus sack, but even so one place can be better than another. And this place smells like trouble to me.

Meanwhile Red goes right ahead mercilessly bugging Cartwright. Not for all the wrong reasons either. In a way he's trying to preach to him. A tough assignment since Cartwright doesn't believe in any god or, if he does, it must be a god like Cartwright. A mirror image of himself complete with clip on bow tie, straw hat and a ruinous smile of yellow teeth.

Red is saying: "Then one fine day I came along to save you. I took you up into the mountains where the air was thin and clean. I got a tumbledown shack in a high meadow and I tied you down to the bed posts and then I talked you through the worst part. I talked and prayed and sang night and day. It was a regular filibuster. I read from the Scripture. I sang to you like a baby. And all the time you were lying there screaming, hollering, puking and cursing God's name. Which old Job – who had it worse than you ever will – never did. I ministered unto you and when I finally turned you loose you were free, or anyway as free as you will ever be. Healed up if not reborn. Maybe not saved but anyway a new man. And you can't deny that."

"No, sir."

Red looks away from him, past us, not seeing us or anything really, the brightness of his eyes dimmed with a cast of thought. Then drinks and turns back to Cartwright.

"Where do you expect old Dreama is now?"

"I wouldn't know," Cartwright says. "I haven't heard tell."

"God knows," Red says. "And one of these days He is liable to point out the way to her. His Invisible Index Finger is going to point right at you wherever you are. We'll probably be just hanging around like this somewhere, talking trash, passing the time of day, and all of a sudden, lo and behold, there she'll be, Dreama the Denver Bombshell, fire in her eyes and murder in her heart, and a lawyer right behind her carrying a whole stack of legal papers. . . ."

Red is only kidding him lightly now, but Cartwright reacts true to form like one of Pavlov's drooling dogs. Punch the right bell or button and he'll do it every time. He can't help sneaking a quick look over his shoulder just to see if she's coming across the field after him right this minute.

"Look at him!" Red booms. "The sonofabitch has done turned *green* on us!"

Which is quite enough to make all three of us laugh, the picture of that woman, imaginary to us anyway, named Dreama of all things, picking her way toward us across the lumpy field, walking in the highest of high heels, delicate and awkward at the same time, swinging her purse like a lethal weapon, and behind her, skipping to keep up, comes the Lawyer, a solemn and distressed owl, arms loaded with papers all written in the precise chaos of legal jargon over which poor Cartwright can wrinkle his brow, can ponder with the perfect incredulous bafflement of a monkey trying to read a music score.

Faced with all that sudden laughter, Cartwright has to grin a slow and sheepish grin and shrug with an eloquence worthy of any of the tribe of Abraham.

"You know why I keep you around, Hookworm?"

"No, sir, I don't guess I do."

"On account of you're a symbol, a walking, talking, living, breathing symbol of the undeniable fact that there is no man so low, so worthless, contemptible and lost that he cannot be chosen to be a servant of God. Hookworm, you continually restore my confidence in my vocation."

45

"Seems like you might take a look at your ownself some-time," Miami says.

A mistake at the moment and she knows it as soon as she speaks because I read that in her eyes as clearly as if she had clapped both hands over her mouth. And Red, still smiling, has the sudden hard glinting light of anger in his eyes. For a moment they look at each other, poker-faced and unflinching.

"As long as we're on the subject," Red says, "let me tell you about the time I found Miami."

"Shut up," she says.

"There she was, without stitch one on, unless you could call cigar smoke a kind of clothing, up on top of a table in a room full of men. She had already done her dancing and now she was doing her stunts and tricks. Oh, she had her tricks, too. When I walked in the room the men had made a stack of quarters on the table and she was squatting down over those quarters. . . ."

"I'll scratch your eyes out," she says.

She lunges at him, her nails set like the claws of a cat, her teeth gritted. A hissing sound from between her teeth and a move as quick as a striking snake. But Red is quick too, very quick for a big man. He steps to the side and his hands come up seizing her at both wrists, though not quite quick enough to stop one finger nail from flicking his cheek with a razor-fine line of red. Grinning, he tightens his grip without effort and sweat pops out all over her face at once and shines in the sunlight. Then her hands, suddenly as white as chalk, go lax and limp. And he lets her go.

"You have a dirty mouth," she says. "A dirty mouth that goes with a dirty mind."

"Where would you ever find another one like me?"

He drinks, tilting his head back to do so, gulping now and

46

letting whiskey spill over his chin. She has turned away and moves slowly, head down toward the trailer.

"Miami!"

She stops. The line of her shoulders, even beneath the shapeless bulk of the bathrobe, droops as if she were carrying a heavy weight on her back.

"Your brains may be in your ass," he says. "But I like to look at the eyes of somebody I'm talking to."

When she turns back to him her face is set and calm. She lifts her chin and the old fire of pride is there again in her eyes.

"You look like hell wearing my bathrobe," Red says.

"Why don't you buy me a new one?"

"Take it off."

"I will not."

"Take it off and do us a little dance."

One giant step and he is next to her, seizing the sash of the robe in a gnarled fist, yanking her to him, cheek to cheek like a pair of dancers. And he is speaking to her, a soft, lewd, reedy whisper not for my ears or Cartwright's. I do not know the words he shames her with, do not hear them, yet I can read them in her eyes over his shoulder, not by expression but by the absence of any. She is staring at me over his shoulder and her eyes are as blind and blank as glass.

"That's enough, Red," I say.

He turns back to me now, astounded.

"You better get rid of that bottle," I say. "You've had enough."

"Why?" he says, genuinely puzzled.

"What if somebody should come along and see you?"

Red laughs so hard that his body bends and he slaps his bare thigh. I see Miami tighten the sash of the robe. She does that, but does not move away, not yet. She smooths the robe and

47

pats her hair in place. Then she moves away, easy and unhurried toward the trailer, self-conscious, remembering all of her body now and hiking back her shoulders so that she can be tall and straight as she walks.

"I'm a star," Red is saying. "I am just like a godamn freaking movie star. Ain't that right?"

"That's the truth, Red," Cartwright says.

"You told me that one time, Moses, remember?"

"Yes . . ."

"Well then, if I am a celebrity or some kind of a star, I can do anything I please."

"You're the boss," I say.

Miami is now inside the trailer.

CARTWRIGHT

"You mighty right I am the boss around here!"

Now for the first time Red has noticed the cages across the field over amongst the pine trees. I've been wondering when he will see them. Big rusty iron cages, some of them set up on slabs of concrete.

"What's all that?" he says, pointing.

"Evidently there used to be a zoo out here," Moses says.

Red keeps staring at them, shielding his eyes to look. "I guess they got the right idea in High Pines," he says. "I bet they didn't put them cages up for no ordinary animal zoo. No, sir, they aren't intended for wild animals. Those cages are probably for us. All these years they've just been a waiting for us to get here. Well, here we are at last."

"What are you talking about?" I say.

"High Pines has got the right idea, Hookworm, old buddy. High Pines is the town of the future. One of these days every city and town in the world is going to have to build cages like that. They'll start throwing them up, acres and acres, then miles and miles of them. In the end everybody will be in cages. The last man in will have to lock his ownself in. Then they can give the world back to the real animals and they can all come out of hiding and stand around and look at us."

I have to laugh. I mean, troubles or no, a fella can't help laughing and being tickled at a notion like that. Red must be kind of tickled too because all of a sudden he ain't mad anymore. He laughs too and pats me on the back like I really am his old buddy.

"Boy, you better be careful," he says. "I hear you're number one on the reservation list."

We all hear it at once and turn at once to look. We hear the loud bumblebee noise getting louder and coming toward us.

"Would you just take a look at that!"

Here she comes again. Not much more this time than a blur like a smear of blue paint flying down the highway. Down the road and then screeching in a turn under the arch and bouncing across the field already without slowing down. Dust boiling out behind it.

"*Wa-hoo!*" Red hollers. "*Yee-ha-ha!*"

He is running as fast as he can, running and waving his arms, yelling, laughing, running and all kind of leaping and jumping and dancing all at the same time. Like a raving lunatic somebody just turned loose of.

It looks for sure they're going to meet that way, head on and both going wide open. Like she is going to run smack into him and drive – *crunch* and *crack* – right on over him and keep coming. He keeps running for it and she keeps driving straight for him until I just know they are going to crash and I open my mouth and yell but don't a single sound come. I'm thinking maybe he will just run right over top of that blue bug and crush it, and her too, flat like you step on a cockroach.

Then she stops and he does too. But he's going too fast to pull up that quick. He falls over top of the hood and rolls over quick on his back and rolls off it (must be hotter than a tin roof, middle of July) and lays on the ground next to the car, still laughing so we can hear him, looking straight up into the sky. Up goes the bottle and he takes a drink. Flat on his back.

"Come on," Moses says.

And away he goes too, running (not thinking cause we could've easy drove in the car and got there quicker). It strikes me mighty strange to see him run. Waddling real fast would be the best way to say it. I don't recall ever seeing old Moses run for anything the whole time I've known him.

I'm running too now, right behind Moses. Sonofabitch is moving too! He goes faster than it looks cause he's going to get there first.

We come running up longside of the car, puffing and blowing. Red is stretched out there on the grass, kicking his feet and laughing to hiself. She is just sitting there, that's all. She don't look happy or sad or glad or mad. She don't look anything. Now that we're standing up close enough to see what makes her have such a wild pair of eyes. She has got all this crazy eye makeup around them. Like she was in the show business or something. The funny thing is she ain't got no other kind of makeup on her face. Nor even lipstick.

"He's ill," Moses is telling her.

"Yeah," I say. "Don't pay him no mind. He's a sick man."

"Am not ill," Red says. "I ain't even sick."

I bend over to help him.

"Come on, Red."

He ain't about to notice me. He sits up, then kneels beside the car, holding onto the door, looking at her.

"Blow the horn," he says. "Don't say one word until I hear the sound of that horn."

She looks at him real serious. Like maybe she's deaf. Or maybe she don't understand. Or maybe she don't approve worth a damn. I figure I better do something or say something quick and it better be the right thing for once, but before I can even think of one remark to make, she has a big smile and then a laugh and commences to toot on her horn. *Toot-toot-toot-toot*! And finally *HONK*! Because she leans forward against it and closes her eyes laughing with her shoulders shaking and heaving.

Moses keeps a straight face. He's mopping it now, mopping the fresh sweat off of his ugly face with one of his folded hand-kerchiefs.

I sneak a look quick over my shoulder behind me to see where Miami is at. She's there all right, standing next to the trailer. Looking at us. Just looking and not liking it.

"I'm drunk," Red says. "I'm drunk and I don't know if I can stand up or not."

"I can see that," she says, still smiling.

Then he pulls himself up and stands over her, right next to the car, looking at her. She looks up and he looks down and all they can see are each other's eyes. Their faces are so close they could kiss each other without hardly more than a nod. I sneak another look back to see what Miami is up to. Which is nothing. She's gone back inside of the trailer.

"You probably don't remember me," the girl tells Red.

"Refresh me," he says.

"It goes back," she says, "quite a few years."

"That's a bad beginning," Red says, "Make me feel like an old man."

They are just batting words back and forth the way some people play ping pong, but already I can see Red is sober as a judge, just listening. He's that way. He can be drunk or he can be sober whenever he wants to. Moses is still standing there like a statue (except who in the hell would ever make a statue of him except for a joke?). He's still got that folded handkerchief in his hand ready to wipe the sweat off his brow when there's enough of it to make the wiping worth the trouble.

And here I stand with my hat in my hand thinking just one thing. Not listening, just thinking. Thinking that any minute now Miami is going to come busting out of the trailer with the shotgun in her hands. If she does, I'm going to be ready. Soon as I see the door fly open and the light strike on that barrel, I'm going to be gone. I'll be gone so fast they can't even catch me in that blue bug.

Me and Moses just standing here like a pair of stuffed birds not moving a feather while Red and the girl are playing this kind of a ping pong conversation game. I'm thinking about Miami and that twelve gauge double-barrel shotgun. It may be old but it still shoots. Birdshot is probably all she's going to be able to find. I hid the buckshot where nobody will ever look for it. After that time in Lexington, Kentucky, who would blame me? Lucky for me I got a good start running because she still had to load it and I only got a kind of a whiff. The Doctor could pick them out with a tweezer. He thought it was pretty funny and maybe it was too. But I sure hate to think what might have happened if that gun had been loaded to start with. I mean, I'm a bony guy and I ain't got too much ass to begin with, but if she'd a got a good shot at me I wouldn't have none left at all.

"I remember you," Red says, all of a sudden serious. "I remember you well. I laid my hands on you to heal you."

She stops talking and nods. Then she bows her head down and he reaches forward and lays both hands on her head like he does when he's healing. But he don't pray or say a word. It's more like he was trying to remember what it was like, exactly, and where it was and when. That must be what he's doing because he's closed his eyes and his whole face is lined like he felt a pain or was lifting something heavy off the ground.

MIAMI

I watch them from the window. Red carrying on like a jackass. Moses brooding and worried. Hookworm waiting, poised like a rabbit or a squirrel waiting to dart away at the first sign of trouble from any direction.

And the girl. Well, she's probably young which is something and sick which is nothing. They all are, the ones that come after him. She's not the first one and won't be the last. If all they wanted was to get laid, then more power to them. He'd dance with them a while. He'd wave his wand over them like a magician and turn them into something. Wake up the Sleeping Beauty, oh smiling sweetly in her dream. But Red's not Prince Charming. Music they never heard will blare in their ears and they wake up from sweet dreams, as empty as cotton candy, to a world of monsters. And it doesn't take long to find out the monsters were all there inside them all along. A little shaky in the knees, they slip on their clothes in the dark and sneak away to Mama or Daddy or some fink husband named Harry. Who'll cuddle, baby them. Croon lullabies and pretend that there aren't any monsters in the real world. Those are only shadows, honey. See I make them with my hands. And pretty soon their little minds heal up more or less and the whole world is cotton candy again and carousel music.

But they don't always want just to get laid.

Being women, they want something more. And being women they want me to leave him or be sent away. They may want that more than anything else, once they get laid a couple of times and get that over with. Well, why not? Why should I think I'm the only one who is right for him? It's the woman in me, crying out in the old woman-language like a cat in the night. Suppose I did get pissed off and leave? Or what if Red threw me out on my ass? The ones I've seen so far, the ones that follow him, would be nothing but bad news for him. Maybe they'd have some money. They usually do. And I don't deny that money could help Red keep going. But they're young and who would he reach for to talk to in the bad, black hours after midnight? Who would understand a word he said to her? There have been times when we lay on the bunk side by side and held hands like a couple of children and talked through until the sun finally decided to come up and chase all the ghosts and monsters home.

I watch out the window of the trailer, standing back a little so I won't be seen, holding the curtains aside with my fingers.

Now he hops in the car with a big easy jump and they drive off slow, just to the edge of the trees, over by those animal cages, where there's some shade. And that's because she's ready to talk, to pour out her guts to him. He's ready to listen. There's nobody who can listen like Red does. And they all want to talk, talk, talk talk! That's the one kind of intercourse they're experts at.

Let him lay her if he feels like it. Let him take her in one of those cages and treat her like she wants and fears to be treated!

The other two, Moses and Cartwright, look at each other, look over here at the trailer but can't see me, then back at each other and shrug. What can they say to each other?

Here they come scuffling along, kicking the dust. I guess they'll start to unpack the truck (which is a job, the way it's packed so tight and neat; we need a new one pretty soon; get her to buy us a new truck, Red; then throw her, bare ass, in a blackberry patch). They'll go ahead and get started just in case he changes his mind and decides to stay here and preach.

Depending on that girl, he may and he may not.

I turn away from the window. The trailer is hot as an oven already. I'll air it out and clean up a little. No, instead I think I'll get all dressed up and go to town. I might even find a store and buy myself a fancy robe – a *peignoir*. Make him eat his words and holler about my wasting all that money. Be worth it for the laugh.

I slip out of the robe and fumble in my suitcase for some underclothes, some nice clean, sassy lingerie. I'll drench myself in perfume so the men will cut their heads to watch me.

But first . . . Like a girl, like a damn fool I have to go look in the mirror. I know what I'm going to see – and it isn't bad at all considering the mileage and the use; in fact, it's kind of a miracle for a beatup woman to look so good. Proves that you can't tell the book by the cover or the package by the wrapping. I could probably find a nice husband and he'd never know he was umpteen hundred in line.

Looking at myself, I feel cold all over. Goosebumps. And the trailer is getting hotter by the minute. What the hell am I looking for? It's all there, just where it was yesterday and will be, God willing, for a little while longer. To tell the truth, I'm not so sure. I don't know what I expect to see. That something had changed suddenly. That every sin, every smile, is now written all over me. Maybe like tattoos. Maybe not like tattoos, but like lines, scars, skin all corrupted and open sores, no nose, rotten with red swollen boils, dripping with pus. I wouldn't be surprised.

Maybe, though, it is something else. Maybe I want a change for the better. To look in the mirror and see a young, thin, shy girl, golden haired, shy as a new moon. The kind who could slip into a satin bridal gown and blush and be pretty while blushing.

I don't know what I want to see.

I don't know what I want.

When he looked at me the last time out there, I didn't see him any more. I don't know who it was, but it wasn't Red. It was a stranger. I was hoping, I guess, that I was the one who had changed and made him change.

Why did he look at me the way he did?

I swear to God I never did anything so dumb in my whole life – to stand in front of a mirror and look at myself.

Why do I love him? It can't be gratitude even though I am grateful but not enough to feel the way I do. Other men have given me more and have done more for me and you can't go around feeling grateful to people and survive. It's all a matter of luck anyway.

I've had my share of luck – good, bad, and no luck. Enough to know it comes and goes and nothing can change that.

He has more than enough faults and failings and I don't, can't envy him. Envy what? All his blind sorrows and blind furies and blind gifts. I do not believe a word of his preaching. I do believe, though, that he is God's crude instrument. I believe that somewhere inside me crouches a naked girl who howls and begs for mercy. She will receive none. She will receive nothing, no gift except a hairy fish wrapped in last week's terrible headlines. I do not believe, yet I do believe that somehow because of him even her howls are holy. I have seen in his eyes sometimes a glimpse, like a flash in a cracked mirror, of what he sees. A reflection of what he sees. Which is only an occasional keyhole view of a garden full of flowers and fountains where all of us are children again and our voices are like birds in spring. I do not believe in this garden and I know that I will never enter into it even if there is any such. But I know he has seen it truly. And I see him. Which is enough.

if I lose him let me die and rot on the frame of my bones

no not die because not believing not seeing not anything still have I seen and known him believed him and never no never can be the same again

so take him or leave him

my heart will mend and break again for hearts are fragile so sweep up the pieces in a dust pan go on living you can live fine without one

will not cry to lose him like a woman a fool a creature of moods and tides and moons

will depart in peace for he has given me what no other man could

I love him it is enough

Somebody is knocking at the trailer door. Through the small window at a distance I see Moses with a box of hymnbooks in his arm. It will be Cartwright up to no good whatever he's up to.

I reach for the bathrobe, then have a second thought. One last glimpse in the mirror a grin and a wink and quick to the door. I jerk it open. He blinks. His knees sag, his eyes pop, his voice is a mumble.

"What's the matter, Hookworm? Ain't you ever seen a girl before?"

I slam the door in his face and leave my laughter to yap at his heels like a dog.

57

2

And when he went forth to land,
there met him out of the city a certain man, which had devils long
time, and ware no clothes, neither
abode in any house, but in tombs.

LUKE VIII, 27

"You probably don't remember the name of the town," I say to him.

"Maybe not," he says, his face not showing anything, blank as a carved mask through which bright eyes peer. It should be a black mask, African, carved out of ebony, but it is white and pale.

"Tell me something," he says. "They told me, but I already forgot. What's the name of this place?"

"High Pines."

"Oh, yeah," he says. "Here's to High Pines. . . ."

And tilts his bottle to drink. He sits beside me, huge in this car, in the skimpy little underpants like panties, with his bottle of whiskey seeming fragile as a wine glass in his large, square, hands. It could be so easily only the end of a crude, cruel practical joke. The joke and last laugh on me. I left John, without a word, asleep in the motel. He will wake up – has woken! My God, that was a week ago – cursing my name, smashing the furniture, the mirror. Then he finds that he has lost nothing, not a penny, not even a credit card, only the girl and her car. In fact he has gained because I didn't even stop to pack. I slipped on my coat and tiptoed out while he lay on the bed like a teddy bear, his mouth wide open. Well, at least he had all the bed for once and woke up to find he had most of my things too.

Now it could end in a joke. Here he sits beside me, a pale Apollo fashioned by Bernini; no, more massive, hewn by Michelangelo from living stone in three dimensions, the Adam of the Sistine Chapel first in paint, now in flesh. I couldn't have even dreamed him this way. I remember only a tall, broad young man, first in a dark suit, later in shirt-sleeves. I remember his voice. Like the deepest of woodwinds and I remember his hands.

He ran across the field toward me laughing, clothed in brightness only and cavorting like a clown. He floated absurdly in the dusty, speckled windshield, blurred even more by the speed. Shouting like a savage. I wanted to run him down and run over him, crushing his bones and spilling his guts and brains on the ground. On and over the other two too, his silly fools, tossing them high and limp like rag dolls. But as he came closer the sound of his laughter sang in my ear, tickled my ears like a pair of tongues. I waked from fury. I knew I could stop just in time.

Now in the shade with him. The blazing field behind and all around the blue mountains like puffs of smoke. So cool, so blue, so light and airy like balloons on a string. I let go of the string. I wink and they go away higher and higher and gone back to the sky. Leaving a world without mountains. Flat as west Texas. Flat and white as driftwood or the bleached skull of a steer.

He looks at me calmly waiting, ready to listen. His eyes brim with light. While I sit here waiting to talk truth, I am alone under spotlights dancing for him, myself shining and free, dancing for joy with no music but the rhythm of my pulse. I am not afraid.

"I want to tell you about it," I say. "I was very sick, sick to death and you healed me."

"What was wrong with you?" he says.

"Oh, they said it was *psychological*, meaning, I guess, it was all in my head and could be cured by pills or electric shock or rest or analysis or what have you. I had given up any hope of ever being healed."

"And I healed you?"

"Yes. . . ."

His large broad brow wrinkles. He wonders.

"It's really very simple," I say. "The doctor called it a classic case."

"How did it begin?"

"Let's begin with the house," I say. "The biggest house in town. Call it my mother's house. Everything in it was hers. Even my father's pipes, his slippers. Everything she ever touched turned into something of hers the way Midas touched and turned everything to gold. The house smelled of her, clean and sickly sweet. Like dying roses. Even the potted plants bowed to her or she cut off their heads. My father lived there, too, of course. A guest, a transient, a small, delicate shadow moving quietly, carefully, on tiptoes so as not to chip or break anything.

"I was an only child. You might call it a sheltered life except there was neither shelter nor sanctuary. It was a prison with my mother the warden. A spell cast by my mother, the wicked witch from a fairy tale. I slept. She kept me under glass, under a vacuum bell the way she preserved her bridal bouquet. It sat on the polished top of the piano. Flowers never fading, but never, except once, real. Maybe they never even slapped me when I was born. I only know I had to learn how to breathe.

"Of course I played games, went to parties and church and school. But somehow none of that was real. I passed among others, friends and enemies and strangers, exactly the way my father moved among the clutter, the neat clutter of bric-a-brac and the potted plants.

"Then there was a springtime in me. I began to change into a woman. I felt a new tingle in my veins, heard new sounds and noises. For the first time I began to listen to words. I had understood them but never heard. Now I heard the babble of a strange, foreign tongue. I was charmed and delighted. The scales fell away from my eyes and I began to look. Everything was new and strange, like digging for China in the back yard and suddenly poking a hole through and *being there* among pagodas and rice paddies and funny hats. And everything was good. I was all so good . . ."

Up goes the swing and down again a girl stands in it a little girl in a white party dress in pig-tails tied with a ribbon

high she goes up and swift comes down it is Clytie pushing me in the backyard swing swing goes up up up and oh oh again down

Clytie catches stops the swing I don't want to stop but she promises to push again and now with quick black gentle fingers undoes my braids fluffs out my hair free & gives the swing a push another another begins

up up up oh ah down again sky is blue grass is green   I am all white Clytie all black except for pink of her palms

breeze in hair   leaves on trees in the breeze whisper my name to each other I will dive up in the sky in the cool bright blue pool sky & sink to bottom of it drown forever & ever be dragged down white in my white dress wrapped in gold of golden hair my hair is red   in the sky it will turn gold

up up up & oh ah now now I step out into air & dive for the deep sky   see the little girl fall to the ground while I fly away fall into the sky numb because it is so cold   she cries out in fear but I cry for joy

while I drown in daze of blue hear Clytie speaking to the little girl dropped and left behind like a doll I am tired of

child child oh Lord what did you do why child did you have to do that what child did you do to yourself naughty doll won't answer

doesn't know how to talk   come then footsteps running shouting & crying footsteps shouting ambulance screaming rubber swish swish of nurse's shoes rattle trays glasses little bottles somewhere phone ringing

ringing voice calling calling monotonous crackle of loudspeaker rattle
of wheels the child wakes screams stabbed with needles sleeps again
wakes to white white nurses white doctors white sheets to cry out
where is Clytie I want Clytie Clytie is black & I am blue   I am all
blue because I was thirsty & drank up the sky it's my fault everything
is white

He waits for me to go on. I can't. He senses that. He knows I
have lost my place. Find my place for me and I will tell you
everything.

"How were you really hurt?" he says.

"In town there were two kinds of people, nice people and
Trash. The Trash came from the little shacks at the edge of
town, no different from and sometimes mixed among the
Negro shacks. Or else they came in from the country in dusty
yellow school buses. And they wore funny clothes, hand-me-
downs, castaways, charity. They never ate in the lunch room.
They brought their food in paper bags. They ate outside together at tables in the schoolyard in the part we never went to.
The boys were mostly barefoot and the girls wore funny shapeless dresses or else tight sweaters and lipstick early and rouge
and dimestore perfume. They all smelled bad if you sat next to
them in class and nobody would, but that time I wanted to and
did.

"One day I followed a gang of them home, boys, and girls,
living on the edge of town. I never thought about them noticing me or paying any attention to me. You know sometimes I
put on dark glasses and I'm convinced that no one can see me.
It's like being invisible.

"I followed them. They waited for me. In front of a burnt
out filling station with fields on both sides. They were all
around me in a ring.

" 'What are you following us for?'

" 'I don't know,' I said. 'I just want to see where you go.'

"They looked at each other, surprised. Then one of the girls, a fat ugly girl named Ida, I'll never forget that, laughed.

" 'You,' she said. 'What's your name?'

" 'Judith.'

" 'Let's show Judith where we go after school.'

"They pushed me into the filling station. There was nothing inside, burnt walls, charred ceiling with afternoon sun falling in beams through the holes, and a dirty floor.

" 'What you going to do, Ida?' one of them said.

" 'Wait and see . . .'

"She came close to me. Her face was full of hate. I wasn't afraid. She never knew that. Right then I wasn't afraid of anything. She touched my hair and my dress.

" 'You look so pretty,' she said. Then to the others: 'Ain't she about the prettiest little girl you ever seen?'

" 'Damn sight prettier than you, Ida,' one of the boys said and some of them laughed.

"The hate in her face and the envy was fear. She lashed out, pushed and I fell down and then she straddled across me, holding me down, pinning my shoulders with her knees. . . ." *

heavy she's so heavy a soft lump made of flour dough she breathes hard   see the blackheads on her nose all over round dough face with little pig eyes gritted teeth like a dog's red lips rosy red smeared with lipstick but never pretty no never pretty poor ugly girl fat ugly girl

see blackheads all over her nose you couldn't count them heavy & soft knees digging face close to mine yelling come on girls what are you waiting on   let's see what she's got that we ain't

"Did they hurt you?" he asks.

"No," I say, "They didn't hurt me. They didn't mean to do that. They wanted to tease me, to shame me I guess. . . ."

hands unseen grab my ankles holding them down   Ida crumples a brown paper bag in a ball & shoves in my mouth so I can't talk or yell for help   I gag & feel skirt flip back high then quick fingers yanks at my panties down yank my pants & over my ankles gone   it's quiet my legs are cool & bare

Ida twists is twisting turns back & says don't just stand there boys come have a look see if she's so special see has it got mink around it then back she looks with a smile no longer hate but pleasure akin to love

the pleasure is hers poor fat ugly Ida's   read in her eyes bright with excitement she dreams we trade places dreams it is she they'd want to see her thighs squeeze she rocks on my shoulders   hurt now I'd cry out but can't   eyes filmed with tears Ida is melting made out of wax

"Did they shame you? Were you ashamed?"
"No," I say. "I should have been but I wasn't. . . ."

hear girl giggle they must be coming one by one to look   boys barefeet soft on the floor then touch tentative gentle a brush against soft down I shiver

this will be all I don't have to be afraid it's like playing doctor we played in the backyard he was the doctor my cousin & got a whipping

touch there the first   I shudder not from fear I see Ida's face above mine mirrors my shudders but eyes are closed   lips are tight she bites her lips & shudders with each touch more   I think she will faint I may faint if they don't stop now   now they stop her eyes are open

Roy she says now's your chance you're always talking a boy's voice says we better go

I close my eyes hear Ida saying pleading she's feeble-minded can't

67

*you see that don't worry she don't even know & I would laugh if I
could but paper in my mouth a boy's voice saying we better get the hell
out here don't you know her daddy's a judge   I feel her weight gone
& hear them running away*

*poor daddy save me I guess they were afraid of you they are gone all
gone thank you daddy   though I was not am not afraid*

*I brush off my clothes walk home slowly the way I came stopping
once to watch a boy fly a kite I run the water in the tub at home &
suddenly laugh remembering they ran away so fast they forgot to give
back my pants*

"So you didn't tell on them?"

"There was nothing to tell. And if I told them, Mama and
Daddy, and I told the truth, I'd be ashamed. They'd make me
ashamed. I would have to confess it was dirty and if I did that it
would mean I was dirty too."

"And you didn't feel guilty?"

"No," I say, "not yet. I didn't know what being guilty was.
Oh, but I learned, though! Didn't I learn about guilt!"

"We always do," he says. "That's one thing we're bound to
learn."

A voice like deepest woodwinds, eyes like springwater, hair
of a ram, body of a statue and a smile like no other I have ever
seen.

CARTWRIGHT

That freaking Moses is going to kill me unloading the truck and
we don't even know if he's going to even preach here. Probably
not. He'll get a wild hair to be moving on and we'll have to
pack up everything again in a hell of a hurry and roll.

Moses is bent over one of the footlockers fumbling for something. I get an idea, a inspiration and step up next to him.

"Gimme the glasses," I say.

"What glasses?"

"You known, them field glasses."

He hands them to me, a set of U.S. Army surplus field glasses with a strap too you can hang around your neck. I slip the strap over my neck and raise the glasses, fiddling with the focus.

Two round foggy circles and then the two of them in the car across the field caught clear in the two circles, now one circle brightly clear. Red isn't sitting too close to her (course you can't get very far apart in one of them bugs either). He's leaning back, his big arm dangling over the side of the car, his hand loose and slack, relaxed. Just listening. He won't hardly listen to me at all even when it's important.

She's talking away a mile a minute. Talks like she drives I guess. I can see her red hair, brighter than Red's, and her suntanned face with eyes that look like black burnt holes at this distance on account of all that gunk she's got around them. She's still got on that black raincoat, buttoned all the way up to the top.

Wonder what she's got on under it? I knew a girl one time used to wear a big old long cloth coat and she didn't wear stitch one under it. You never know. But it do give you something to think about.

It must be mighty interesting or Red wouldn't be bothering to listen. I mean, it ain't like he was on duty or something. He's on his own time and he could be sleeping.

I don't know what I've been thinking about. That little old girl is crazy, that's what. (Red always does like to talk to crazy people). It would take a crazy person to drive a car like that. It don't take no genius to put two and two together and figure out she's crazy as a jailhouse bedbug and got herself a case of the hot pants. People say a drunk woman is heaven in the bed. A crazy one's even better sometimes. First time I ever got any was off of a old crazy girl back of the freight yard down home. Spoiled me for a long time, it was so good. She just lay back singing "Yes, Jesus Loves Me" the whole time and I still can't hear the little kids sing that song without having to bite my lips to keep from laughing. Like you get with a girl and maybe you call one song or another they're playing on the radio or the juke box "your song". "Jesus Loves Me," that was our song.

Red may listen, but he can't do nothing about it because Miami ain't going to let him. She'll cut his throat from ear to ear. Or, what's worse, she'll take off and take her car with her (cause it's still registered in her name; she may be dumb but she's smart enough for that). That would leave us with nothing but that beat up old truck that's got troubles enough hauling itself around without trying to pull the trailer too. And that little blue bug, she may make aplenty of noise and go like the wind, but she ain't up to pulling no kind of a load. What I mean is, Miami, she will tolerate them girls down in Galveston on account of it's their business. They're real professionals. But no little chicken that runs around the country in a blue bug wide open and hell bent for trouble has got a chance.

Moses is out of the running. He's ugly as sin, but, you know, he's got what some people call a soulful look. To me he just looks constipated and maybe he is most of the time. Keeps a whole box full of all kinds of pills and things. Some days he gobbles them pills like peanuts.

The long and the short of it is there's only one candidate around here available to take care of the crazy girl in the blue bug. If she's got problems, old Hookworm is just the doctor. He's got the remedy.

"Look out!" I holler coming up off the ground like a rocket blasting off.

I turn around quick and mad too, expecting to see Moses, but there stands Miami laughing fit to kill. If it had've been Moses I was all set to punch him in the mouth. If it wasn't for Red and the fact that I am a gentleman I'd punch her in the mouth right now. Everybody knows how goosey I am and it ain't funny a damn bit.

Miami is all dressed up, I mean, looking really good. She can look like somebody when she gets fixed up. She's got that expensive perfume on too. She won't wear cheap stuff when it comes to perfume, only the best. And she's right too. The good stuff works, it gets to a man and stays with him a while. You can remember a good perfume.

"See anything interesting?"

"Miami," I say to her serious, "how come you always got to tease me?"

She smiles at me and gives me a friendly pat.

"I tease you cause I like you," she says.

I got to give that some thought. I mean, a woman that picks on you and teases all the time, she might still be teasing right now.

"That's news to me," I say.

"Shame on you," she says smiling, stepping up real close so our two noses just about touch and bumping me with her boobies. "Shame on you," she says all kind of whispery, breathing right on me and her breath smells sweet too like she done *gargled* with perfume. "I always thought you liked me too."

Something funny is going on around here this morning. Everything's crazy as hell. I cut my eyes and see Moses has stopped what he was doing and is just standing watching us with his pokerface, mopping his brow with a folded handkerchief. Why don't he just get hiself a sponge? Be a whole lot cheaper . . .

"Cat got your tongue?" she says, flicking her tongue quick between her teeth like a little red wet snake.

"What do you want?" I say.

She makes a pout and steps away from me, opens her purse and her compact and looks at herself in the little mirror.

"You sure do look good, Miami," I say, trying to make up in case I said the wrong thing. "You look like a million dollars."

That must be the right thing to say for once because she pops that compact closed and looks up at me with the nicest smile she ever give me.

"Where are you going?"

That's Moses for you. He's got to know what's going on every minute.

"Nowhere special," Miami says. "I just got a little shopping to do and I thought maybe I'd go sit in an air-conditioned movie for a while if they've got one. Anybody want to go see a movie?"

"We've got a lot of work to do," Moses says.

"How about you?" she says to me.

Now I know something crazy is going on. She knows how I like the movies. I'd rather sit and watch a movie than almost anything else you can name (not including, of course, *that*). But I happen to recall that Miami don't care nothing about the movies.

"I thought you don't like picture shows."

"I can take them or leave them," she says. "But the idea of sitting in a cool place is just about like heaven right now. Besides . . ." (and here she lowers her voice way down soft where Moses can't hear) "I've got some things to talk to you about."

Cartwright, you may be crazy as hell. I mean, you may be letting your first and last chance slip by. You may be pulling

72

the chain and flushing chances right down the drain. If you had any sense, you wouldn't even stop to think about nothing. Just go, boy, go! You'll never figure out women anyway. There ain't no way. Life's too short. If a chance comes along, grab it like it might be your last one because you never know. But I've known Miami too long and this just ain't right.

"I guess I better stay here and help Moses," I say.

She makes another little pout, but it just kind of interrupts that smile. Then she turns to Moses.

"You boys really think Big Red's going to change his mind?"

I take a look over towards the car hearing Moses say "You never know . . ."

Then she is standing right behind me, flush up against me. I smell that perfume and her hands come over my shoulders and lift up the field glasses. She moves her head just alongside of mine, almost cheek to cheek with her hair brushing against me and looks through the glasses, kind of resting on my shoulder. I can't explain why – maybe it's the same reason I'm goosey, just born that way – but when a woman comes up behind me like that, it drives me wild.

"I don't believe he's going to preach tonight. He won't be able to. He's going to be all worn out from listening."

She lets the glasses go, but gently so they won't pull the strap around my neck and, casual as you please, with her right hand where Moses can't see it, she lets that hand keep right on going down past my belt, down the length of my fly with a kind of a little pinch-squeeze-flick and then gone as she turns away toward the car and *oh Jesus*! I like to have done it right in my pants. She knows, Lord Save us, that Miami knows everything there is about the weakness of a man. You could hate her for it if it didn't feel so good.

"Bye, boys," she says. "Bye-bye, see you later."

73

With a voice like a young girl's, all sing-song and tra-la-la.

I turn my head to watch her go. (I can't turn around for a minute anyway because old Moses will see the state I'm in and laugh. I can't help it. Nobody could. It's *bio-logical* and bigger than me. But Moses would laugh anyway. That's the way he is.) I watch her, swinging her purse, walk to the car and step in. My heart flies up like a dove because I believe she has the most beautiful ass in creation. She hops in the car and turns on the engine, then looks back and smiles, waving her hand. And she's gone with a "see you later" tossed over her shoulder at us.

I take a deep breath and think of cold water, a ice cold mountain stream you jump into and come up blue and out of breath and all shrunk and shrivelled up. My old scoutmaster (I was a Eagle Scout, believe it or not; I can prove it, though; I've got my merit badges right in the bottom of my footlocker in the trailer) he always used to read us that part in the *Boy Scouts Handbook* where it says try not to think about it, but if you just *can't help thinking about it,* then get plenty of exercise and cold showers. Only trouble is there ain't always a cold shower handy. So I use the power of my mind. I concentrate real hard and think about jumping into a ice-cold mountain stream and it works most of the time unless you get tempted right quick again.

Works like a charm this time and I turn around and look at old Moses. He's still got a sad pokerface, but he gives me a shrug of the shoulders. He can shrug like nobody else I ever seen.

JUDITH

"I was still too green, the world was too new and shiny. I could no more conceive of guilt than a child who hasn't been burned can know how a live flame feels. My mother trained me for the

74

practical things like fire. When I was still a toddler she took my hand and put it right in the flame of the gas stove and held it, only a flash of a second, but enough so I thought she might never let go.

"'That's fire, child,' she said, gripping my mouth with her fingers, so I couldn't scream and drown out what she had to say. 'That was how fire feels. Keep away from it.'

"And I did too, out of fear and in knowledge. I'll give her the credit for that. Still, there was something else, something subtle and strange at the heart of my fear. I remember there was a kind of fascination, too, with all flames and fires. I remember how one time I wanted to burn up the garage. They kept old newspapers and cartons stocked in the garage and I took some matches and tried to start a fire. Lucky for me, Clytie caught me. She wasn't even mad. She just took away the matches.

" 'Lord, Lord, Lord, child,' she said. 'Ain't you a mess? Looks like I got to watch you every minute.'

"Then she took me by the hand and led me back to the kitchen and gave me some cookies or candy or something even though my mother didn't approve of eating between meals, especially sweets. That made it a secret between the two of us. I knew when she poured out a glass of milk for me and gave me the cookies that she wouldn't tell on me about the garage and she was proving it to me that way without saying a word.

"So I didn't tell on them that time. I had a nice hot bath and felt good about it. Proud in a way, as if I had passed the initiation to some secret club. And the next day after that I got Clytie to make me a lunch and put it in a paper bag. I used my lunch money to buy candy bars for them. At lunch time I went out and sat down at the table right beside them. They were afraid I was going to tell and get them in trouble, but when I passed out the candy bars they knew I wouldn't. Poor Ida, I

75

knew she'd love candy and there were tears in her eyes when she took her candy bar. She was my friend after that, as much as she could ever be friends with anyone. They all accepted me – maybe not as one of them but anyway not against them. Except Roy. He was the one who knew about Daddy being the judge. He was the one who had scared them away. So he had nothing to be afraid of, no reason to be beholden to me. Everyday I brought him a candy bar too. And everyday he left it sitting on the table, to melt for all he cared. (Ida would usually end up eating it.) At first I thought he was just proud, but then it began to dawn on me that he was ashamed of something. None of the others were ashamed, only afraid. But he was ashamed and I was making him feel ashamed. So I stopped offering him a candy bar. (I always had one for him with me in case, he asked, but I stopped offering it to him.)

"One day at lunchtime he was waiting for me by the door when I came out. I smiled at him.

" 'I got to talk to you,' he said. 'I got something to say.'

"I walked over under the shade of a tree far enough away from the tables and the others so no one could hear. I leaned back against the tree and looked at him and waited. He was a great big hulking boy with hands like hams and he never knew what to do with them. When he was nervous or shy or awkward he would stand there and crack his knuckles. He stood there in front of me, not wanting to look me in the eyes, kicking at clods of dust, and cracking his knuckles.

" 'All right,' he said finally. 'I'm the one that did it.'

" 'Did what?'

"Stumbling, awkward, painful: 'I'm the one that swiped your panties' (Then quickly) 'Don't nobody know but me. Nobody saw me and I ain't told a soul.'

76

" 'Thank you for telling me,' I said. 'I wondered what happened to them. (Trying not to laugh right out loud) 'What did you do with them?

" 'I got them right here,' he said, patting a bulge in the pocket of his levis and it crinkled with a sound of tissue paper. *"He had them all wrapped up in tissue paper!"*

I see him start to laugh, a ripple of the beginning of a laugh along the corded neck and I touch his hand.

"Wait," I say. "That's not the best part."

" 'You can have them back if you want them,' Roy said.

"He said he had washed them himself with Camay face soap he bought at the drugstore. They were all clean and he hadn't even touched them again. He wrapped them up in tissue paper and he was ready to give them back.

" 'I don't want them back,' I said.

"And I could see he felt worse than ever. So I told him I had quit wearing them after that day because it felt good without them and it didn't seem worth the trouble of putting them on if people were just going to come along like that and yank them off again."

"That was the woman in you," he says. "The woman taking over in command."

"It was pretty mean," I say. "I didn't want to hurt or embarrass him, but I couldn't help it. And he blushed, I swear I made him blush and he couldn't look at me anymore."

"A woman is born with a sense of irony," he says to me. "A man has to learn it."

"So I told him I wanted him to do me a favour, just like the knights of old in the history book. I wanted him to keep them for me, to carry them always just like that, wrapped up in tissue paper and clean. That they were our secret and he must never tell anyone or touch them again or else I would make him give

77

them back. He didn't laugh or anything. He just looked right at me and said it would be a privilege.

" 'One more thing,' he said. 'I reckon I'll take a candy bar now if you got one for me.' "

Now he cannot control himself any longer. He laughs so hard he grabs the sides of his waist to hold himself together. And I explode with laughter too, letting it all go. Out of control I lean against the horn and, never mind the blast of it, we laugh together wildly.

MOSES

I am trying to work without benefit of Cartwright aid when the sound of that horn makes me jump and twitch like a rabbit.

"Slow down, Moses," Cartwright says. "You may have a heart attack or something."

"Give me a hand, will you?" I say. "We have a lot to do to get ready."

"He ain't going to preach."

"Maybe he will change his mind."

I bend over the footlocker trying to sort out the mess. He comes over and finds the field glasses. I don't know why we need those field glasses or what on earth we can use them for. But he talked Red into getting them and I guess we're stuck with them.

"What do we need those for?"

"Birdwatching," he says.

Well, Red must be having a time, listening to that girl. He likes to listen to the wild ones, the mad ones, the lost ones, And it's part of his job. How else can he learn? Which is why he listens. He's always looking and listening even when he's talking. He wants to know. Maybe that's the power that keeps his gift alive. He will not let his mind set like concrete. He is all questions, always questioning, storing it all up deep the way a poet or an artist does.

Here comes Miami out of the trailer. She's got on her best dress, her sexiest outfit, looking for trouble. Which is exactly what I've been afraid of all morning. Trouble we've got enough of. More trouble we don't need. I look at her hoping she'll read the "please don't" in my eyes, but she winks and sneaks up behind Cartwright and gives him a goose that would raise a hippo off the ground.

When he whirls around he's face to face with Miami. He literally sags in the knees.

"How's the birdwatching?" she says.

"Why do you have to tease me all the time?" he says.

"I like you," she says. "Didn't you know that?"

Maybe she's made up her mind to leave. In which case Cartwright has always been part of at least one plan. Or maybe she's ready to go now. That dangling purse may be crammed with money. She hops in the car and drives away for good and all. But she would have to open the safe. Which would put me in a hell of a spot, as the only one here, who officially knows the combination. It's no defence to say that a woman like Miami couldn't share a trailer with any safe in the world for a week and not know the combination. If she never opens it, still I know that she knows and could open it as easily as a bicycle lock.

She has opened her purse now and stands checking herself in her compact mirror.

"Where are you planning to go?" I say.

Pop shut goes the compact and she flashes me a look. *Don't worry, I've got plans all right,* the look says, *but you'll know when the time comes. I owe you that much.* Meanwhile chattering along about window shopping and maybe the movies, knowing that Cartwright would give his soul to go to the movies, especially with her; and knowing he can't, won't, wouldn't dare. But doing it well, doing it nicely. He may be suspicious. But he hasn't got the sensitivity to detect the cruelty she has. He can't, locked in a mad world where all women are flowers, a garden of nudes in the sun, a dream of that garden, high-walled with himself the sole proprietor and gardener and not even a bee can sniff or a bird nest in their hair without his permission, a childish, happy, tawdry dream, he isn't able, so self-crippled by his own illusions, to use his mind and see her in abstraction, sexless, another human being, a soul, a mystery to be reckoned with. He's lost, I'm relieved. Whatever she's up to includes him and includes me, but later, not now.

Virtuoso always, she borrows the glasses and standing behind him, leaning against him, looks at the car and Red and the girl in the shade. Poor Cartwright, such indignity, such swelling and groaning he must endure till the day he dies. A puppet not only of any woman who touches him, but a puppet of his own glands, led like an ox with a ring in his nose by a few shabby inches, less than a pound of flesh. His only salvation would have been, long ago, a life in rags on the burning desert, a bed of nails and the sun to stare at until his eyes went blind and rotted out. It's too late now. Take him as comic, you can hardly help it. Or see him as pathetic, the archetype of the folly of being a man, a folly that offends so because all of us share it.

Thinking of Cartwright, I always remember something from the *Symposium*, the crude little myth Aristophanes tells to explain the origin of human love and desire. That once we were whole, neither men or women, sexless and happy, one creature. Until the gods punished man for some disobedience or pride by tearing him in two. We became two separate parts as if cut in half, each incomplete without the other. And then the gods laughed, the laughing white gods lounging in nude and ideal beauty against the splendid theatrical backdrop of Olympus. They laughed and will laugh still till the end of the world as these fumbling, grotesque, amputated creatures, stumble through days and nights in vain seeking their lost other halves, meanwhile condemned to be freaks, monstrosities, fools. Condemned to the blind and burning impulse without knowing why or what for, only able to give it a name while they burn. And able, of course, gifted with just enough fragments of broken Truth, to delude and deceive themselves. To wander a lifetime through a hall of mirrors, not like Versailles and the strut of powdered and elegant charms, but naked in a Glasshouse, like one in an amusement park, where you see yourself in so many poses, fat and thin, short and tall, but never truly, until in the end, frantic you run from mirror to mirror and see only a shiver of lewd poses flash past like the face cards of a gambler's shuffled deck!

See Cartwright and you can believe in those gods and almost hear the cruel continual music of their laughter. He, too, must hear it constantly but, like poor Caliban, he cannot give it a name.

Then away she goes with a fine handsome strut and a bye-bye for both of us. My God, what a woman! You can believe every fairy tale you ever read. She's witches and wicked stepmothers and cruel stepsisters and always, too, Cinderella, Sleeping Beauty, the enchanted helpless Princess to whom, alas, no charming Prince will ever come.

She drives away and after a moment Cartwright turns to me like a living, animated question mark.

What can I do? What can I say to him?

I shrug.

He says nothing, only smiles and nods for me to go on. I see myself with wonder now, as if I were a wooden dummy sitting in my own lap and clacking words. Why do I do this? Layer by layer to peel away oneself. It hurts, but his smile, the bright eyes in the mask, tell me he knows that it hurts and knows about pain. He is here beside me. I am helpless anyway.

"Began not even then but before that, somewhere long before even memory. In the first shriek of my birth or before that even. Maybe when the little, twitchy tadpole of sperm shot out, fired like a circus acrobat out of the cannon and found the fertile egg. You can go back before then to Daddy and Mama, young and burning, beyond that even, back through generations, a wilderness from which strangers glare back, back, back . . ."

"To Adam and Eve," he says quietly. "Where it began and ended for all of us."

He looks away from me, squinting across the bright field toward the trailer. I look too and see the woman come out of the trailer. She wears a red dress. She teeters on high heels. She is talking to the other two.

Then he looks back to me, his face calm, all his attention for me. He nods and I go on, impelled.

"And then, then suddenly it was summer. School was over and that was all over for me. I was tired of everything. We were going away to the beach later on and that would be fun. So I spent the lazy days of June in the Library reading. I read everything I could because books were all new too. They were beginning to mean something that summer, to be about something."

I hear the car drive off and see she is driving it away, but he has never taken his eyes off me.

"There was a boy who lived on the same block we did. Edgar was a nice boy, very sweet and thoughtful. Polite to grownups and very correct, but shy. At dancing class he would always dance with you at least once. His palms sweated when he danced. I cannot tell how much that disgusted me or why it did. But it did. He was fat and pale and wore thick glasses and was terribly intense.

"That summer Edgar was at the Library too, reading and studying to prepare for his College Board Exams, he said. He'd usually walk home with me in the afternoon. We talked about schoolwork and books and things. It was nice to have company and nice to have somebody to carry my books, that's all. There were two or three different ways to walk home from the Library and we'd try one on one day and another the next. One way to go passed by a park where we all used to play when we were little.

" 'Let's look at the park,' he said one day.

" 'Why?'

" 'Just to do something different,' he said.

"So we walked in the park and looked at the swings and the see-saws. They seemed so small now, the way things are when you come back to them after a long time, smaller and kind of sad. But I was happy and I let him push me in the swing awhile.

" 'Let's go look at the old haunted house,' he said.

"At the edge of the park was an old house we had always called 'haunted'. An old lady lived there alone for years and nobody except the maid ever saw her. She died and the house was empty and slowly falling down. She had lots of plants and shrubs, some of them from as far away as India and China,

83

strange, beautiful plants. When she died, they grew wild in a jungle all around the place. It was all green and dark and shadowy. When we were little, playing in the park we used to sneak up as close to the house as we dared and then always run away yelling because someone would say they saw the ghost of the white-haired terrible old woman looking at us from a window.

" Edgar dared me to go inside.

" 'Don't be silly,' I said. 'There's nothing inside that old house.'

" 'I dare you,' he said.

"That always worked with me, a dare. They could dare me to do anything, once upon a time, even things the boys wouldn't do, and I'd do it. So we went in and it was just a dusty place, empty except for a few broken things that might have been hers or somebody else's. I looked around and felt sad. Our wonderful haunted house wasn't haunted at all. There weren't any ghosts left in the world. I think I would have been happy if only the old lady had come running down the stairs cursing us and shaking her cane in a rage.

"I remember I picked up a piece of broken glass, a piece of a mirror, all tarnished and dusty. I looked at myself to see how sad I could look, to see if I looked sad enough to cry. Could I just cry if I wanted to for all sad things? Edgar's face was in the glass too. He looked sad, too, but it was hard to tell because he had taken off his glasses and without them he had to squint and strain to see.

" 'What's the matter, Edgar?'

" 'Nothing, I just . . .'

" 'Did you lose your glasses?'

" 'No, . . . I took them off.'

" 'Why?'

84

" 'I can't kiss with my glasses on,' he said, still looking sad.

" 'Are you going to kiss somebody?'

" 'I love you, Judith,' he said. 'Kiss me.'

"Then he closed his eyes completely and puckered his lips and I couldn't help laughing even if it hurt his feelings.

"He stood there pouting like a spoiled baby. I thought he was about to cry. I didn't want to have to see that, so I hugged him and gave him a peck on the cheek.

"That was enough, I guess, more than he hoped for, because he smiled again and put on his glasses.

" 'I really love you,' he said. 'You have no idea how much I love you.'

" 'I'm glad,' I said.

" 'I suffer,' he said. 'I can't get to sleep. Sometimes I see the light in your window late at night when you're reading or something. . . .'

" 'Do you *spy* on me, Edgar?' I said, only teasing.

" 'Oh, no,' he said. 'I wouldn't do something like that. But I see the light and I think of you up there. I think of you and I ache and I can't go to sleep.'

" 'I'm sorry if I've caused you aches and pains.'

· " 'We have lots of things in common,' he said. 'We both like books and things.'

" 'It's getting late,' I said. 'We'd better go home.'

" 'Don't you even love me a little?'

" 'I'll have to think about it,' I said.

"That seemed to suit him fine. He picked up my books and we went home."

Now he laughs at that and it's funny all right. But it stops being funny. Maybe he knows it's the last time he'll have a chance to laugh at my story.

It's lunchtime and the store's pretty quiet right now. I'm thinking about maybe going out now myself and having a good lunch. Fellow gets to a certain age and three good meals a day is about all he's got to look for.

I am just coming out of my office, when I see the woman walk in, a woman in a red dress and really stacked, built and put together like you don't see them often. I can see that much clean across the store without even going back for my glasses. Which, as usual, I forgot. You can tell by the way that they walk, the way they can walk a race horse past you and if you got any feeling and experience you just know whether that horse can run or not. It's in the way she's built and the way she walks. Ten years maybe since I seen any woman walk like that.

It's a crying shame to see it all wasted on Mr Percy. He comes up to her knowing enough to put out his friendliest greeting and I can tell the way she's standing she had him zeroed in before he said a word.

Now they come down the rack of the summer dresses, the first class merchandise. She takes one off the rack and holds it up to her chin and looks at Mr Percy. He's nodding and smiling as well he might. That's a easy customer to please. She looks good in anything or nothing and she knows it. They ain't made nothing in her size yet she won't look good in. She'd stir up folks dressed in black as a widow.

Hold on Howie. Get ahold of yourself. You're a big boy now. You don't want to have a stroke or something before you have lunch. Don't just keel over dead on a empty stomach.

She's going back to try on the dress and Mr Percy, he's got a armload of dresses she's pulled off the rack.

I go back in the office to get my glasses. But I don't put them on. I know I've seen that woman someplace before. I can't remember where it was . . . (must be getting senile too) . . . but with or without my glasses. But where would it be and when?

I know I never spoke to her or she to me. I'd sure as hell remember that. I never forget something like that. Where was it . . .?

I sit there raking the ashes of my brain and coming up with nothing at all. . . .

A while goes by, *must* have gone by, with me just thinking and trying to remember, when here comes Mr Percy swishing in the office and waving dollar bills in my face.

"Five dresses!" he says. "The lady bought five dresses just like that, cash sale!"

"That's nice, Mr Percy."

"Nice?" he says, puffing up with pride and righteous indignation.

I hate to always be the one to disillusion Mr Percy about his charm and talent for salesmanship. When that lady came in, she was intent on blowing her money, her own or somebody else's (more likely the latter) on the first things that caught her eye. The plain truth being that old Percy couldn't give her the stuff if she hadn't already made up her mind.

"Anything else? Did you sell her anything else?"

"Well!" he says, huffy as a old maid. "She almost bought the robe."

"What robe is that?"

"The gold lamé one," he says, "you know the one that's snug in the waist and then kind of falls in an elegant line like this . . ."

I wish to hell I had a picture of Mr Percy when he talks about ladies' clothes. He gets so enthusiastic. You can almost see him in whatever it is. If I had the energy, I'd sell the store and just manage him. Book him into nightclubs and just let him stand up and describe women's clothes. Funniest thing since Will Rogers. I could die rich on ten percent of that.

"That thing's been hanging around here for years," I say. "Who ordered it anyway? Did you?"

"No, sir, I did not. I certainly know better than to order a thing of beauty like that for *High Pines*."

"What are we asking for it?"

"Cost," he says. "Two hundred dollars."

I whistle through my false teeth.

"You mean to stand there and tell me, Mr Percy, tell me with a straight face we got a item of clothing just hanging out there on the rack in the store that *cost us* two hundred dollars?"

"I don't take any responsibility for it," Percy says.

"Didn't you even try to bargain with the lady? That's half the fun, Mr Percy, the bargain. Don't you like your job? Don't you *want* to have fun?"

"Mr Loomis, you are perfectly aware that when an item of merchandise is reduced to cost, I haven't got the authority to . . ."

"Is the lady gone yet?"

"I don't know," he says. "They were wrapping the packages . . ."

"Don't stand there like a nanny goat! Go get her and bring me the robe . . .!"

He's gone. That's one good thing about Mr Percy. You yell at him loud enough and he responds. He responds very well once he's broke in good. His mother, of course, she don't do nothing but yell at him. But she can't help it. The old lady's been deaf as a gatepost for years.

I open up the desk drawer and reach for the box of cigars I

save for salesmen and special customers. No, I ain't going to offer her one. I'm fixing to smoke one myself, first one in a week or ten days. On account of this is a special occasion. Doctor's order or no, you only live once.

I get it lit good and here comes Mr Percy, bowing her in, carrying the robe in his hands. I stand up, pull in my gut, and shake hands with her.

"How do, m'am, I'm Howie Loomis, the owner. Won't you have a seat?"

I turn and take the robe from Percy.

"Thank you, Mr Percy. That'll be all."

That really burns him up because if there's one thing he wants to know it's how much or how little I'm fixing to give it away for. And, know something? Percy ain't ever going to know. I'm going to die without telling him. From the look on his face as he goes out, I reckon he suspects it too.

I toss the robe across the top of the desk where the light can catch it good. A real fine piece of merchandise all right. She don't even cut her head toward the robe when I toss it. She's got a blank face, cautious but not worried, calm caution you'd have to say, and she keeps her eyes on me. I take a puff on my cigar, I smile and sit down behind my desk.

"I hope you don't mind my smoking a cigar," I say.

"I've smelled a cigar before."

Flat, monotone. Tough. I wouldn't want to get in a card game with this one, not if you was playing for anything real.

"Well now," I say, "we're mighty pleased to have your business, Miss . . . Excuse me, I didn't get your name."

"I didn't say my name."

"Well now, we're just mighty pleased. Are you going to be with us long, here in High Pines?"

"I don't know."

"I was going to suggest, if you was planning to be in town any length of time, you might be interested in one of our charge accounts."

"I usually pay cash," she says.

"That's fine, but you got to admit it's kind of unusual in this day and age, the age of the credit card. Looka here . . ."

I whip out my wallet and dangle a long row of credit cards like the flags on the mast of a ship.

"Isn't that nice?" she says. "You've got all kinds of credit."

I'll be a monkey's uncle if I'm going to miss my lunch and smoke a cigar and everything and then let Percy have the last laugh on me for the first time in his life. This woman is walking out of here with that robe if I have to give it to her. Hell, I may end up paying her to take it off my hands.

"Mr Percy tells me that you like this robe."

"It's too expensive."

"I don't see why we can't work out something."

"Look," she says irritably. "I come in your crummy hick store and I buy five dresses right off the rack and pay cash for them. Is that some kind of a crime around here? I said I don't want the robe. It's too expensive."

"What are you willing to pay for it?"

"Nothing. I don't need it."

"Would you just sit down a minute, Miss? Just do me that favour."

"Why?"

"Because I still think we can work something out, something to our mutual advantage, so to speak."

She looks at me, then she sits down again and crosses her legs.

Smooth girl. She could sit like that and face a firing squad.

"I wonder if you have a cigarette?" she says.

90

I put on my glasses and reach in the desk for a packet of cigarettes.

JUDITH

"The next day I had to go downtown to do some shopping. I ran into Roy on the pavement. He was delivering packages. I smiled and said hello – and I was glad to see him. But he was acting strange. He mumbled and wouldn't look at me. He cracked his knuckles and sulked. I asked him what was the matter. Nothing, he said, but I kept after him.

" 'It's that boy you go around with,' he said.

" 'What boy?'

" 'The one you walk home with from the Library every evening,' he said.

"I was pleased (what girl wouldn't be?) to find out he'd been spying on me. And it was there, right on the tip of my tongue, to say the right thing. I could have laughed and made him laugh too, if I told him all about Edgar. But, even so, something else moved inside me and spoke for me. I told Roy it was none of his business and I didn't like him spying on me. I said Edgar was cute and smart and clean and he loved me, the kind of boy I'd probably marry some day. And then I prissed away and left him scowling.

"I knew what would happen. And it made me feel all light-headed to know that something would happen for sure because I willed it and had the power to make it happen with just a few words and glances. I was drunk with the idea of that.

"But not really. I mean, yes, I was intoxicated with myself growing up, but at the same time I, the real me, wasn't there at all. I was somewhere else, outside of space, if not out of time, watching a girl spend the afternoon in the Library, sitting next to Edgar at the reading desk, idly, accidentally brushing against him, carefully checking out a whole armload of books for him to carry, and walking down the steps with him as they closed the doors behind us. I guess you'd have to say there were three of me then, divided in three the way a single cell multiplies and divides. There was the one who watched. There was the girl walking with Edgar, calm, cool, and even a little coy and flirtatious. And there was another I was beginning to know, a drunken savage, a wild creature fierce with wordless knowledge.

"I asked Edgar to go back to the haunted house with me. He looked a little nervous, as though he sensed my malice without being able to believe it (for what reason could I have to want to be cruel?). He said he was sorry about the day before not that he hadn't meant what he said and not that he was really ashamed of thinking it or saying it, but that he just hadn't been able to help himself.

"We stopped and he stood facing me with all that load of books in his arms. I took off his glasses and kissed him on the mouth and then I ran away from him across the playground toward the house, I looked back and saw him, floundering like someone running in deep soft sand, blind without his glasses, burdened with my books. I laughed and ran faster, ducking through the tangled plants.

"As soon as I shut the door behind me I saw them there just as I knew they would be. Roy was angry and the other two tried to look casual, unconcerned. I even knew that he would not be alone. I laughed. He raised his hand to hit me across the face, but I caught his arm and I winked.

" 'He's coming ' I said to him.

"I walked away with my back to the door looking to see if I could find in the already waning light (it was green with the sun low, shining its last through branches and brambles and bushes, and undersea light; I was walking on the bottom of the ocean searching for a dropped jewel) the broken piece of mirror I had looked into yesterday, knowing I would find a perfect stranger, wild and beautiful, waiting for me in that jagged glass. Hearing as if far away the sound of him or someone running up the front steps heavily, the door banging open and then a gasp, just a gasp, not a cry or a word, and the sound of the books tumbling. I picked up the mirror, listening to the sound of scuffling, panting, a large soft sound as his body struck the floor. Then I looked. I hadn't changed at all. Which made me feel cold, goosepimples, that I could be so changed and yet my face, my eyes, the little smile, remain the same.

" 'Don't please. Don't please. Don't . . .!' Edgar was saying.

"I heard the sound of the zipper and the rustle of cloth. . . ."

I stop talking. I don't want to tell anymore not any of it. I want to say, *it never happened nor any of the rest of it I made it all up I made it all up to shock people to shock you. . . .*

But one hand grips my hair and he yanks my head around to face him again, then that hand lets go and the other, holding my chin as if it were an eggshell, lifts it and I have to look into his eyes. He is not smiling now, his brow is furrowed, his lips pursed a little as if to spit . . . or kiss. . . . I will tell him. I'll tell him and the rest of it too and how he healed me and then be done with it.

"You have to understand," I say. "I was fourteen years old, going on fifteen, partly a woman, already able to bear children, but partly a girl – a little girl in a white party dress and my hair in pigtails and black, patent leather shoes. . . ."

There is no nod, not even a blink of the bright eyes behind the mask, nor any slackening of the vice on my chin.

"I had never seen a man like that before!"

Still nothing from him, neither pity nor anger nor contempt.

"I looked in the mirror, making faces at myself.

" 'Come here,' Roy said.

"I turned and saw how two of them were holding him down and Roy was standing over him.

" 'Come here,' he said.

"I heard Edgar gag and thought, poor Edgar, *they're not going to hurt you they don't really hurt you they only pretend there's nothing to be afraid of.* . . .

"I looked into his eyes. I smiled. Nobody was holding his mouth closed. They knew that whether he yelled or not nobody would hear him here. His face seemed a long way away, small. He opened his mouth wide, but no sound came. I wanted it to be right; so I took one of the books and carefully ripped out some pages, balled them up, then stuffed the wad of paper in his mouth.

"Then I came around and kneeled between Edgar's spread bare legs.

" 'What kind of a man would that be to marry?' Roy said.

"I didn't choose to answer him. I knelt there between his spread, stubby, fat, pale legs, sprinkled with fine, dark hairs. I looked at the downy patch of dark between his legs, fascinated. He started thrashing and gagging on the paper, so I got up again and looked down at him. Tears in his eyes and trying to shake his head, to plead with his eyes.

" 'Don't worry, Edgar,' I said. 'It's just like playing doctor.'

"The boys laughed, but I wasn't trying to be funny. He twisted his head away as far as he could and closed his eyes.

"Now, I thought, *now* I will touch him. . . ."

kneeling my fingers tentative exploring a wrinkled bag like a fig leathery feels two grapes peeled grapes within   the other part white & soft round a cigar butt lit with pink tip   touch the tip it moves it

94

moves   see look I cry it even grows it's growing how big does it grow
laughter in my ears like listening in a seashell   miraculous elastic
plant why do they laugh   stop laughing   go away   Roy haunted
house all but me & this in the world elastic to touch   up up up goes
the swing & oh ah down that's fire child how fire feels keep away
  white fire Edgar's on fire
up up up oh ah down   Clytie's black sky is blue Edgar's burning
  how fire feels   put out fire smother fire   put out fire with a kiss
up up up oh ah I step free fall over & over into sky vanish forever to
rise again   rise up from my knees tall full of fury fire joy   I am
powerful my hands burned to crisp I hold them high   oh juice of the
world be sweet on my hands be always sweet

"The others had gone. Edgar was moaning and the others were
gone. I wondered if someone had hurt him. I wouldn't like that.
I remember I was very calm. I looked at the books and decided
to come back and get them some other time.

" 'Come on, Edgar. It's time to go home.'

"He wouldn't look at me.

" 'You don't have to carry my books. Let's leave them and
come back tomorrow.'

"He turned over and hid his face and sobbed. I remember
thinking how silly he was being. I tried to think of something
nice to tell him, but if he was going to act like a baby, I'd walk
home all by myself.

MIAMI

This old guy is not to be believed. He's a character and shrewd.
But a hick, a hayseed, a rube to the core. Once one always one.
He opens a fresh pack of cigarettes, offers me one and holds the
desk lighter for me where I have to lean well forward to light it.

"Keep the pack," he says. "Were you ever in Atlantic City? I go there or I used to some times on conventions."

"No," I say. "I've never been there."

"I never mistake a face or a voice," he says. "I know I've seen you somewhere."

"Maybe. I've been here and there."

"I'd know and remember if I ever had the pleasure of meeting you."

"I used to be a dancer," I say. "Maybe you saw me dance somewhere."

That usually works. The world's full of dancers of all kinds. He shakes his head, puffs on that cigar and thinks. Then his eyes brighten and he snaps his fingers.

"The movies!" he says. "Were you ever in the movies?"

"Mr Loomis," I say. "I don't know what all this is about. I am here with Big Red Smalley's Gospel Troupe. Maybe that's where you saw me."

"Doubt it," he says, very cocky now, flipping the ash of his cigar on the floor. "I wouldn't go to a tent meeting if it was the last form of entertainment left on the face of the earth."

"Maybe you're missing something. You ought to come out tonight. I'll leave you a ticket."

"I got all the tickets I can use already," he says. "And I got ten percent of the show. I don't need to come out there."

Look out, Miami. Time to exit with a sashay and a great big smile.

"Well, I hope you change your mind," I say, standing up, smoothing my skirt as demurely as possible. (How about this red dress for a *tent revival* girl?) "We have a mighty good Christian evening planned."

"I remember you!" he says. "I even remember the name of the picture – *Sinner's Revenge*."

96

Blue movies, damn it to hell that I ever made one! They follow me everywhere. It's worse than being a movie star. If I had any sense, I'd get a good nose job and die my hair.

"I'm sure I don't know to what you're referring. . . ."

"Midgets!" he says with a big, hearty laugh. "It had all those midgets in it. Funny as hell. I laughed myself sick. You know, considering the circumstances, you weren't bad. Maybe you missed your vocation. Maybe you *could've* been a movie star. I mean, look at Joan Crawford. . . ."

"Thanks," I say sitting down, beginning to feel like a jack-in-the-box. "I'm glad you enjoyed it."

"I feel better," he says. "You don't know how much better I feel. I've been trying to place you since you walked in the store."

He takes off his glasses and puts them on the desk. He's beaming and happy. I imagine ten-twenty years ago he was a sport.

"Tell you what," he says. "I'm hungry and I bet you are too. Let's go have lunch and celebrate the triumph of human memory. All things conspire towards forgetfulness, but patience worketh against all things. Or something like that."

"What do you want out of me, Mr Loomis?"

"All I want you to do is take that robe."

"I bought the dresses. I paid for them."

"The profit on them dresses don't mean a thing to me," he says. "You can buy out the whole store and it still don't mean a thing. I'm getting old, Miss. Death has done touched me once. I'm a marked man. Do me a favour and take the robe."

"Why? Just tell me why."

He looks at me and the grin fades away, a dissolve like in a picture. It's funny watching him as the grin goes away because all of a sudden I think of that story about *Alice in Wonderland* or in *Oz* or *Through The Looking Glass* or wherever the hell it was when that cat just vanished *except for the grin.* Which is something I always liked. The idea of that. Everything going except the grin. Of course, with my kind of luck, the only thing left would be you-know-what.

"I'll tell you something else," he says to me. "The ten percent off of your gross don't mean anything to me. The Jew and the Worm in the Hat, they're going to cheat me anyway."

"Why don't you just send somebody to count . . .?"

"I'm not finished yet," he says. "I was saying your tent show don't mean a thing to me. I'm only doing it for a joke anyway. *Me* sponsoring a religious show around here. That's a mighty fine laugh and worth it even if I had to pay for the privilege. Which, in a way, is exactly what I'm doing. I ought to get a tax cut for what they steal from me . . ."

With that he stops talking, swivels in his chair and lifts the phone off of its cradle. It's so quiet I can hear the dial tone. He probably expects me to jump in and say something quick. Which is exactly what I'm not going to do. I don't know where you're headed, old boy, but I've gained one step on you because I know what you expect me to do next. Which is exactly why I won't do it. Until, of course, you get used to that and think you've got me nailed down again.

Still holding the phone off the hook he turns his head, not the chair, just his tilted old foxy head so he can see me.

"We got a Sheriff in this County," he says. "Great big fella name of Star. Now old Star, he's not dumb, he's smart. He just takes some things too serious for his own good. His job is one of them. Now, I'm just wondering, speculating so to speak, what would be old Star's reaction if I was to give him a call."

Well, if the old fart had jammed a poker up my ass, he couldn't get me to holler *Uncle!* any quicker. Not that I'm afraid for myself. I can tell him to go play with himself and walk right out of the store and roll. I got my car and I got some new clothes. I'd do it too. It would serve Red right the way he's been acting lately and treating everybody. But the one thing he really don't like, the one thing that bugs him out of his mind, it's the police, the law. He's got his reasons and don't we all? But on Red, I don't know, I'd rather spit on his Bible, and use his crucifix for kindling wood, I'd almost rather kill him than to sic the law onto him. I believe in my heart he could stand burning at a stake or being nailed up to a cross, but I don't think he's got it to take the bright lights and the questions, the fingerprints and the picture with the number, the typewriter clacking and then that iron door clanging behind him. I would not like to see him wither and die in bits and pieces. He deserves better than that.

"You want me to give him a call?"

"No," I say. "Mr Loomis, you can hang up the phone. You drew to a royal straight flush and you win the pot."

"I like a gambling woman and a good loser," he says. "I like class in horses and women."

"Thank you kindly," I say. "What do I do next?"

"Well," he says, "I guess I have ruined the chance of a pleasant lunch together. Why don't you pick up that robe and get the hell out of here?"

"I never got something for nothing in my whole life."

"There's always the first time."

"And I never gave something for nothing either."

"If I was ten years younger," he says, "I'd take the dare. But even if I could, the Doctor wouldn't let me."

"There must be something."

"Beats me," he says.

"I tell you what," I say, standing up and kicking off my shoes. "You never saw me dance. I was good."

I take a turn in my stocking feet around the room.

"You missed something."

"I imagine," he says.

"Let me dance for the price of the robe."

He looks at me, then he grins. "A man can never stay ahead of you for very long. I'll give you credit for that."

"Just one thing," I say. "I do it better with music."

"What kind of music?"

"You got a radio out in the store?"

He goes out. I unzip the red dress and slip out of it. I sit down and start to unroll my stockings. *Red*, I think, *this is for you, a dance to end all. And if the old sonofabitch don't keel over dead from a stroke before I'm done, it won't be my fault.*

JUDITH

"I looked and everything was washed, freshly laundered, blessed with an ineffable sweetness. And I felt good and clean, blessed too, for in some way I had shared in all the marvellous goodness of Creation. All that slow, steady, growing, thrusting, blooming, finally blossoming (for something like that, like a perfect flower had bloomed and opened under my care, at my touch, by my ministry) proved beyond shadows and doubts and once and for all that all things made were intended to be good and fine and strong and beautiful. Just then I know I could have kissed a leper for joy.

"I know now most of the causes of my elation. I know, am aware, that simple, and, in this day, incredible ignorance triggered my inner explosion; that there was, no doubt, a confused marriage of revenge and penance for the earlier humiliation that had not seemed to be that at all, that self-hatred was involved, for wasn't I acting out the role of my mother (as she seemed to me then) again and punishing my father (Edgar), yet through punishing him trying to awaken in him pride in himself as a male so then I could offer myself as a sacrifice, full and sufficient, to that pride (?); that there was textbook envy (oh, I have read the books) of the female for that little drop or dangle of flesh that frees him from all of the things a woman must live with, *unjust*, *unfair* that he or any man by some accidental fusion, some action of chromosones and genes, should be always more free and more fearless than I, not chained to the journey of the moon and the struggles of the tides; oh yes there was that; that also there was pride that I was chosen to be the receiver, the taker, the vessel without which that drop and dangle of flesh would wither and die; power, knowing that I had the choice to offer or not, to tease, to withhold, to tug him (or any man) like a pet on a leash, to make him crawl and sit up or jump through hoops of fire, to make him content or to make him curse the day he was born; for I, no, not I, but the least humble parts of, love's mansion set in the seat of excrement, was all of his hunger and need.

"Of course all this is true enough, but somehow leaves us still on the outside of the sideshow, merely imagining the feats (sword swallowers, fire eaters, magicians, boneless wonders, strong men) and freaks (fat ladies, bearded ladies, alligator girls, one-eyed, three-eyed, pinheaded, limbless creatures) and fakes (the headless girl all made by mirrors) which compose a human soul.

"Sex, yes, it was and is all about sex, I suppose. Much, much ado about the commonest impulse, one we share with coupling dogs in heat, goats and monkeys, and even certain kinds of worms. Much ado about sex in a universe in which copulation *thrives*, world without end. They reduce everything to what they believe to be the naked truth of sex. Look closely and you see that the lady has tights on, flesh coloured tights. Can't we take sex, even the hunger and desire which seem at last the exposed truth, can't we take all this as merely a sign, another veil cloaking the Mystery?"

"The early church fathers did," he says to me. "They knew all about burning and weren't afraid to look into the flames either. But even that was only a fitful shadow on the walls of a cave."

Then he laughs to himself. "Maybe," he says, "we made our biggest mistake when we came out of caves. When we threw off our animal skins, which I guess, are our true and proper clothing, in favour of armour, satin and lace, gabardine or what have you. They'll probably have to drop the Bomb and send us all back to the caves so we can begin again."

Now he drinks again and for the first time passes the bottle to me. I drink and look around at this quiet bright field with its crazy, opulent arch, at the trailer baking in the sun, at the two of them, his men, trying to put something together with tools and gesticulating wildly and furiously at each other; and here the tall evergreens with patches of shade and the piney smell, litter of pine needles and pine cones, and here and there about us the curious, forlorn cages, empty. It's almost noon now by the sun and so quiet and still. Earlier, even as I talked and remembered and he was listening, I heard birds in the trees and the scrabble and scuttle of the little squirrels on the limbs and the ground. Now nothing is moving except far off a lone black speck, floating like a piece of ash on the air, a lazy buzzard circling, circling.

"I knew all these things," I say, beginning again, "as you know the beat of your heart or the life of your bowels even without the words for any of it. And it didn't matter at all.

"I came in the front door and the house seemed happy too. I could hear from upstairs the sound of water spilling into the tub for my mother's bath. I smelled good things cooking in the kitchen and heard Clytie humming to herself the droning little tune she always used for rolling dough to make biscuits. I pictured her strong hands kneading the dough. Then I listened to the soft *tick-tock* of the grandfather's clock. *Tick-tock, tick-tock, clic-clock*. I stood in front of it smiling, watching the long lazy round-headed pendulum perform. I smiled and tipped my head in time with it. In the living room, where no lamp was burning yet, and only the last flare of the sunset and the first muted wink of the street lights shone, the big oriental rug glowed like a garden of exotic flowers. I looked smiling on the heavy uncomfortable furniture.

"Now the house was funny and happy. I may have laughed. Something in the shadows groaned and stirred. It was my father stretched on the sofa with the evening paper open over his face. He rose, blinking, yawning, stretching and padded toward me on soft slippers. He smiled and kissed me on the cheek.

" 'Hello, baby girl,' he said. Then glanced at his pocket watch. 'Better hurry. It's almost time for supper.'

"I went skimming up stairs, light-footed, two and three at a time, humming Clytie's biscuit tune myself. At the top I turned and saw him standing at the foot of the stairs, grey little man, slump-shouldered, in soft slippers, smiling. I waved. He waved the hand with the newspaper and made a crackling sound.

"Later, it is after supper, I am alone in my room, propped up by pillows, reading. Keats was my favourite then, and best of all, 'The Eve of St Agnes'. Only the reading lamp over the bed is burning. The door opens and the overhead lights turn on. I see their faces (my mother's skin grey and stretched tight over her high fine bones like a Halloween mask, a skintight mask over her skull; my father as if carrying a heavy load in his empty hands and the dull, wet luminous eyes of a dog about to be punished) and I can tell at the glance they know what has happened. (What has happened? what really happened?)

"I feel my lips form a smile.

" 'Don't just stand there,' Mama says to him. 'Speak to her!'

"He comes to the edge of the bed and talks in a whisper. I close my book and put it aside. My mother stands over us both. I keep my smile for awhile to help him. For he has trouble to find the words and compose them. Bit by bit, in fragments and pieces he tries to ask me.

"I smile and deny everything. He seems greatly relieved. But Mama won't let him. She's asking me questions, keeps asking me questions. I am very sleepy. Don't want to answer any more questions ever.

" 'Yes,' I say, 'yes it's all true all of it every word just the way he says the way he said it so it must be must have happened that way I don't remember it must have happened that way if he says so.'

"I feel better about not having to lie. His face is grey as a ghost's and a great vein pulses at the edge of his hair.

" 'She has to be punished,' Mama says.

" 'Let me talk to her,' he says. 'There must be more to it than that. She's confused.'

" 'Talk!' my mother shouts. 'Give me the belt.'

"She yanks his belt free from all loops in one whistling motion. The two of them, speechless, tug for it, play tug of war, round and round my room, while I lie back against the pillows relaxed, watching them whirl and tug and trying to keep from laughing. Finally they stop face to face, each hanging onto the belt for dear life, fury at each other in both of their faces, panting.

" 'All right," father says, 'all *right!*'

"Then they give me a whipping."

she comes quick & pulls me out of bed twists me around throws me
across the bed on my face
  how strong she is how strong no wonder she's taller & stronger no
wonder   I feel the slap sting of the belt not hard   she shouts at him
he shouts at me now harder each time harder until each time a wince a
pain of spasm both legs jerking
  my eyes fill with tears I spit out all the dirty words I know vomit
them up in the sheets can't stand it anymore can't stand it then I'm
away someplace else now seeing all three of us calm clear a camera
lens hovering invisible high   watch it all feeling nothing pity his
pent up fury pity hers pity not the cry-baby girl in pajamas   pain is
good pain an eraser mispell a word erase it write over again   pain is
good silly girl in silly pajamas pity her not at all
  Pain is good everything good pure clean fine exalted again powerful
free
  bloom I bloom now see Edgar how I can bloom too

" 'Yes,' I told them. 'Yes, I did it because I had to. I did what
I did because Roy and the other two made us do it. They had
knives. And yes it was ugly and awful and dirty and filthy. I
didn't want to but they made me. Yes, I only lied before
because I was afraid they would kill us. They said they would.'
  "They went away then and left me to go to sleep. Mama gave
me a pill."

everything blurred soft melting
  everything furred fuzzy downy nothing bad not even lying every-
thing good   God makes it good   God made Edgar Edgar's & Roy's oh
ah up down more marvellous   grow bloom like wildflowers in moss
  flowers in a garden   I dance for flowers make them happy or sad
turn to them like the sun each blooms its white flower & then dies

poor flower now a lion tamer with lions now a serpent charmer basket
full of snakes sway in the time to music of time tick-tock now
Salome I dance for Daddy he smiles now Clytie humming bringing
the silver roast platter with Edgar's head

at table we bow our heads say grace Daddy stands up whets the
carving knife Edgar's head rolls over on the platter so he can see me
better pleads with his eyes poor Edgar smile sweetly for Edgar smile
nicely at Edgar at last asleep

"They sent me away first to a hospital and then to a kind of a
school. I talked to doctors, took treatment, talked more until I
learned to say the right things and they sent me home. Free, the
first night home I wrote a long letter to Edgar in college. I said I
was well now, all well, that I loved him and wanted to thank
him and pay him back. We would live together in the haunted
house, keep all the doors locked, the windows closed, never go
out, let nobody in and let the green things in the yard grow
higher and taller than Jack's beanstalk. Edgar would be my
giant, my god. I would worship him day and night. I would
bow down to his marvellous marvel. I would keep him always
happy. Then I sealed the letter and slipped out of the house to
mail it. After the letter dropped out of sight and the red and
blue box clanged shut, I remembered I had forgotten to put a
stamp on it. So I ran away.

"They didn't find me for quite a while. And maybe they
would never have found me at all except for the police. They
found me, arrested me anyway, then found me in one of their
cells with the others."

cities how many cities are there across the land & then there's the
world too to get there some day

cities strung out like beads of light in the dark I know you by heart
by dark

your bus stations train stations airports subways   your bars night-clubs hotels motels rooms

men too men   hungry they walk hunters at night smile & walk with them soldiers sailors marines young boys old men fat thin short tall deformed beautiful all beautiful sick well rich poor cruel kind good bad   neon bathes the bed my body's red green white again red he is a shadow who curses or kisses spits or prays at my shrine the gate to my garden

"I came home again. Sick now with all the diseases. Drugs for all that did fine, but the doctor said I ought to be 'fixed'. Like a cat. At the hospital my mother cried and cried and called me her poor baby. Who had to be fixed and was fixed like a cat.

"Then, I came home again, freed once more by the doctors. I had learned how to live like a shadow myself. How to smile and talk and read books and listen to music. Everyone said how well I was doing and wasn't it wonderful. Mama and Daddy were already old.

"I knew how to move and live among others like a shadow. Except that *I* was never there at all. Even the doctors never guessed that or knew where I was. I was far, far, away, always a little farther. While a shadow fooled them all, I was elsewhere. Elsewhere I still lived naked in a dark garden, drenched, sticky, shining. I cared for them all, the plants in my garden. Tenderly embraced them, clung to them, kissed them for joy and fainted again and again. . . .

"When Daddy died, only then and briefly, I rejoined the shadow. We came back from the funeral and Mama went up to bed. I wanted to cry but had spent all my tears in dreams. I went to the piano and looked at the vacuum bell with the bridal bouquet. I smashed it to pieces. Now! I thought, *now let's see who's afraid of the fire. At last I'm worthy of fire.* In the kitchen I turned on a gas jet high and thrust my hand into the flame and held it there without anybody making me do it. Then Clytie came in the back door.

" 'Look Clytie!' I said. 'I'm not afraid of fire any more.'

"She pulled me away from the stove and held me in her arms until the doctor came.

" 'Baby,' she said. 'Don't you lose heart. We are going to get you all well again soon.'

"It wasn't a bad burn. There's only a little scarred place left to show for it. See?"

I show him my hand. He takes it lightly in his and holds it looking carefully. Then he lifts it and kisses the tips of my fingers.

"I remember you now," he says.

HOWIE LOOMIS

She's quite a woman, quite a gal. A robe and a lunch (and well, yes, she talked me out of the transistor radio too) is cheap at the price for that dance. Not that I'm much on dancing. Never could dance a step myself. And what's worse, I couldn't carry a tune in a five gallon can even on my harmonica. So when it comes to dancing to music, it's just movement as far as I'm concerned. Might as well be setting up exercises or something. Anyway this girl can move. Lord she can move! And, tone deaf or not, I ain't blind yet. I can tell a first-class piece of merchandise when I see one and once in a while, if I'm in the right mood, I can even appreciate something beautiful whether it's got a price tag on it or not. What gets me the most is the *novelty*. I built that old store and I've sat on my ass in that office for many a year. Through ups and downs and into a time when a store like mine is like a museum. A man with any sense or any future would get shed of it in a hurry. The worst thing about getting old is how after a while anything new stops happening. All of a sudden you wake up and see it's the same old thing happening again that did before and always will. You get in that frame of mind and you're just a natural sucker for novelty and surprise. You keep waiting for it to come along, the way a young man waits for opportunity, to knock on your door and open up a sample case full of brand spanking new tricks like nobody ever even dreamed of. Nothing happens, so you put your imagination to work and picture something happening. That's a temporary solution to the problem, like a pain-killer. Trouble is you either run out of things to imagine or when something new or interesting or unexpected happens it just can't live up to what you already imagined.

But I'm telling the truth when I say that I never once dreamed, imagined, or pictured a gorgeous woman doing a dance like that in my office, turning and spinning, leaping and wiggling all different ways and even hopped up on top of my desk and tromped on all the invoices and letters with her bare feet. When she was done and took a bow I give the swivel chair with me in it a whirl and clapped for her until my hands were hurting. That old office will never be the same again. Neither will Mr Percy either, I guess, judging by the look he gave me when I came out of the office and told him to wrap up the robe and the radio too.

"Tell you what," I say. "Why don't you marry me and I'll give you the store? At least you'll have a good judgment to get rid of it."

She's sitting across the table from me spooning away at her chocolate sundae. She smiles at me and shakes her head.

"You don't even know my name," she says.

"Don't have to. I'll marry you and never even ask you your right name."

"You're a character," she says.

"So they say. Tell the truth a couple of times and they'll put that reputation on you."

"Are you married, Mr Loomis?"

"Yes ma'm. Married thirty years to one woman, one good woman until she died. She died of cancer and took a long time doing it. A long time. . . ."

Not days, not weeks, not months, but years. . . . They kept taking away parts of her, inside and outside, to try and keep her alive. I couldn't even look at what they had left of her. *I couldn't even eat at the table with her.* That's how bad it was and I loved that woman. I tried, but all I had to do was to watch what was left start chewing and I had to run. At the very end, and even that lasted a good little while too, she screamed and screamed and kept on screaming. They tried everything they've got to kill the pain until there wasn't anything left.

"She was a beautiful woman," I say to her, "and she took a long, long time to die."

At the time I asked myself: if there is a God – and I want to believe it – how can He just let all these things happen. Maybe He just doesn't know how it is. Let him come down and walk through the hospital in the middle of the night and see how His children are doing. Let Him take a look at the Children's Ward and see what's happening in there. Don't come around telling me His eye is on the sparrow. When I think about all the suffering and the misery I've seen all by myself and then multiply that by all the other people in the world and then multiply that by the number of generations as far back as you can go, then I too get a picture of the world the way it must look to God. I see a globe, all eaten away like my wife's face, a horrible hurt thing. I come in closer, focus down, and see it's crawling with corruption. I put on my reading glasses for a real close look and now I see the whole globe is a muddy, excremental mass of human bodies all packed together and whirling in a dark empty sky.

If there's a God and out of His Will came this Creation, then I do not ever wish to see the face of the Creator. They're wasting their time with prayers and hymns and organ music. They ought to be filling the air with howls and screams and curses until He can't help but hear us. And then if He won't listen, blow up the world. Maybe that would teach Him something.

Or maybe not. The God I'm thinking of would just laugh. I mean, wouldn't that be a perfect ending? Just the way He planned it. And wouldn't He be laughing right now at me? Letting myself get all crippled up and bent over and lame, like somebody with arthritis in every joint, because I am so full of hate for Him. If you get far enough along to figure out the others, calling themselves true believers, are true damned fools, then you ought to be smart enough to see that even the hate you've acquired from a little knowledge and a little experience is only part of His plan too. Then what? What can you still do? Go crazy or kill yourself, that's all. Those are the only free choices you've got from the moment they yank you out of your mother's womb and slap the first of a long series of howls out of your throat.

So I said no. No, Sir, no! I won't settle for hate. If God is good, the way most people believe, or anyway tries to be good, means to be good, then He don't need worship. He needs at least one day a week set aside for pity. If He's hateful, then you still don't have to knuckle under and give Him what He needs. Don't hate Him. Live, hang on, hold on to the last little bits and pieces, and spite Him.

"Some people around here think I'm an atheist," I tell the pretty girl who's still finishing her sundae, spooning away at the last drops of sweet in the bottom of the dish. "I wouldn't know about that. I reserve judgment. Agnostic might be the better word for it. Let's just say I lived enough and long enough to be sceptical. The older I get the more things I can doubt. And those I don't doubt I don't care nothing about anyway. . . ."

She's looking at me with her hands folded in front of her. She's listening. She's got on one of the new dresses she bought from the store, and if it don't quite show off her figure the way that red one did, well I guess I know what she's got already (and it's mighty fine; exceptional you might say) and she looks just a whole lot "nicer". Not that clothes do a whole lot for any of us, but it tickles me. Here in the space of, say, an hour I've seen this woman in three different states, one natural and two artificial, and all three as different as night and day. I don't know which one is real, if there is a real one. But it tickles me that sitting across from me at the table with her hands folded demurely and listening politely to an old man's conversation, wearing that nice print summer dress off the rack in the store, she looks every inch of her a lady, somebody's well-brought-up daughter (could be my own). Like she never even had one little naughty thought or saw one ugly thing in her life. I could hug her.

"Yes," I say, "I was born to doubt. But right now there's one thing I'm sure of."

"What's that, Mr Loomis?"

"I'm a damn fool to be sitting here talking, when I could be looking at you."

She laughs. She has a pretty laugh now to go with the dress, I guess. A pretty, tinkling little laugh. Course she's an actress, but talented. She's come a long way since *Sinners' Revenge*.

"Laugh again."

"Why?"

"You've got a nice laugh. I'd like to remember it. If you'll laugh again for me, I'll give you something, anything your heart desires."

She frowns and looks down at the empty desert dish.

"All right," she says. "It will cost you another chocolate sundae."

"Hell! I'll join you," I say. "Even if it kills me."

I snap my fingers for the waitress and she laughs again even prettier than before.

JUDITH

"Clytie was the one who showed me your picture in the paper and told me about you. I looked at your picture and I knew you could heal me if you just would. You would be the one to put the different parts of me back together again.

"A doctor could only cure me by setting one or the other free. No one could heal me so they could all live together. Except maybe a man of God, some stranger chosen by God, elected by Him to be dragged down deep through all the filth and shrieks of hell to the bottom of it all where the devil sits and plays with himself. Then sent back again to the world, cammanded to tell what he had seen and heard.

"I studied your picture, your face like a map. I looked at the eyes and I knew they had seen everything I had and much, much more. But you weren't blind. You hadn't turned to stone.

"Clytie told me she was going to take her grandchild, a little crippled boy, to see if you could help him.

" 'Take me with you,' I asked her. 'Please take me with you!'

" 'All right,' she said. 'It may not do any good but it sure can't do you no harm.' "

RED

The rain came down that night. It blew up from nowhere. There had been clear skies all afternoon right up until sunset. Not a sign, not even a whiff of rain in the air. But just before time to begin it started coming down, sheets and buckets. Raining bullfrogs. I was tired and my voice was almost gone and now I was going to have to shout over the patter of the rain on the tent.

"I remember it rained that night," I tell her. "The rain kept lots of people away."

JUDITH

We sat in the back with the niggers. We were soaking wet and the sawdust was wet. There were lots of sick people and crippled people all around us. I never knew there were so many. They were the ones who would come rain or no rain.

I remember being worried about when it would be time to go up and get healed.

"Don't worry," Clytie told me. "I'll let you know when the time comes."

"As soon as you walked in and started to lead us singing a hymn," I tell him now, "I knew you were the one to heal me. I *knew* it! You had the power."

RED

I, too, could feel it coming over me as soon as I looked at that crowd. But you can't be sure. It comes and goes like a fever. It waxes and wanes. You are nothing. You may be happy or you may be sad, you may be in a state of grace or crawling with the cruddy itch of sins. It doesn't matter. It takes command of you. It is as if and much the same as when you feel your tongue turn into flame just saying, repeating the old familiar words of the gospel. You start a simple prayer with less thought than a man spinning a prayerwheel or maybe you begin to preach conscious only of the sound of your voice and the little signs of response in the crowd. When all suddenly, before you know it, you are speaking words of fire with a tongue of fire. All power is with you, all glory. And then you know that the words, the Word is real and for a little while you are permitted to be real too.

"You had the power that night," she is telling me. "You really had the power."

I was singing the first hymn when I felt it. Thunder and lightning outside and the old tent waving in the wind and my words dwindled away as if the breath were squeezed out of me by a huge fist. Raindrops fell from a hole in the tent and splashed in my hair. I bowed my head and tried to think of a text to meditate on, to pray on. For a moment the rain fell on me and ran down my face and my mind was a blank. Empty. My breath was all gone and with it my memory. My skull, inside, was a cave, a cell, whitewashed and empty. So empty a man could shout his name at the top of his voice and there would be no answer, no echo. The rain in my face tasted of salt, cool salt, rain and sweat mingling, and then the text, whether a voice in my ear or a great hand with a paintbrush daubing and scrawling the words across the whitewashed wall:

Abba, Father, all things are possible unto thee; take away this cup from me: nevertheless not what I will, but what thou wilt.

From the Gospel of Mark. It came to me from Mark, Mark who feared not to record the miracles and the hard sayings. You find it in Luke and Matthew too, and maybe most beautiful in (in our language) in Matthew: "O, my Father, if it be possible, let this cup pass from me. . . ." But it came from Mark, strong Mark, the Lion. Then think on this for a moment of time. Our Lord in the Garden of Gesthemane praying in vain while the others slept. And wasn't this vanity, vanity, vanity of me to think on this now, to think of myself in the words of Jesus?

Then another text, also from Mark, but now as a memory, a thought, as my mind came back and the vision of that white empty place faded, a thought in words and with words:

And these shall be the signs shall follow them that believe; In my name shall they cast out devils; they shall speak with new tongues; they shall take up serpents; and if they drink any deadly thing, it shall not hurt them; they shall lay hands on the sick, and they shall recover.

"I remember," she tells me now, "how you stopped singing and bowed your head. The others stopped singing too one by one. Some of them bowed their heads too and some of them watched you and wondered. Then you raised both arms high and smiled the brightest, wildest smile I have ever seen.

" 'Praise be to God!' you said. 'The healing Power of God, the Son and the Holy Ghost has possessed my soul.' "

JUDITH

And then you said: "I am only God's instrument, the least of his unworthy servants. But I know, I know I have His Power, His Presence, His Command to heal tonight. I can speak to you for Him. I can speak to you all – the crippled and oppressed and lame, the halt, the blind and the deaf, all of you suffering. I'm talking to those most pleasing to God – the broken in spirit, the contrite of heart. Because it is His Will tonight for all of you to be happy. God wants you to smile tonight more than anything else. He's been a long time watching and brooding, a long time without smiling. Be happy and make God smile to see you. He has wept enough for one day. Come forward, bless you, all those troubled in body and soul and let God's Power flow through my hands and make you whole again. . . ."

You held out your hands in front of you and looked at them. Even in the back where we were sitting I could see them tremble. Then Clytie was standing, trying to help the little boy get up and slip into his crutches and get out of the aisle. I moved out into the aisle and waited while they passed him along. I waited to follow behind her, an old coloured woman with white hair, helping, hurrying the little boy towards you. She looked back at me once.

"Come on, child," she said. "Now's the time. Don't be late."

RED

I look away from my hands. I look up and see the first ones coming up the aisle between the folding chairs. I see an old woman and a pitiful little nigger boy coming to me. I can see all the shame and all the hope in his eyes.

I should be coming to you   I should fall down on my knees & crawl through dirt to you let me wash your feet I am not worthy

forgive me   Dear Lord Jesus Christ in heaven listen to me   I spit on you make a mock of your name every day of my life crucify you in my heart nail you up   jam on a crown of thorns squat down & shoot craps for your clothes & stick a spear in your side hang on a cross

dying myself saying if thou be the son of God come down from the
cross daily I bury you

  make my living at it spitting on you digging your grave making
mock of your name   no health in me no health

  sick to the marrow of my bone & not to be healed myself don't want
to be healed   please please please God & Jesus who walked the earth
two-legged like a man lived & died like a man   please Jesus please
give me this cup of power once   let me borrow your power to heal
this little boy

"You had your eyes tight shut," the girl beside me now says.
"Sweat popped out all over your face. Then you opened your
eyes to look at the boy, kneeled down in front of him and laid
your hands on his head. Your lips were moving. You were
trying to talk to him, but there wasn't a sound except the rain
on the tent."

"No!" I say. "No, you're wrong. I was shouting at the top of
my voice. Didn't you hear me?"

take it all away God   take everything   dry me up let me rot in pain
fire in tribulation but Great God let Power pass through my hands to
tips of my fingers into this child love him

"Then I could hear you," she says. "We could all hear you
then. You spoke to the boy."

I said: "Little boy, the Lord God in heaven looks down
tonight shining on you. The Lord is looking shining down on
one little crippled up boy with a black skin. He looked down
and smiled at you and then He spoke to me. Said. '*Tell that
little boy,*' the Lord said, '*tell him for Me, My son, he's my son and
I'm well-pleased, tell him he has borne his tribulation well. Tell him I
don't want him to have no more of tribulation. Tell him I want him to
get well. It's My Will. Tell him he can make Me happy and all the*

118

bright angels will clap their hands and sing and shout for joy if he will throw away them old crutches. Tell him all he's got to do is throw those crutches away and stand up tall and walk right like a man."

I leaned down and let him hand me the crutches. He teetered there, dizzy, loose-limbed, clumsy as a new colt. Then very slowly he tried a step without them, jerky and awkward and stiff like a marionette or a wind-up toy. Then another and another, each one stiff and jerky, but he was moving.

"By God, he walked," I say to the girl. "He walked without those crutches. Didn't he walk?"

JUDITH

Clytie, with tears streaming down her face, fell on her knees and kissed his hands, the blessed hands that had healed her grandchild. And he stooped way down and kissed her white hair. Then she hugged the boy and he was smiling. People were yelling and shouting and singing. Some women fainted and grown men cried and called out praises of God.

RED

I stood up on the platform and looked at them, not seeing any of them. I have been lonesome all of my life, but this time, seeing it happen like that, was the loneliest. All the noise and commotion was far away from me. I was bathed in sweat, a cold sweat, head to toe. I wanted to laugh or cry but couldn't do either. I was cold, cold on my skin, in my muscles and joints, in my veins, my guts. The centre of cold, a frozen place, was my heart. I might as well have been a corpse.

JUDITH

Then it was my turn.

"I knew you were there, standing in front of me," he says, "even before I looked down and saw you."

"It must have been the perfume," I say, "the cheap perfume. I borrowed it from Clytie and drenched myself with it. I don't know why, because I had bathed myself and scrubbed myself as clean as I've ever been. Maybe I was afraid that nothing would hide the stink of myself from you. I didn't mind for you to see and hear. You could have played a movie of all my life and I wouldn't have been ashamed. But to smell the stink of it!"

"No," he says, "no it wasn't the perfume."

RED

odour of woman primal original archetypal woman   but more than womansmell

odour of strangeness old & new intoxicating dangerous   something touched by fire or smoke if not flame then smoke   cured by the smoke of the fires of hell

You look up into my eyes. Your eyes are green, green and light-thrilled, cloudless as a sky in spring.

Your eyes are green and on fire. I ought not to look. I should turn and run away. I am afraid. I want to run out of the tent. But I won't. I won't! I will be fearless for once.

I see in a drab corner of a dirty room hunched down a sick bird a thin girl thin barely more than a boy with all over soft smooth flesh of girls' smooth long-muscled sinewy frail-boned you cover your high little breasts with one arm

120

knees tight together hair long hair uncombed dirty leaves & twigs wild as empty bird's nest hair tumbles forward over your face your shoulders   yet behind that waterfalling hair red hair see how your green eyes glow like a cat's in the dark   reach I reach so careful to touch your hair to brush it away from your eyes   you snarl you cry you yowl like a cat in the night

JUDITH

I smile   smile at the god statue of a god hewn carved out of hardwood chipped in rough stone cast in bronze enormous straddle-legged over me where I crouch hope to hide   where is his face his head
   in clouds in sky among white clouds ringed by clouds doves hawks whirling wheeling for halo golden your flesh ripple of muscles like racehorse bulk knot of muscles like plough horse draughthorse
   where is the rider   foxy red & brown I foxy run away scoot go to ground or stay a girl kneel down reach up to kiss tip end of gold if you dare   oh ah open my mouth to beg mercy beg love take you golden by surprise then   draw like a straw from you quicksilver fire all of you leave only husk of you tattering tattered scarecrow tormented by crows soared over by bald heads buzzards with hunger to pluck out grapes of your eyesight   sweet sight sweet grapes all gone   destroy gold ripple power
   give me a trophy   knife in my hands   shriek whose mine of joy dream two hands mine my own streaming dark blood holding this high
   thus I atone this sacrifice for everything

RED

reach like a man into fire hands in flame trial by ordeal
   let my palm rest on the skull the soft smooth shampooed brushed shining hair her crown

grips my hair in huge fingers this giant's entwined

    yanks each tender root sends fire to my toes snatches my hair I am bald bald as a monk oh hide my bald shame thrusts stuffs in my mouth hair that hair mine

    I gag now spreadeagle on burning sand & he painted an Indian dances now played out on green earth hillside you he now a boy wearing the skin of wild beasts he sits beside me now lies down beside me now lies down beside me bright hair young face propped on open hand elbow on earth looks into eyes mine tender sad flute music playing somewhere a flute tinkle of soft bells sheep graze here may safely graze above below around bells tinkle I cannot anymore your sad & tender look bear upon myself to look into centre of sky blue as flame's heart look see clouds like sheep untinkling shepherdless run cavort

    when I die will turn into a cloud

    now pain oh no stop now gone

    sky goes red round the socket of gouged eye he not moving still languid propped on elbow still sad & tender idly a boy with stems of grass playing

    he you one by one each fine tender soft hair there pluck out wake up

    I cannot cry out cannot cry not there no sound yes sound tinkling bells flute playing softly not there would be touched ever again not ever not there

    you he whistling tune flute tune softly now feel feel & dare not look myself a new creature feathered am I head to toe all covered with feathers have wings but can't fly you he he you idly my feathers one by one pluck out

RED

*my hands in fire   lay resting in fire burning soon will I catch fire &
burn all over a sparkler so brightly   soon will be ash   who will my
ashes come blow upon*

JUDITH

*where is the boy now hiding behind a broken column is that laughter
or sunlight   where is the flute where has he gone   ah I am featherless
hairless   stranded & staked & splayed & stark & smooth who will
have me now   sheep sheep nuzzle sniff tickle   a ram horned a green-
eyed red curly ram looks now no longer tender & sad looks now on
fire   the boy hides in fire in skin and coat and horns of red ram gone
    now a snake bracelet of beads with fork tongue twines my thigh will
I sleep now*

RED

*not fire not I burning no   not fire my hands rest softly on her red
hair   this is the hair of a girl who kneels and looks to the preacher
who has healed before and God willing in God's time will heal again
this is a bad preacher bad man God has chosen who willed not to be
chosen who asks not to be chosen who asks most and only to be left
alone*
    *Abba Father all things are possible unto thee   this is a preacher who
runs like the wind from a lion*
    *this preacher is not saint Mark is no saint this preacher is among
sinners a chief   take away this cup from me   this girl is also among
sinners a member she smells of sin not sickness   why how should I
heal her   if it be possible let this cup pass from me   why should I*

heal her when I am not healed heal me first then her how can I heal
what I cannot see   nevertheless why should I   not what I will let
me burn in the fire   but what thou wilt why thy will be done
    this is a preacher that is a girl   see how she kneels see how he prays
    thy will be done

JUDITH

warm good   float drift toward sleep   snake on my thigh moves inch-
ing no not there inch not stop don't no   up up up oh ah down not stop
don't stop now no
    up up up oh ah down oh ah down oh ah ah   now look at the sky
again I dare blue & empty   empty save for one speck circles lazy &
slow a blur smudge smear in the sky turning descends
    no stop now I am healed healed healed no more sky is black rushing
feathers   bald head beak and talons stiff groping eyes must go too to be
healed be blind to see   take them take them   now can I lie here in
peace to rot in the sun
    not yet not done yet
    come then rodents & small birds pick me clean   now bones only
so frail small thin to carry all me all hungers   hear how they tinkle
keep time with the wind   my bones piano keys make his your hands
let play on them make music
    o make let us a joyful noise unto the Lord for He is a great God
above all gods praise Him

RED

"Bless you, my child," I said. "I believe in my heart that you
are healed."

You nodded with your eyes bright with tears. You rose and
turned back toward your place, walked away down the aisle

with your back to me, facing the others. Shaken, weak, but feeling maybe like Jacob when he wrestled an angel all night and won after all, I turned to the next uplifted, urgent face.

JUDITH

Now, weary as if it had all happened only a moment before we stroll together under the shade of the trees. I slip off my tennis shoes and leave them, first one then the other, hopping one-legged, so I can walk barefoot on the soft pine needles. The woods smell sweet with pine and dry. Now I can't see the mountains, their blue and the sky's blue mingles and both of them seem whitened by the sun.

We walk together, both barefoot, in shade on soft pine needles. He stops, and, turning away from me, leans against a tree, his face hidden in his arm, making not a sound but his great back heaving.

"Why do you feel that way?" I say to him. "It doesn't matter, you know, how you feel. God picked you out. He choose you."

"Who asked to be chosen?"

He whirls around glaring at me, one fist clenched and his eyes dry, reddened with pain or fury.

"I don't want it," he says. "I just want God or whoever or whatever it is to let me alone. *Why won't everybody just let me alone?*"

"I understand," I say.

"I'm no good," he says, "no good! I never said I was. I'm a bad man, terrible tempered, mean and full of evil right up to the tip of my tongue. Why did He have to pick me? I don't want to preach anymore . . .!"

"But you will."

"I won't do it."

"You're going to preach tonight. For me, if for nobody else."

"Why?"

"You owe me that much."

"I don't owe anybody anything!"

Then suddenly the mask cracks to pieces and he laughs loud filling the woods. He tosses his hair out of his eyes and laughs. I stand quiet, amazed, waiting.

"Does it really matter to you?" he says.

"Yes."

"All right, by God, I'll do it!" he says.

We walk on, side by side now, not touching, but side by side, not going anywhere, just walking a loose circle in the woods. The field glares. Heat waves shimmer, are cellophane between us and the trailer.

"Well," he says softly, "what are you going to do now? Keep driving around like a maniac in that car? Are you going to stay with us a while or go back to whoever it was you left in a hurry?"

"My husband," I say.

"I didn't see a ring."

"I left it on top of the bureau for a souvenir."

"You are a mess," he says. "Just about a mess."

We walk a little farther. He stops and leans against a pine tree scratching his wide back lazily against the rough bark. Broad shoulders, heavy muscles, a big neck, a flat ridged stomach, and a bulge like a fist at the crotch of his underpants. I feel the old sap rising in my limbs. A feeling so real, so exact, it's easy for me to believe the myth of Apollo and Daphne. Maybe one day I'll offer a prayer to God and He'll turn me into a tree. I should be a tree with green leaves and birds nesting in my hair. But not yet. Not yet. . . . .

"Tell me something," he says, grinning, his curly hair like a satyr's, his eyes glinting now. "Don't you ever get hot in that raincoat?"

"Sometimes."

"Why don't you take it off?"

"Because," I say, "it's all the clothes I've got. There's nothing under it."

He hurls the bottle away among the trees, backhanded. It smashes and shatters. I hear it but am not looking. I am looking at him.

"Just like launching a ship," he says. "I christen thee Judith."

We look at each other a moment unsmiling, coldly, appraising. Then he laughs and tosses the curls on his head.

"Don't just stand there," he says. "Come here, you crazy girl. Don't keep the preacher waiting!"

3

I am gone like the shadow when it declineth: I am tossed up and down as the locust. My knees are weak through fasting; and my flesh faileth of fatness. I became also a reproach unto them: when they looked upon me they shaked their heads.

PSALM CIX, 23–25

Nothing worth talking about ever happens around here. So I wouldn't exactly call my job adventurous. Police work ain't bad, though. You wear a clean uniform and you carry a pistol and all kinds of people say sir to you. There may not be a whole lot of Crime, but there's always enough to keep you from going to sleep on your feet and it beats working for a living.

I'm sitting around with a couple of the boys playing poker. Couple of prisoners from the County Jail. It's kind of funny. The Law, I mean. Here they got an ordinance against gambling of any kind whatsoever. They can fine you or jail you or both at the same time depending on who's on the bench that day and what did he eat for breakfast. And one of these here prisoners is in here for just that reason. A stranger around here, he came in town and tried to get a poker game going in the Thomas Jefferson Hotel. Did all right for awhile too. Let 'em win a little, enough to keep coming back. Then, being smalltime (they'll do it everytime), he got greedy too quick. Took everybody for all he could get and had it in mind to hightail it out of the County. Bout that time somebody come along and swore out a warrant against him, and me and Jack jumped in the car and went down to the T.J. to arrest him. He was long gone, checked out, paid his bill and everything. We took a look down to the Bus Station. He wasn't there. Then old Jack got an idea. We hopped in the car and took off down the highway hauling ass. Caught up with him just this side the County line.

He's walking along the road carrying a big old suitcase. When he hears a car coming behind him, he drops his bag right on the spot and turns around with a great big friendly smile on his face, and his hitchhiking thumb is about halfway up when he sees what kind of a car it is and who is in it. I'll give him credit. He never lost his smile completely. It just kind of blinked off and real quick like a light bulb when something like an air-conditioner cuts into the power. He didn't drop his hand, he just drooped it a little.

"I sure am glad to see you, Sheriff."

"How come?" Jack says.

"Somebody done switched suitcases on me."

"What did they leave you?"

He kicked the suitcase. "This old thing," he said.

"What's it got in it?"

"That's a good question, Sheriff," he said. "I don't know why I didn't think of that myself."

"Well," Jack said, "let's take a look. You never can tell. Maybe you got the best of the bargain."

So we get out of the car and all three squat down around the suitcase and just look at it, lying on its side.

"You better open it, Sheriff," he says. "I just don't feel right messing around with somebody else's property."

"Aw go ahead," Jack says. "We won't tell." (Turning to me): "You won't tell will you, Rosebud?" (That's his nickname for me.)

"No, sir, you know me."

"That's why I'm asking you."

So we all squatted around there looking at it a while longer, nobody saying anything.

"Sheriff," he says finally, "ain't you ever going to look inside?"

"Well, now," Jack says. "I don't know. I just can't make up my mind. I mean, here you are way out on the highway all by yourself toting a suitcase. What if you're lying to me?"

132

"Sheriff!"

"What if you swiped this suitcase off of somebody else?"

"Why would I do a thing like that?"

"People do all kinds of things and I don't understand a half of them."

"Me either," he says.

"What if I was to open up this here suitcase and find something suspicious in it?"

"I don't know, Sheriff."

"Let's just suppose, for the sake of argument, that this suitcase is cram full of some kind of stolen goods. . . ."

"Sheriff!"

". . . or illegally acquired contraband, merchandise and so forth and so on. . . ."

"You sure do have an active imagination."

". . . why then I'd just have to impound it and take you back to town to answer a whole lot of questions."

"I don't know nothing about nothing."

"That appears to be the case," Jack said. "Nevertheless I'd have to do my duty. Put yourself in my shoes."

He sneaked a look down at Jack's big old number 14 boots, cowboy-style with a point on 'em and I could tell that right about then he was contemplating how the point of one of those boots, applied with a good share of Jack's two hundred pounds behind it at the approximate place where his mouth ought to be, if he just gave up on thinking he was goodlooking and shaved his ass and walked backwards, would feel. And he was thinking that it wouldn't feel good. And he was no doubt thinking from experience, boots of one size and another having been applied there most of his adult life.

"Why don't you open it?" Jack said.

"I would just as soon, not, thank you," he said.

133

"How about you, Rosebud?"

"It don't make no difference to me," I said.

"What do you reckon we ought to do, Sheriff?"

"Well," Jack said. "I've been thinking here while we been squatting down. I always think better that way. The blood rushes to my brain and I start thinking. . . ."

He waited about two or three seconds to see if either one of us was dumb enough to crack a smile or laugh.

"We got two alternatives," he said, "the way I see it. Of course, I'm always open to suggestions, but I only see two. We can leave this suitcase out in the field and forget it. Maybe somebody will come along, you know, finders keepers, and pick it up and then it would be their problem wouldn't it?"

You should've seen that fella's face. Only expression I ever seen to equal it was a guy that got the skin of his pecker caught in the zipper of his fly. He couldn't zip up and he couldn't zip down and he couldn't just go around like that the rest of his life.

"What's the other one, Sheriff?"

"The other what?"

"Alternative, damn it!"

"Well, now," Jack said, standing up and shaking the kinks out of his legs. "It looks to me like you can just leave it safe in storage, all banded and sealed where nobody can open it and look. Then you'll have a nice surprise waiting for you when you get out, just like those toys they used to put down at the bottom of a box of crackerjacks and you had to eat your way down to get at em. Course there was always some damn fool that would pour out a whole box of crackerjacks cause he just couldn't wait long enough to chew up and swallow all that stuff."

"Get out of what, Sheriff?"

"The County jailhouse," Jack said, serving the warrant on him. "Come on, you all, let's go."

That's what old Jack did, too. He put bands and seals on the suitcase and put it in the storage bin for the duration.

"What do you expect is in that suitcase?" I asked him.

"Money," he said.

"How come you didn't open it up and see?"

"I got two reasons," he said. "If I opened that suitcase, I would've had to take that money and give it back to the ones that lost it."

"You don't approve of gambling?"

"They knew what they was getting into. I don't like anybody, never did, that plays a game of marbles for keeps and then when he loses starts hollering about it was all funsies."

"What's the other one?"

"Put yourself in my shoes," he said. "One of my duties is to run this jailhouse. Now, I like it to be nice and clean and quiet. I want all my guests to be contented. You think I want that fella moaning and crying around here for ninety days? I'd rather they lock me up and trade places with him."

So here I am, been playing poker three days running with the fella with my own deck and losing steady until this afternoon. I'll give the fella that much, he don't have to cheat. But along about noon today my luck changed and I'm hot, baby, hot! So come on cards! Keep running! Come to your old daddy! Come on home!

"Rosebud?"

Come on Lady Luck! Be with me now and I'll be your slave the rest of my life. I'll paint your toenails and brush your teeth and wipe . . .

"Rosebud!"

There stands Jack with his hat on his head, buckling on his belt, ready to go.

"Where we going?"

"Out to the Fairgrounds."

"How come?"

"You'll see."

I give that gambling fella one last look.

"Don't take it so hard," he says. "It's all in the breaks of the game."

I don't even get a chance because Jack is already saying: "Don't you lay a finger on that man, Rosebud. He's a guest of the County and a ward of the State."

Lady Luck, you've done done it again. Just let a fella tell you how he really feels and you'll do it every time! You're worse than my wife, Ruby.

MIAMI

I sit on the steps of the trailer, smoking a cigarette, thinking. I'm wearing my shorts and a halter to keep cool. I watch Hookworm and Moses fuss over the last little things. The old tent is up now. The generator for the lights is all set up and tested out. Somehow between the two of them they put that little portable piano together one more time. (Moses can play it, but he sure can't put it together for the life of him.) They got the card table set up under an umbrella for selling tickets. They got the hymn books all laid out ready, one on every other chair. They got the boxes of photographs of Red (and me too) all ready to sell. I can't remember when we've been this close to being ready so early with still plenty of sunlight left.

Of course, they're not all the way ready. They've still got to have their daily fight over how neat the tent is, how tight the ropes are and if the stakes are all in deep and lined up even, etc. And whose fault it will be if the lights go out or the piano falls apart. And who's going to drive tonight if we go on. We'll get to that shortly.

Red's in the tent alone with his Bible. This is his quiet time. He sits in a chair reading, searching for a text. But not really reading the words. Instead he just lets them happen to him, sees them, his mind takes them and drops them like coins into a well. He's listening for the splash. What he's really doing that way is asking himself again and again can he do it, should he do it, is he able. He's wondering if when he gets up there and starts to talk God will strike him deaf and dumb or turn his voice into a cackle like an old hen's.

Meanwhile Miss Nympho Bitch-Little is inside the trailer rummaging through my footlocker and my costumes, looking for one to wear for tonight. Because Red's got a bug about working her into the act too and I've got to figure out something she can do and not look like a damn fool. Well, when it comes to skits and routines, I've got a million. And if I don't know one already I can make one up. Right now she's having herself a ball trying all the different costumes on like a little kid playing in Mama's closet. Mama's tired right down to the tips of her toes and Mama's tired of kids and costumes and skits and almost everything.

She is trying to kill me with kindness and sweetness, that girl. Well, I can play that old game together with the best of them. We went in the trailer arm in arm, giggling, like a couple of girls going off to the Ladies Room to compare notes on our dates. We got in there and she looked all around at everything oohing and aahing. Like I just asked her into my living room. It was so *cute, clean* and *neat* and all like a yacht, she said. (Honey the times I've been on a yacht, it wasn't clean, it wasn't neat, and it wasn't a damn bit cute. They get you far enough out so you can't swim and then it's every man for himself.) Then she took my hand between hers and looked me right in the eyes.

"I know we'll get along," she said.

(Sure we will. Because the day we don't one of us is leaving.)

"Yes," I said. "I hope we will."

"It's so important," she said.

"I know what you mean."

Then I pulled out the footlocker and opened it up to show her the costumes. You would've thought I was opening up a jewel box full of treasures. She clasped her hands together (bites her fingernails) and just sighed.

"They're so *pretty*!"

"They've seen better days," I said.

"Could I try one on?"

(You better, baby, cause we're two entirely different sizes and you stand to lose if you walk out there in a costume fitted for me. Not that a few laughs wouldn't pick up the show.)

"Help yourself."

"Any of them? I mean, don't you have one you want to wear?"

"I've worn them all one time or another."

So she turned her back to me and slipped out of that black trenchcoat. That surprised me a little. I just didn't figure her for the kind to run around wearing a trenchcoat and that's all. She has a kind of a slim, long-legged figure a little like Brigit Bardot in the movies, suntanned all over, just to show off I guess, and a nice, high, tight little ass. . . . Then I saw the marks of the pine needles and I had to bite my tongue to keep from laughing. That old Red! Wouldn't you know? Well, at least she did it flat on her back. A girl like that, you would expect, more likely, she'd prefer hanging upside down on a tree limb or something.

"You just try them on," I said, "and pick out the one you prefer."

She turned around half-way to smile thanks to me. (Well, Sweety-pie, you may never win a titty contest, but at least you don't have to worry about sag.) And I smiled back and left her to her fun.

I wish to hell I had thought to bring the transistor radio with me when I left. But I'm not going back in there and have to talk to her to get it.

She raps on the trailer door from the inside.

"Everything all right?" I say.

"It's awfully hot in here," she says. "Is there a fan or some way to open the windows?"

"Turn on the air-conditioner. It'll work in a minute."

Then to the two of them, standing by the tent, arguing over a tent stake: "Hey! Put on the generator."

"Are you crazy?" Cartwright hollers.

"The lady in the trailer says it's too hot."

He grins and nods. You know, if old Hookworm just had a halfway decent set of teeth, he'd be perfect for a pimp. Next time we're in Galveston I'll plant the seed of that idea in his head and see what happens.

MOSES

"Take care of it, will you?" he tells me. "While I get this stake in right."

"There's nothing wrong with that stake."

"Do you want the whole tent to fall down? Is that it?"

"A hurricane couldn't blow this tent down."

He leans on the sledge and grins at me. If you look very hard and very closely you can see what might pass for a faint flicker of cerebral activity behind his eyes.

"You still don't know how to start the generator, do you? After all this time. If you had the mechanical sense that God give a low-grade moron . . ."

"Show me."

"Hey!" Miami calls. "Do I have to come do it myself?"

"Keep your pants on!" Cartwright yells back.

He goes over and gives it a couple of tries. It sputters and dies on him. He starts cussing it and this time the first time it sputters he gives it a hell of a kick and it catches. Naturally he almost busted his foot. So he's hopping up and down still cussing through gritted teeth and Miami's laughing herself sick.

"What's so funny?" he says to me glaring, hopping toward me furiously, still holding that foot in his hand.

"I'm not laughing."

"You were too. I saw you."

"I don't like to see anybody suffer."

"Especially you," he says. "For you work is suffering."

Now the first smarting of pain is gone. Gently he lowers the foot to the ground. Tests it, gradually increasing his weight on it, looking down at it intently. Now takes a step. Another. Looks up and grins with pride and satisfaction.

It is true. I do not like to see people suffer and I do not like pain, the sight of it or my own pain; but Cartwright's incredible snaggle-toothed grin presents me with an intricate moral dilemma. In my heart of hearts won't I have to concede that if it comes down to pure, simple and absolute choice, I prefer the vision of Cartwright holding his foot and hopping around, his whole face screwed up into an eloquent expression not only of anguish, but also of the brutal injustice and ingratitude of inanimate objects, to the other – Cartwright of the Indescribable Grin, Cartwright rampant, triumphant?

"I guess we know who you can depend on around here," he says.

"I guess we do."

"Did you watch how I did it? Do you think you could start the motor all by yourself now?"

"Maybe," I say. "But I'd rather not."

"See? I told you you was no good."

Ah, Cartwright and the idol of Self-improvement, the great American panacea for *ennui*, frustration and emptiness. Cartwright has taken all kinds of extension courses to improve himself. Courses of every conceivable kind. Those being advertised in the back of certain second-rate magazines. He has studied: piano, guitar, and accordian, electronics, how to be a real estate broker, meat cutting, how to turn songs and poems into dollars, how to be a detective, commercial art, hypnotism, how to earn Big Money, how to repair any watch or clock, how to make any window into one-way glass, photography, how to investigate accidents and sell shoes, how to write shorthand, be a fingerprint expert, plastic sealing and laminating, how to use a transistor metal detector to search for buried treasure, drawing, how to be a motel executive, welding, body repair, air-conditioning and refrigeration, karate (including a life-size practice dummy only 99 cents). He has even written to the Rosicrucians for "A Secret Method for the Mastery of Life". If they told him, he is keeping the secret well. He has also studied, figure drawing, hotel management, has improved his English, has practsied judo and jiu-jitsu, dynamic tension and isometric exercises; he has credentials and the documents to prove that he is a trained detective, a television repairman, a famous author. Miami has lately been urging him to learn a new language, preferably Swahili, a suggestion which inevitably touches two delicate nerves which, struck like guitar strings, emit the sound of rage and irrationality – the niggers and the United Nations.

Now he stands and looks at me.

"I can't hop around on one foot as well as you can."

"That ain't all you can't do as good as me."

We shall now, no doubt, resume the subject of the tent.

"You were in the Army, weren't you?" he says.

"Yes."

"I bet you had one hell of a time in the Army."

"That's a pretty accurate description."

"Didn't they even teach you about *tents*?"

"They tried to."

"I'm 4'F and I still know more about tents than you."

I avoid bringing up his carnival days at this point, a digression which always prolongs this argument to a point beyond endurance.

"What's wrong with it?"

"Look at it!" he says. "I guess it's about the worst looking tent I've ever seen."

"It's going to be dark outside. Nobody will even see the tent."

"It's the freaking *principle* of the thing!"

"Speaking of principles, Cartwright, I'd like to say here and now, that it offends me to see you, a *business manager*, performing manual labour."

"It ain't always going to be like this," he says.

"Really?"

"The trouble with you, Moses, is you got no vision of the future."

"Do you think things are going to change?"

"Listen here," Cartwright says, "I know how it looks now. It don't look too good sometimes. But I foresee the day coming, I *predict* the day will come when we'll have dozens of young strong men – fulltime, permanent, first-class roustabouts, working for us, putting up tents two and three times as big as this old thing. Ten times as big! Big, brand new tents, air-conditioned, capable of seating thousands at one time. We'll have loudspeakers and a portable pipe organ. We'll have a choir and maybe even a big brass band. People like brass bands, and when we come rolling down the highway it won't just be one old dusty trailer and a half-ass truck that you can drive right by without even noticing. When we come down the road, it will be in a procession, a convoy of trucks and trailers with a police escort. It will be a parade wherever we're at. I know the day is coming when Big Red Smalley's Old-Time Tent Revival Meeting will be famous and celebrated from coast to coast!"

"How about Europe?"

"Why not? Asia, Africa, remote islands and distant places . . . !"

"Paris," I say. "That would suit me fine."

"What's so special about Paris?"

"You know what I mean."

Glimmers now, begins slowly to glow in his eyes, shows also in the sly yellow snaggled smile that spreads as if reflexively, and and all of this ending in a wink as blatant as a slammed door and a laugh like the snort of a horse. Cartwright's expression of a subtle, awakening feeling, the feeling of mutual, shared, complete conspiracy of something not *evil* (he wards off that word by deleting it from his own dictionary of practical usage), not *vice* (because, for him, that's a tool you use and a metaphor for what you get them caught in), not even *frailty* (for that con-

143

notes something else, perhaps like the teacup and saucer he will never learn to balance on his knee), but what he persists in calling his *Weakness*.

"Moses," he says. "I believe you're turning into a dirty old man."

"What's wrong with women?" I say, a picture of sudden righteous indignation.

"Nothing," he says quickly.

"Don't you want to go to Paris someday?"

"Sure, but . . ."

"Why?" I demand. "To see the Eiffel Tower?"

"It's just that I never did expect to hear you come out in favour of – you know – sex."

"Maybe you never really knew me," I say.

"Maybe not . . ."

"Stop for a moment to consider," I say. "We're different, it's true. We dress differently, talk, think, act differently. Our pasts are remote and alien to each other. Who knows what the future will be for either of us?"

He opens his mouth to make a sound, meanwhile protesting with both hands.

"No," I say. "We may be as different as night and day, but we have one thing in common, we are both men. I, too, am a man. Do you imagine seriously, that I am immune to the pleasures of beauty? Do you think that you alone, of all living creatures, have suffered the pangs of desire?"

He pauses for due consideration.

"I'm glad you said that, Moses," he says. "I never thought of it exactly like that."

"Well," I say, addressing him with the saddest expression I can muster up, "when a man reaches a certain age. . . . But there is one thing they can never take away from us, the boundless, limitless freedom of the human imagination. *That* is the answer! Grow old with me and so forth. Cultivate a full, rich imaginative life, Cartwright, and you'll always be a happy man."

"Is that like a racial characteristic?" he asks puzzled beyond either malice or irony. "What I mean is, do most Jews as a rule have a good imagination?"

"I wouldn't know."

"No offence meant, Moze."

"How about you? What do you dream of? Where does your imagination roam?"

Ah the smile again! The wink that bangs like a loose shutter in the wind.

"Don't be shy," I say. "We're all big boys together."

"Well," he says "the truth is I *do* think about women a lot. I mean, they give a fella a lot to think about."

"Indeed they do."

"I guess I think about women most of the time."

"You're young and red blooded. It's natural."

"That's the way I look at it," he says.

"How do you picture them?"

"Well, it's kind of hard to put it into words."

"Try," I say. "Every man has some vision of how he would like the world to be if he had the power to make it that way. Some men dream that they are great rulers and emperors. Some are heroes, cheered by the adoring crowd. Some dream of a peaceable kingdom where the lion and the lamb lie down together. I suppose there are as many kinds of dreams as there are men."

"You mean if I had my *druthers*."

"Yes."

He concentrates. I wait. It would be a lie not to admit that it gives me some satisfaction to tease Cartwright, to expose him, if not to himself (and that is his redeeming core of strength, God's gift to fools, he will never know . . .) at least to me, a reminder that often for all his narrow, small minded, smug offensiveness, he is a pitiable wretch. But it is small pleasure and less satisfaction to be reminded continually of the obvious. No, there's a reason, a simple, defensive reason. If not this, then the tent. We will continue to argue and fuss about the tent until night falls otherwise. Today I do not choose to discuss the tent anymore.

"You'll laugh," he says.

"You know me better than that."

"Well . . . The way I see, it's kind of like a wheat field . . . a great big rolling field of wheat as far as the eye can see in every direction. Only, see? it's not really wheat. It's women. A whole godamn field full of naked women just smiling and swaying in the breeze. . . ."

"Where do you fit into the picture?"

"It's like I am the owner," he says. "Like I'm the farmer that owns the field."

"It sounds beautiful."

"Yeah, it's great. I mean, it probably sounds crazy to you . . ."

"No," I say. "I understand you."

Then his whole expression changes. His eyes go glassy like a fighter's. His knees sag. Breath, not words, explodes from his lips becoming at last a kind of choked half-whistle.

"Holy shit!" he says. "Look ayonder!"

I look, see a striped car, its small red roof-light catching the sun, turn off the road and under the arch and head over the field towards us. I glance back at Cartwright, but he's already half-way to the trailer, bent low, hunched and bent at the knees like an infantryman under fire. But not running. He goes with a kind of quick, stealthy walk which suddenly reminds me of Groucho Marx.

CARTWRIGHT

Miami, coming up off the stairs of the trailer, walks right past me saying to herself: "I'll be a sonofabitch. He turned out to be a dirty old man after all." Which don't make a damn bit of sense, but I'm not stopping now to ask her what the hell she's talking about or even slowing down to think about it. It's up the stairs and inside quick, shutting the door behind me, able to breathe again anyway, leaning against the door and listening.

If that's old Dreama, sitting in the back of that car with murder in her eyes and papers in her hand, my ass has had it.

"Hello!"

If a man could really jump right out of his skin and run off and leave it, I'd be the one. The first thing that pops into my head is that she's here, been in here just waiting for me to run and hide, knowing me the way she does. And then when I turn around and the first thing that hits my eyes is skin and the flashing of sequins, I'd faint dead away if I could.

"What's the matter?"

It's the girl, the godamn girl. Only she's done shed the raincoat for one of Miami's costumes. In which, making allowance for her size and shape, she don't look too bad, not bad at all.

"Scuse me, ma'm," I say. "I forgot there was anyone in here."

"Do you like it?"

"Yeah," I say. "On you it looks great."

"Why are you whispering?"

"On account of," I say, keeping right on whispering and hoping like hell she will too, "the po-lice has arrived."

"What do they want?"

"I don't know," I say. "But I ain't taking no chances."

She wrinkles her forehead, wondering.

"I don't want to get caught with this on me."

I ain't got time to explain all about Dreama, and anyway that seems to cause some women to bust out laughing when I tell them. I got another reason which is just as good as Dreama. So I open my coat and show her the .45 pistol stuck inside my pants.

"Oh," she says, looking at it. Then she gets that frowny, puzzled look again. "Why do you have that?"

"We take in a good deal of money," I say. "You know, contributions and offerings and so forth and so on."

"What kind of gun is it?"

"It's a Army surplus item," I say. "Here, have a look." I hand it to her.

"Oooh!" she says, giggling. "It's so heavy."

Then she's got both hands wrapped tight around it and her hand over the trigger and the barrel is pointing straight at me.

"Bang, bang," she says. "You're dead."

"Be careful, lady," I say, trying to sound calm, cool and collected so as I won't frighten her into accidentally squeezing that trigger and blowing me straight to kingdom come. "That sonofabitch is loaded."

"Oh," she says. "I'm sorry."

"Don't never point a gun at somebody unless you're fixing to use it."

She stops pointing it, just lets it dangle loose in one hand, but she don't offer it back.

"Tell you what," she says. "I'll keep it for you. Then you won't have to worry about getting caught."

"That's mighty kind of you, ma'm. But I don't think that's such a good idea. I mean a gun is like a dangerous weapon. What if it was to accidentally go off or something? What if you just happened to hurt yourself? I'd never forgive myself."

She turns her back to me, picks up that black raincoat and fumbles in the pocket. She comes up with a whole fistful of green bills. They were just in there, loose all the time.

"I'll buy it from you," she says. "You just name your price."

"Why?"

"I don't know," she says. "I never owned one before. How about two hundred dollars?"

"That's mighty generous, ma'm," I say. "But you'd be getting robbed."

"I don't care."

She means it. She's done made up her mind she wants that gun and she's going to get it. And I don't like it even a little bit. I mean, I could use two hundred dollars, and if I wanted guns I could get a whole arsenal of them for that kind of money. But it just ain't right. Something's wrong somewhere.

"You're just kidding me, aren't you?"

"Make it two-fifty," she says. "That's how much I'm kidding."

I knew she was crazy all along. I mean, you start giving guns to crazy people and then you better look out. If that girl has a gun, somebody around here is liable to get hurt. I don't care about the rest of them, but I don't feature getting cut down by a .45. That thing makes a hole in you as big as a fist and there aren't too damn many places on one man's body where he can stand a hole as big as that being added. Anyway, she might kill herself, accidentally or on purpose. What if she was to aim at one thing and hit another? She might take a shot at one of us and miss and hit somebody else. With my luck that's just what would happen to me, gunned down, shot down like a dog, and it wasn't even me she was aiming to shoot.

"I sure do appreciate your offer, ma'm. And don't think I don't. If I was to sell that gun to anybody it would be to you. But that gun is kind of special, you know. It's got like sentimental value."

"Don't give me that shit."

I like to keel over. Well, what do you expect from a crazy person? She sits down on the bunk and looks at the floor.

"I wonder what would happen if I pulled the trigger right now."

She looks up right at me with a great big smile, the happiest smile in the world.

"Can't you just see all the police and everybody running in here."

"Don't even *think* like that."

"What would you say?"

"I don't know. It all depends."

"I know what I'd say," she says, still smiling. "I'd say this man (you) was trying to rape me."

"Are you crazy or something?"

"I'm just crazy enough to shoot you right now."

And right then up comes that barrel pointing it at me again and she's got both hands gripping it and her finger is on the trigger. The barrel is very steady.

"I flipped off the safety," she says. "In case you're wondering."

The smile is gone. In that crazy costume of Miami's, with all that red hair falling over her face and the gun pointed right at me, she looks like some kind of a monster. Like she just turned into a monster right in front of me.

"I wish you could see yourself," she says. "You look scared to death."

I can't work up enough breath to make an answer, even if could think of one.

"Come here."

"Lady," I say. "Listen Lady, I'll give you the gun. I'll pay you to take if off my hands. I never did like guns anyway. *Only please quit pointing that thing at me.*"

"Come here!"

"Pretty please?"

"I'm going to count to ten. One-two-three-four . . ."

I sit down on the bunk beside her keeping a respectful distance.

"What do you do?"

"Who me?" I say. "I mean, what do you mean?"

"Around here. With the show and all."

"A little bit of everything, you know. I take up tickets and help people find their seats and all. Me and Moses, mostly me, we get everything set up and then pack when we're ready to leave. We go ahead and make arrangements, business things. . . ."

All the time she is inching to her left down the bunk very slowly sliding down the bunk towards me and I am inching to my left, trying to do it so slow that it won't look like I'm moving. She's smiling, looking right into my eyes like she's listening, even interested. Her left hand is free and her right hand is up against the little flat bulge of her stomach just below the navel that's got a rhinestone winking in it. That right hand has still got the Colt .45 pointing right at me.

About this time I am up against the wall.

"Is that all?"

Her free left hand moves over and kind of tickles me on the inside of my thigh. Naturally I can't help twitching a little bit.

"Sensitive?"

"I'm a little bit goosey, anyway, Lady," I say, "but under the circumstances . . ."

"You're sweating, too."

"It's a hot day."

"The air conditioner is on," she says. "Don't you feel it?"

She leans across and kisses my ear. She lets her tongue aloose to run all around in there. I try and sit very still with both my hands on my knees, looking straight ahead. I figure she's going to blow my head off any minute now.

"What else do you do?" She whispers in my ear.

"Different things," I say. "I used to look after the snakes when we had 'em."

"What did you have snakes for?"

"Country people, you know. Some of them get so worked up when they get saved they like to have snakes crawling all over them just to prove it. It says something about it in the Bible."

"Isn't it dangerous?"

"No," I say. "We didn't have no poisonous snakes. And anyway I had me some stuff to give 'em that would make 'em all kind of sleepy and relaxed."

"Do you like snakes?"

"Not specially. I mean, I can take 'em or leave 'em," I say. "Please ma'm, don't do that."

On account of her left hand has done strayed up just enough where she's fixing to give me trouble and embarrassment.

"You know what you are?"

"No, ma'm."

"Trash," she says.

Zip goes the zipper and I feel the cool air, only I don't want to look and see if what I feel is really so.

152

"That may be so, ma'm," I say. "But it ain't a nice thing to say to a fella you don't know well."

"I'm not a nice girl," she says. "Are you comfortable?"

"No, m'am."

"Get comfortable."

And she gives me a pretty good shove, I'd say, for a little thing, and I kind of topple back on the pillows of Red's bunk.

"Ain't you got no shame at *all*, woman?"

"Nope," she says, curling up close beside me.

"What if Red walks in here right now?"

"I'll kill him," she says, putting the point of the pistol on the bridge of my nose between my eyes and just leaving it there. I sneak a crosseyed look at it and it looks terrible. It don't feel too good either, kind of cold and oily.

"Do you ever perform?"

"I ain't got a whole lot of talent for the show business."

"That's too bad," she says.

"I used to whistle pretty good. You want me to whistle you a tune?"

"Just tell me about the snakes."

"That's a pretty big subject, m'am. There's all different kinds. . . ."

Then she busts out laughing right in my face, laughing so hard I'm scared shitless she's going to forget and squeeze off a round. Right between the eyes, poor boy! Maybe the last thing I'll ever see of this world is the face of a crazy woman laughing at me. Well, we all got to go sometime and I'll be a sonofabitch if I'll let her *laugh* me to death.

"What's so funny?"

"You've still got your hat on!"

Sure enough I do.

"Excuse me," I say.

153

"Didn't your mama teach you to take off your hat when a woman gets in bed with you?"

SHERIFF JACK STARR

Here comes a fat one that looks like an Arab or a Jew running up to us.

"Afternoon gentlemen," he says. "Can I be of assistance to you?"

"Are you the one they call Red Smalley?"

"No, sir, I'm the business manager."

"I was fixing to say you don't do a lot of justice to your picture if you're the one."

He tries to smile. That's all he can do – stand there and smile. It's kind of a weak smile, but you have to give him credit for trying.

"You don't look much like a preacher neither," I say, still looking him over, not looking at Flowers when I say: "Do he look like a preacher to you, Rosebud?"

"Not like a Christian preacher," Rosebud says.

I climb out of the car and square my hat and hike up my belt.

"Course you just never can tell nowadays," I'm saying. "The way folks advertise things is a crying shame."

"He has a new picture of him made every year, Sheriff."

Rosebud gets out on the other side. First thing he does – clink, clink – is shake his pants legs. Rosebud was an M.P. in the Army and got in the habit of wearing boot chains inside his britches, still wears 'em bloused like that over the top of his boots. Like to look sharp in his uniform. I can see what's he's got his so-called mind on. There's a woman kind of strolling over towards us.

"He's got more nerve than I do," I'm telling the fat guy. "I won't let nobody come near me with a camera."

"Yes, sir, Sheriff," he says. "I know what you mean."

I just bet you do, you little old fat ugly man, you. You've got yourself a great big round belly and a face like a Halloween jackolantern; just a butterball. Kind of a fellow it would be a pleasure to put on the road gang for thirty-sixty days and see if you just don't melt and disappear in the hot sun. All that would be left of you would be them suede, nigger-style shoes. Kind of a soft, sneaky, rug-merchant kind of a guy it would be a pleasure to boot in the butt.

"How many more of you are there?"

I see the trailer, the truck that looks like it wouldn't make it from here to the highway and the big old Buick they use to pull the trailer. Over across the field, just under the trees, the sun blinks off of the point of a brand new sports car.

"Just the other manager, Mr Cartwright."

He would be the one that took off quick as he saw us turn off the road. A man that runs that quick ain't got nothing worth hiding.

"What's that over yonder? Looks kind of like one of them *foreign* cars to me. Belong to you?"

He doesn't even look when I point. He's got his eyes right on me.

"No, sir," he says. "It belongs to a lady."

"This one?" pointing at the woman with the skim milk complexion and the way of handling what she's got that just doesn't fit a brand new car or the definition of a lady either.

"No, sir," he says. "A young lady who drove here to see Reverend Smalley."

"People come from far and wide to see a preacher," I say.

"Sometimes they do."

"Rosebud," I say. "Take a run over there and check the licence on that car."

He is just making the acquaintance of the woman, got his hat cocked a little, talking to her and she's smiling and listening and looking at him with those big old, baby-blue eyes.

"Take the lady with you," I say. "Maybe she'd enjoy a ride in a police car."

I turn back to the fat man.

"All right," I say, "Where's he at?"

"In the tent," he says. "I'll go get him."

"Don't bother," I say, starting for the tent.

"He's meditating, Sheriff. Maybe I better go tell him you're here."

"I'll only be a little while and then he can meditate all he wants to."

Inside the tent it's kind of shadowy after the bright sun and hot, too. It'll be hot tonight too. Some people don't seem to mind the heat when they come to one of these things. Like some of them have got to get good and sweaty before they can start to feel religious.

There he is, sitting down at the far end, reading his Bible. Big enough too, big enough and red-headed enough to live up to his name. Reading along slow, word by word, following his finger across the page, moving his lips too. Well, I guess he can read anyway, Which is a damn sight more than most of these travelling so-called preachers.

"How do," I say. "Are you L. J. Griggs?"

He looks up quick and surprised, even mad for a flash of a second, mean looking. Only a second, though. He sees the khaki, the leather, the light on the badge and the butt of the pistol, and the broadbrim hat and he's already blank faced, wary, on his feet and fighting a reflex to reach for a hat he isn't wearing and yank it off his head. He's been trained. Somebody trained him a long time ago.

"Hello, Sheriff."

"Star's the name, Jack Star, County Sheriff."

We shake hands. He has a heavy-boned, strong, calloused grip.

"Is your name Griggs?"

"I haven't got anything to hide," he says. "Yes, sir, that was the name I had before I got the call."

"Still is too, ain't it?"

"I guess you're talking about in a courtroom with a judge and a lawyer and papers and so forth."

"That's exactly what I'm talking about," I say.

"Big Red Smalley is the name I go by and work under."

"Like an alias."

"I never gave myself the name in the first place. The Smalley part was a mistake. The first time I ever preached a tent meeting we borrowed some paper fans, like we always do, from a funeral parlour. The fans had *Smalley* printed on both sides in great big letters. Some people just naturally took it for granted it was my name and the name stuck. The other part was bound to happen. I just kind of acquired it as I went along. The first time I recall anybody referring to me as Big Red, like it was my real name, was in Murfreesboro, Tennessee."

"Now tell me something," I say. "This L. J. Griggs, the one you used to be and still are as far as the Law is concerned, did he ever get into any trouble with the Law?"

"I don't deny I've got a record, Sheriff. My past ain't no secret. It's an open book. I read it and weep. But that man you're talking about, L. J. Griggs, he's dead. In a figurative sense, he's dead and gone. Saint Paul tells us all that we must put off the old man and put on the new. That's what I did.

157

He also said. 'Thou fool, that which thou sowest is not quickened, except it die. . . .' So, in a way, you might even call me a murderer. I killed L. J. Griggs. And I dug his grave with pleasure and buried him deep."

"I can see you're familiar with your scripture," I say. "So am I, as it happens. I read my Bible too and pray, even if I don't make my living at it. Right now I'm making my living and I just want to get a few things straight. This Griggs has been busted on some pretty serious charges."

"He did his time, didn't he? He took his medicine. He took the worst you people could hand out and come back for more!"

"Take it easy," I say.

You know better than that, big boy. There's always worse. There's no man alive that can't be broken down to jello sooner or later by the Law. We could break you. If I was a cruel man I could make you curse God before morning. And don't think I'd mind doing it either. I'd like to see just how much faith you've got, you paid preacher, you jailbird making your living claiming to be a preacher of the Lord. Like to see how long it would take to turn you against Him.

"The last time I ever saw Griggs," he's saying, "was in the jail at Forth Smith, Arkansas. I walked out of there and left him to rot."

"Facts," I say. "Facts are my business. You can't convict a man figuratively in an imaginary courthouse and send him to an imaginary jail."

"Good men, Sheriff, better men than you or I, have acquired a police record. Saint Paul himself was thrown into a Roman dungeon. Our Lord and Saviour Jesus Christ was hauled and dragged up in front of a magistrate by the name of Pontius Pilate. That's in black and white too. You might even say Jesus Christ had a police record."

"You might," I say. "You got a point too. I might even agree with you except I didn't get called or chosen for my job. I got to stand for election every few years."

He laughs at that. He's got good teeth or else a damn good set of false ones. His curly goat's hair shakes when he moves his head. All those little curls, a wild looking head of hair that looks like some kind of a wig and isn't. And the eyes. The eyes are green, pale green with a strange light in them, a light without a source. They cloud over and then get clear again. He sees you, but he's really looking at something else. Not in the tent or the field or the County. Maybe not in the world where we live out our time and where, whether it's a dream or a fact, when you kick a rock you stub your toes and it hurts. He may be looking at some place where you could kick boulders like footballs and never feel a thing. It isn't the first time I've seen a light like that in somebody's eyes. I have seen it in the eyes of men wrapped up in straightjackets, foaming at the mouth like mad dogs.

"Sheriff," he says. "I know you're a busy man."

"I won't be long," I say. "I've just got a couple of questions."

"Ask me anything you want to."

"What are you doing here?" I say.

"Sheriff," he says. "All we want to do is hold a religious service."

"There's plenty of places. Why pick this one? This is only a little old town drying on the vine. There aren't enough souls worth saving for you to even slow down, let alone throw up a tent."

"We just want to have a tent meeting. An old fashioned revival. My only plan is to preach the word of God. Is that a crime around here?"

"No, sir," I say. "I guess you could say we tolerate the word of God as much as the next place."

"What's the problem, Sheriff? Will you just tell me that much?"

"That's why I'm here," I say. "You hold your meeting. You sing and shout and pray and preach as much as you please. That's your privilege. This spot is County property, but you're welcome to use it. You have your revival and then you pack up and get out of here and don't ever come back. You hear?"

"Yes, sir."

Now he cuts his eyes away and looks down at the ground. That's all I wanted, but I'm sick of myself for wanting to see that happen. When he looks up, he's got tears in his eyes.

"Do I look like a rich man to you?" he says. "Am I sleek and fat, living off the best fruits of the land. Why don't you look around you? Take a look. This is all I own in the world. I don't even own a blade of grass. All I want and all I need is enough strength to keep on doing the Lord's work."

"You're either a liar or the luckiest man alive."

"You don't give a man much choice."

"You made your choices a long time ago," I say.

"Why don't you come tonight?" he says. "Why don't you come and see for yourself?"

"I guess I'll have to get along without it."

"Aren't you a religious man, Sheriff?"

"Let's just say I read my Bible and say my prayers and go to church on Sunday. I don't feel the need of a circus tent."

I start back up the aisle, knowing he's watching me, following me out with hate and anger burning him alive. I stop and turn around on him.

"Griggs?"

I'm going to wait until he answers to that name if it takes until Judgement Day.

"Yes, sir?"

"You don't have any snakes with you, anything like that?"

"No sir."

"You sure?"

"You want to see? I'll show you around myself."

"I'll take your word for it."

I step outside the tent and stop a moment to mop my brow and breathe the fresh air. I take a look at the mountains. Well, they're still there. They haven't moved an inch.

I go back to the car. There's Rosebud standing with his hat on the back of his head trying to sweet-talk the woman. She's heard it all, boy. She heard all the sweet talk there is in the world while you were still running around in diapers. Here comes the fat man running up, all smiling again, to open the door for me. I get in.

"Rosebud!"

"Sir?"

"Let's get the hell out of here."

He hops in behind the wheel. He gives a little wave to the woman and she gives him a smile and a nod, then he scratches out across the field. Just as we get to the arch, he flicks the switch that sets the red light blinking and cuts on the siren full blast. We make a squealing turn.

"What do you think you're doing?"

"I'm just giving the lady a thrill," he says.

I twist my head and see the three of them standing in front of the tent, the big one shading his eyes against the sun to watch us disappear.

"Cut it off!"

"What's eating you?" he says.

"Why don't you just shut up and drive the car?"

"Where's Judith?" he says, not even looking at me.

"In the trailer, I guess."

"Go get her."

Out of the trailer comes old Hookworm without his hat on and looking like he just saw a ghost. He stumbles down the steps and right past me, doesn't even see me. He just says "*Je-e-e-e-sus Christ,*" to himself and then takes off at a dead run across the field for the woods.

I go inside and there stands Little Miss Nympho Bitch in front of the mirror. She's got that black trenchcoat on with the collar turned up, and she has on Cartwright's hat and it's pulled down. She's got his pistol in her hand. She turns and sees me and smiles.

"How would this do for a costume?" she says. "I could be a lady bandit."

"Yeah," I say. "It might be a brand new way to take up the collection."

"Do you really think I'm silly?"

"Red wants you."

"What for?"

"He didn't say."

She tosses the hat and the gun on the bed. She slips out of her raincoat and looks at herself in the mirror like she was the first woman in the world. Like nobody else ever had one but her and if she could figure out some way to make love to herself it would be the most, the end, better than the book of Revelation. I got news for you, chickie-babe. It would be a drag. You wouldn't like it.

"What do you want me to tell him?"

"Tell him I'm taking a shower."

And with that she slips into the little cubicle shower and draws the curtain.

"Be careful," I say. "Don't use up all the water."

On the way out I take the clip out of Cartwright's .45, empty it and then put it back. She can play with it all she wants to now.

Moses is waiting for me outside the door.

"You better talk to him," he says.

I can hear Red inside the tent cursing and yelling and throwing the chairs around. I go quickly and stand in the entrance of the tent. He's throwing the chairs all over the place.

"Godamn!" he yells. "Godamn them to hell! Son of a bitches! Godamn their eyes! Let me *alone* . . . !"

He takes a running start and knocks down a whole row of chairs.

I laugh as loud as I can and he stops and looks at me.

"Godamn you too!"

He comes toward me. I pick up a chair in both hands and let him have it over the head. The chair splinters and he sits down, dazed, shaking his head.

"I can break chairs too," I say.

He's crying now. I kneel beside him and hold his head in my arms.

"You're going to have a lump on your head," I say. "But it won't show."

"Call it off," he says quietly. "I can't do it."

"Never mind. . . ."

"I won't preach in this godamn, god forsaken place."

"Just sit still. Everything's going to be all right."

"One of these days I'm going to have to kill you," he says.

"One of these days you may not get a chance. One of these days you'll wake up and find me gone."

He laughs now. "That will be the day," he says. "That will be the day!"

We stand up and he brushes the dirt off himself. He looks around the tent and shakes his head.

"I guess I kind of made a mess."

"I guess you did."

"Listen," he says to me. "I'm sick of the whole thing. I'm sick to death of everything. All I want to do is puke. I hate them all. Why don't they ever leave me alone?"

"I'm not too enthusiastic about the cops either."

He turns to me and lifts my face in his hand, looking into my eyes.

"Miami," he says. "You're a good old girl."

I wait for him to kiss me, hoping he will now, knowing his need. It's all I can do for him. Maybe all I'm good for.

"Where's Judith?"

"I was wondering when you'd get around to that."

"Where is she?"

"Taking a shower."

"What for?"

"I don't know," I say. "Maybe she likes to be clean. Maybe she likes to feel all clean and fresh."

"What do you think, Miami? You think a shower bath would make you clean and fresh again?"

"What don't you try one and see what it does for you?"

"You know something?" he says. "That's one thing I never did in my whole life. I never took a shower with a woman."

"There's room enough for two. Course it will be kind of crowded. But you'll figure out something and if you don't, she will. She's got a very active imagination, that one. It might even be good, all slippery and soapy . . ."

"You've got a dirty mind."

164

"We're two of a kind. We belong together, Red. We're both dirty from head to foot with the kind of dirt that you can't wash off in a shower bath."

"Speak for yourself," he says and he walks away from me.

At the entrance of the tent he turns around with a big smile. He throws up both hands in the air like he was preaching and his big voice booms out and fills the tent.

"And it came to pass in the eveningtide that David arose from off his bed and walked upon the roof of his house: and from the roof he saw a woman washing herself; and that woman was very beautiful to look upon."

"Red," I say. "You're forgetting the most important part."

"What's that?"

"David was a king."

"Well," he says, "a man can't have everything."

"You better hurry," I say, "before she uses all the hot water."

I set up a fallen chair and sit down in it. He's gone. I feel like crying and I might even do it. Except that I used up all my tears a long, long time ago. Isn't that something? Can't even cry when I want to, when I need to, when I really feel like it. Can't even cry. Anybody can do that. It doesn't take much talent. It's the easiest thing in the world. . . .

"Can I get you something?"

Here's old Moses, good Moses who can't stand to see anybody suffer. Moses, you overstuffed, ugly clown, you good, good, man. Now I feel them. You see? I do have tears. I can still cry!

"No," I say. "Everything's going to be all right, all right . . ."

He pats me on the shoulder.

"Are you sure?"

I nod, still crying, but smiling at him now. Smiling and crying at the same time.

"I never was so sure of anything in my whole life," I tell him.

4

I sought in mine heart to give myself unto wine, yet acquainting my
heart with wisdom; and to lay hold
on folly, till I might see what was
good for the sons of men, which
they should do under the heaven
all the days of their life.

ECCLESIASTES II, 3

Now it is late afternoon and the shadows of the western mountains fall, splash and spread dark stains across the patterned pines and fields of the valley. As if the Flood were coming on as steady or sure as those massive shadows. As if soon they will all be drowned and from the bottom of the sea look up where bright stars bob and wink like buoys, far, far beyond the reach of townsman or traveller, remote, indifferent to their unheard cries, supercilious as the lanterns of Noah's ark, riding the crest, floating calmly towards Ararat and the inevitable, beautiful assignation of the dove and the olive branch.

Meanwhile each is alone with himself, with heart and guts, with the long pilgrimage of blood to nowhere and back, with memories like a tribe of ghosts, with hungers, furies, fears, and losses, with a mind that schemes and works equations like a slide-rule, with the imagination which is at once the hunter and the hunted, and with the soul (wherever it is) speechless, naked, in chains, wallowing in every conceivable filth, yet always dreaming of a purity so bright and dazzling clean and shining it would strike a pair of mortal eyes blind to behold it.

Behold Cartwright, hatless, dishevelled and sore distressed, as he crouches on all fours and stares into the pale blind eyes of the sports car.

CARTWRIGHT

But as for me, I am a worm, and no man; a very scorn of men, and the outcast of the people.

Take that you freaking blue bug! Take that you mother-freak of a mongrelized syphilitic cockroach! Your daddy was a

169

cross-eyed, blue-balled beetle. Your mama was a spastic cock-roach. And you! Look what you come up with-wheels! You freak, you got wheels on your ass!

There! I slash the tyres with my trusty knife. It ain't no boy scout blade neither. It's five inches of steel and can cut whiskers as good as anything Gillette has come up with yet. Crawling around on my hands and knees and getting them one at a time. Then hunching back on my hams and panting like a dog to watch you settle down comfortable on your rims with a big long kind of a sign like a fat old lady getting into a hammock.

She never even knew about the knife. How dumb can one person get? Any time I could have reached down in my pocket and come up quick (specially when she just grit her teeth and closed her eyes and said *don't stop, you bastard, if you come before I do I'll kill you*) and fixed a brand new place for her to smile right underneath her chin and all the way from ear to ear. Or I could have, if I wasn't a gentlemen, tried out some *Karate* on her or some of my judo. Except I never did learn any defence for when a woman has got you flat on your back and got a cocked .45 jammed right between your eyes.

Nobody makes a fool or a monkey out of me! Nobody . . .!

except Dreama did from that first unlucky night   I left Miss Snead & walked inside the tent to see what I could see   first two was well-built & already had me ready to compete with Rev. Bob Richards famous vaulter and wheaties-eater then she come on with record player playing "Blue Moon" big round firm stacked blond named right because if something had've jumped right out of my dreams said here I am big boy it would've been her   she must have seen the look cause she done it all for me & I stood there watching her navel with the rhinestone & g-string with sequins swaying like a cobra snake

me hypnotized   paid $1 for private show $10 for very private
where I passed out cold maybe a mickey only not sick just the knockout
drops & woke up husband pimp addict more asleep than before until
Red come and got me free from anyway that
  many a lowdown mean trick she pulled on me first to last being a
puppet on strings namely one string dancing
  none worse than the first the honey-ha-ha-moon we began in
apartment her friend she said oh very nice apartment we could use
  oh honey I'm so excited says she I never had no husband before I
mean it's special I'm so hot & excited & I'll do anything you ask or
ever even dreamed to make you happy only first you must promise the
same   sure, baby
  no matter how silly & I'll do same for you for marriage is mystical
union of two makes one no secrets allowed & so forth   sure baby
first then something she says I've always wanted   anything anything
  take off everything I'll stand on the table on top of the table & you
go round and round table on all fours barking   like dog till I tell you
sit up & beg   aw honey   you promised you said so don't you love
me do you or don't you
  so bow-wow bow-wow round & around bow-wow now sit up &
beg then suddenly laughter gales of everywhere baffled befuddled I find
out the audience sits behind a one-way mirror   so later she calms me
saying don't bitch baby doll we got $100.00 for that dumb trick   a
fine way to start a honeymoon
  $1,000,000.00 not enough for the dumb trick of marrying Dreama
laugh Dreama laugh only look who's laughing now

Standing on two feet like a man I slash the seats and smash the
mirrors. Yank up the hood and jerk every wire I can get my
hands on. The smartest thing of all I do, the Trick of Tricks, is
cutting the fan belt about half in two so the Bitch will get the
whole thing fixed maybe then start driving off like the maniac

she is, 110 miles an hour and then *bam*! *pow*! *blam*! *blooey*! the freaking radiator boils over and the engine burns out on her 1,000,000 miles from nowhere.

Now I piss happily upon her licence plates (would crap in her blue tennis shoes if I could and maybe I will too later). And now, Blue Bug, I am fixing to blind you. I will kick out your eyes. Take that . . .!

"*Oh, ow*! *Godamn*! *Oh sweet Jesus, my foot*! *I've done busted my foot* . . .!

3.

He is left there, hopping on one foot in a little circle near the wounded car, a mad dance which only the car itself, one-eyed, but unvanquished, views. No doubt the car has seen worse. The car won't tell.

Assume a camera, a lens invisible to human eyes, forever watching and recording. It would turn away mercifully from this, pull back and up first to the level of the limbs of the pines, look down brief and dispassionate upon the wounded beast and the hopping, furious hunter, then, not dissolving, not cutting even, but panning across the theatrical backdrop of mountains. Then drop to the level of the field, move in a smearing rush through the tall irregular jungle of grass, seeing as the ant sees, hostile, infinitely dangerous and without limit, the field still brilliant, dazzled, dazed with sun. Above the clear air waves with vague presentiment of coming dark.

Cut now and follow in air the ribboned grey-white streak of a mocking bird, a flash and flutter, a rush, zoom, sweep of wings from the trees to the tent, coming to rest on the ridgepole and pausing there, wary as a weather vane, head cocked, a grey-white parody of an old time preacher in a frock coat,

172

listening observing, then gone again toward the far trees, an impulse so abrupt it dazzles the eye of the beholder.

Drop from the top of the tent to one who rests in the shade of the truck, leaning back against one of the great smooth tyres.

The camera comes now for a close-up of the face. The man in the moon is smoking a cigar. His veiled eyelids droop more, the corner of his eyes crinkle into deeper crow's feet, against the grey smoke of the cigar and the blaring, blazing Technicolour of the ever-fading sun. He is thinking not of himself now or the truck he leans against or the tent or the mountains or even the town called High Pines out of sight. Thinking instead in a free, easy flow of images, a vague and uneasy blur of himself younger, so long ago it seems now, seeing it without pang or pain, sorrow or guilt, merely as something that happened to a young man long ago in a story he barely remembers.

MOSES

Deliver my soul from the sword, my darling from the power of the dog.

A deuce and a half comes down the rutted road fast, bumping, boiling dust behind it. The driver is running scared because from near here on he will be under observation. He's running for the trees in the distance carrying the danger with him there. Only they do not see that, men in back, packed in tight along the bench, gripping their rifles, heavy in all their newly issued gear, helmets jouncing with each bump. They see the dust behind them and the field growing wider and longer under the bright half-oval of the tarp. Then the truck slowing down, double-clutching as the gears go down, grinding and growling, and then the field behind them is gone. Trees are all around them.

The truck stops. Someone calls his name. He rises, fat and clumsy then as now and always, looks briefly at the row of faces on the bench opposite, deadpan faces of strangers all turning the light of their eyes on him. He tries to smile, knowing as he does it is a weak one, a poor meaningless little hail and farewell, then bent low, but not low enough, for he strikes his head on the overhead rib, his grin more foolish now, as if in apology, and heavy and awkward steps over the strap and the tailgate dropping down, landing hard, stumbling, pitching forward as the truck moves away behind him. His helmet rolls, his rifle clatters. He looks up, still grinning weakly, lifting his head which now seems so light without the weight of the helmet, looking up past the tips of a pair of boots, up past faded fatigues, buckles and buttons into the high far face of M/Sgt. Elwood Roberts. The lips are grinning but the little eyes are bloodshot with fatigue.

"Get up you freaking pig," Roberts said.

Then gathering his gear, he stumbled with Roberts through the trees, past strangers in fox holes. Roberts all the while talking, speaking to no one and to everyone: *look look boys what they done sent us they call it a replacement for Christ's sake a warm body I call it a big fat slob Jesus what next. . . .*

They and the Captain, a thin man, grizzled, needing a shave, his bright eyes ringed with black circles. He looks at him (me), looks me up and down and cusses me and says in the same way, the same flat monotone addressed to everyone and no one

this is an assault company by God & we don't count socks here & we don't sit behind no freaking typewriters all day long & goof off or never no never sing & dance with the U.S.O.   we fight that's all we fight & I give you maybe 2 days at the most before I turn your fat ass over to Graves Registration who will cheerfully jam one of your dog-

tags in the roof of your mouth which is what the notch is for & tie a bow on your pecker if you still got one & then sew you up inside of a mattress cover & drop you in a shallow hole in the ground where the worms can get at that good fat meat & maybe ten years from now if we win this freaking war your little old Jew-mama & Jew-papa can come over here having saved up their dough & visit a green place with a headstone among thousands that's got your name on it & mine too & Roberts here too & all the rest of us with the wrong bones underneath but who the hell cares one set of bones is pretty much similar to the next one & maybe they'll spell our names right & maybe not & who gives a fist-flying the best gospel good news I got for you is they can't kill you but one time only as far as we know.

Not stopping then either, going on to the bitter end, the chewed-slick bone of his knowledge and experience:

so bid farewell to whatever it is or was you loved about living food maybe well we got lousy chow mostly cold & you can figure to die with a crummy meal in your guts if you're lucky if it's comfort forget that too you'll die tired & dirty with wet cold feet & dirty underwear if it's beauty forget it forever you done had all you're getting from here on even shit will look like wildflowers if it's pussy you've had your last of that too it's a waste of time to even think about it & as far as I'm concerned it's waste of my time to put you on the Morning Report understand understand???

    Yes, sir

    goodbye fat boy I don't even want to know your name but one thing more you might think about chew on when you get ready to throw down your rifle & run that's if we lose this war they're going to take mama & papa & cook them down to make soap for some pretty fraulein to wash her ass with her blond shiny ass all glowing with mama & papa so forget about running too better to be heels up in some filthy foreign field than that that's the choice you've got carry on. . . .

175

I outlived them all and saw the end of it, always afraid and never a hero, whatever that may be, though somewhere is a piece of paper, more than one in fact, about me with the purple heart I won for giving blood, with the unit citation and with the final bronze thing the ten of us left got for taking that village. Say what you want to, but never forget a fat man who gave up the ghost and thus was able to spur his foolish body to go when they said to go forward; my poor foolish body never failed me.

body my horse & I the rider who never rode a horse in his life before or since but tamed one once & for all to never falter   Hector Tamer of Horses Achilles Tamer of Horses   I too then Tamer of Horses funny fat ugly horse I tamed & brought back for a souvenir seeing Roberts go off in butcher's fragments screaming in vivid air   seeing Captain go down like a tree fall from one slug the size of a cigarette butt fired by a sniper seeing them go down one by one while I cold hungry sick tired went forward squeezed off my rounds on the run stepping over their bodies kraut G.I. until they said stop it's all over

Lucky or not, I am alive and am still breathing. I learned then, knew and know still a few things worth knowing. I know that pain is bad and life is precious. I grieve not for the fallen any more than I ask them to grieve for me. I curse nobody, being drained of curses. *This is an Assault Company, by God!* over those wide fields, through trees and deadly streets of villages, towns and cities I ran and I run still, bent low, forward, not backward, holding my weapon, until my time comes. Asking for nothing, not even silence, peace and quiet, or the grace of a clean speedy death. If I must howl, then howl I will. Brave men can howl. If the mind goes, decaying with the body, both of them rotten, still I will ask for nothing. Beg neither forgiveness nor mercy.

176

if we meet again some place beyond place some time beyond time I will help you bind your many fragments M/Sgt. Roberts & hold hands on that twilit playground telling you don't be afraid fear not the Captain poor Captain was right as rain they can't kill any of us but once . . .

4.

Now to the tent, a stifling and gloomy cave where a woman sits alone on a chair, rubbing *Noxema* on her shoulders. She is sunburned from the folly of standing in the sun too long with the young, muscle-headed Deputy Sheriff. She could do that much for him, then, keep the young one preoccupied with her attention, batting her eyes as if he were the first, young, tall, flat bellied, well-hung young stud she had ever seen. Thus burned her shoulders and back pink and painful in the sun.

MIAMI

I am poured out like water, and all my bones are out of joint; my heart also in the midst of my body is even like melting wax.

All we have to do now is wait for the dark to come. Then we'll hear the sound of the first car or pickup truck coming, all jammed with its scrubbed, damp-haired, cargo of a country family in clean clothes. Then a sound in the tent like the buzzing of insects. Rising and falling. Inside the smell of humans close together. Finally Moses at the piano and the music begins. They quiet down, waiting. At last he appears, tall broadshouldered, serious. He opens his mouth to sing. His big voice booms in the tent and they all rise to sing too, following him. He will smile then to encourage them, nod, and to many it will seem that sudden smile is a sign of God's love.

Now I try to be empty. Not to think. To wait. But have

never learned that trick of thinking of nothing at all. I try to think of something funny to kill the time. Gags and one-liners, I know a million of them. They tickle me not. Anecdotes of flesh and spirit, I know books, true ones of absurd desires, crazy positions, and rituals more foolish in word and deed than any hottentot's. But not now. I keep my secrets, some of them anyway, like a priest, a doctor, a lawyer, an Indian chief. I'm in a mood for less than truth and more. I smile recalling the plot and synopsis of *Sinner's Revenge*, a Technicolor blue movie starring among others – you-know-who.

beginning with rich lady beautifully dressed coming down the steps of a mansion to waiting car where waits the Chauffeur James in uniform tipping his hat opening door   car drives off
   nervous light a cigarette then speak through speaking tube to James never mind the party James let's go hunting   yes mam   cruise the streets in limousine back streets sidestreets of City   James sees something REACTS   there's one madame   a midget on the sidewalk we pull over stop
   with midget in back seat drive off
   neck with midget whispering nothing's in midget's ear promising bliss midget bouncing on back seat
   in basement boudoir of mansion play with midget till he's wild & frantic   cometh then James the Chauffeur suddenly drawing aside curtain revealing a cage into which midget is shoved & locked up
   then James & I on the bed make out   midget screaming rage & frustration whilst we two laugh happy together   through similar sequences the cage fills up with more midgets also hunchbacks clubfeet cripples fat & skinny   meanwhile James the Chauffeur has hots for the Maid a dainty French-creature name of Fifi   Fifi bring me my robe my bath salts Fifi paint my toenails brush my hair massage my back etc.   James to me with a plan as Plot thickens

*Let's get Fifi dainty Fifi down there for the show make her perform
then throw her to the Freaks   delightful idea James just when I was
getting bored we seize Fifi strip her protesting enjoy her both of us
tormenting with feathers & ticklers & tricks of all kinds   but Fifi &
James not noticed by me have reached a wordless agreement for Fifi is
young not dainty after all but merely biding her time   I draw the
curtain open revealing the cage full of howling freaks this is how it
ends Fifi dear I say come James   but instead I am seized and shoved
in the cage screaming help help but Fifi and James. draw the curtain
again & clinch like lovers at the final FADE OUT*

*I laugh because it's so absurd the unleashed human erotic imagina-
tion oh rich with folly   how many laughed not but sat silently
sweating glued to these images believing it truly to be a keyhole peek
at Hell*

how many know what hell really is

*neither ecstasy oblivion or endless ultimate orgasm but only know-
ledge the simple knowledge that we are all shadows not flesh by nature
unable to love ourselves or each other.*

hell is the knowledge of gods

*hell I have lived in will live in world without end amen   but Jesus
let me laugh at "Sinner's Revenge"*

Her laughter from the tent surprises Moses. He looks toward
the tent with wonder and compassion, thinking: *poor girl how
can she a whore-horse ridden by all the untamed & ever unable to be
tame or tame herself endure?*

5.

Now to the house where Howie Loomis lives, once a fine house,
a showplace in High Pines, now a sagging hulk in need of paint,
in need of glass for the windows, a place where loose blinds

flap like broken wings in the wind. Inside he sits in the dusty library, among books and old photographs with no light on, only the last afternoon light filtering through the west windows. He has a bottle of whiskey and drinks in spite of the Doctor's orders.

H. J. "HOWIE" LOOMIS

All they that go down in the dust shall kneel before him; and no man hath quickened his soul.

Sure, I'm getting drunk. Drunk as a skunk and who cares? Not me. If it be not now, it will be, and if it be not to come it will be now; readiness is all. They won't find me for a week and won't I be something to look at then? Won't this old house stink? Or maybe I'll just wake up in the morning with a hell of a headache and have to begin again. Back to the store at least clean again and wait for the Angel of Death to show up like a timid salesman new to the territory.

I came back to the store feeling good, feeling fine. In the office I sat down in my old swivel chair and smiled. Full of lunch and ready to catch forty winks, I laid my head on the desk amid the invoices and letters her bare feet had trampled, and I dozed. Closed my eyes at least and seemed to doze. I will just run back the reel on that dance, I said to myself, just to be sure it's all there and that I can summon it up until the day I die. Now begin, sugar, dance like you danced for me!

how white how round how firm she is as she moves & glides to the radio's tune   she smiles & turns & twists for me & her body hot in the airless room sways like a flower in breeze white as gardenias or easter lilies   her shadow looms on the wall maybe flashes past the frosted glass of the door who cares

how white how round how firm she moves & glides rejoicing
then now the film changes first the music   the music is shrieks &
screams still she dances proud & smiling not hearing or if hearing not
caring now there's a cage in the room crammed with the sick &
deformed   they scream but to her it's sweet music in the cage my wife
calls my name
   now she my wife my beautiful wife young again is the dancer
   she dances I sigh with relief the cage is gone   & she will do a strip-
tease but how not having a fig leaf to take off   begins a striptease of
flesh of skin coyly peeling instead of clothes parts of herself my wife
is dancing to music of screams not her own but smiling & smiling &
peeling until I gag & cannot bear to look   stop please stop dancing
God make her stop please stop

I woke covered with cold sweat, The first thing I did was reach
for the phone. After that I blundered out of the store and walked
home not seeing a soul though I know that the pavements were
crowded with the faces of friends and enemies.

6.

To the Fairgrounds again. Off the highway and under the arch,
across the field to the trailer. Where inside the large man sprawls
on the bunk, spent, empty, limp as a drowned man tossed on
the sand by the nuzzling tide. His eyes are closed. He reaches
for something. The girl standing beside smiles offers him her
small, thin hand. His closes over hers, powerful enough to
crush the little bones to powder, but lightly, gently. She sits
down on the edge of the bunk, holding his hand, and looks at
his face. There is a faint smile on his lips as he breathes deeply
and begins to sleep.

JUDITH

Save me from the lion's mouth; thou hast heard me also from among the horns of the unicorns.

All day long he stumbled towards sleep not able to find it. Now he sleeps like a baby, smiling. I did that! I charmed and enchanted the restless giant. I look at him in wonder from the soles of his feet to the crown of his damp, curly hair. I could kill him so easy now in his sleep. Carry his head proudly as Judith took the head of Holofernes back to her city. What if I carried it back to John in a little canvas bag. "Here, John here's a souvenir of my travels." I could snip off his hair like Delilah and then put out his eyes. Then he would always need me. He would lean his weight against me. I would spoon him his food. I would teach him to dance and do tricks like a bear on a chain.

I stand guard over him, holding his limp hand lightly, looking at him and wishing my eyes were hands and mouths. I should have as many mouths as a fly has eyes! See his face in repose is like a child's, unlined and untroubled. I have the power to put him to sleep. I can erase the lines from his face and give him the gift of silence. I will keep him safe always. I have power and he has the power also to wake me from my deepest dreams to the shining shudder of glory.

o I am an orchestra tuning & tuning waiting waiting he arrives & raises his baton I follow his least signal to make music
o I am a wild horse & he the riding master boots & spurs & riding crop   I balk & buck but he breaks me breaks me   teaches teaches till I jump high leap through rings of fire for joy
I am the puppet & he the master
he jerks a string another I dance dance all splintery & my wooden throat screams joy joy & my glass eyes cloud with tears

he bends my body like a bow I cry out until his arrow sings to the target's shiny eye

he maketh of me an harp strung with fretted nerves   plucks them each & all together & of my shrieks makes harmony

once I was a tree but he touches me I shudder out of bark leaves birds fly & roots ungnarl & I am flesh again holy flesh. . . .

o my beloved comes brighter than morning dew to my little garden his eyes are cruel as hawks his hands are pairs of white doves

I am not milk & honey I am bitter & more secret than the thorny rose bush

o my beloved comes to the rose like dew   I drink & drunken open open

he is the hawk & I the dove

when we lie together he is the lion & I am the lamb

he is the sun & I am the moon

I am the water he turns into wine

listen o my beloved I will bathe you with tears & clothe you with kisses always always

7.

Now it is twilight. The sun blows a last faint echoing trumpet call behind the western mountains. The light is suddenly bleached and vague. We are at the bottom of the sea. The dark flood spreads like a stain. There is a sudden startling quiet. Then the noise of crickets tuning.

Moses, behind the small, satisfactory glow of a cigar, mops his brow with a neatly folded square of handkerchief. He slaps a mosquito on his arm and stares, half-amused and half-terrified, at the blot of blood among the dark hairs.

Then there is the sound of an engine groaning on the highway. He listens to it strain and cough, then looks out across the darkening field to see the headlights flick on and grope across the field as the truck, slowly in low gear, heavily loaded, feels it way toward the tent. He drops his cigar and stamps it out, even as he does looking up into the sky to see the first pulsing of the evening star like a small, good diamond in the light. Thinking: *Now it's too late to worry about doom. Wait long enough and the doom comes to you.*

5

Now therefore be ye not grieved,
nor angry with yourselves, that ye
sold me hither: for God did send
me before you to preserve life.

GENESIS XLV, 5

I am on the platform looking into their upturned faces, listening to them sing an old gospel hymn and singing along with them. Not just to lead and direct them note by note, but so I don't have to listen myself if I don't want to. There are many inequities in the Lord's gifts to his creatures, but none so radically different to my way of thinking as the human voice. God or some absurd combination of genes and chromosones gave me a good one. A man takes his own gifts and attributes for granted. A man judges from his own gifts, feelings, habits, ideas and ideals. It's the nature of a man to do so. A virtuous man, a good one, will see good within and behind your most blatantly malevolent action. And a bad man will sniff the stink of himself behind the charity of a saint. Maybe that's why they say a bad man makes the best Judge. Since every Judge I ever come up before was a first class son of a bitch, I must've come before some of the better ones.

Maybe that's what God intended too. For every man to be bound and shackled in the prison of himself and his own little padded cell of self-knowledge. Else where would you ever get sheep and goats? Else where would the inexhaustible supply of suckers come from. Let copulation thrive and let one be born every minute.

Adam was the first Sucker. And ain't we all a bunch of the same?

For the longest time, longer than I care to admit, it used to drive me to the sheer edge of distraction to hear most people sing or pray or even talk. I blamed them for the sounds which emerged from their throats as much as for the stupid words which came forth coated with the slime of the tongue. It used to make me sick at my stomach to hear a congregation singing. "All things come of thee, O Lord. And of Thine own have we given Thee." Making the sound like a flock of crows in a tree. Making it like a huge bronx cheer in unison. But then I would every once in a while hear a human voice so beautiful, so rich and true to tone, pitch and rhythm, and it might be anywhere, lost somewhere amid a crowd of blank insipid faces, that I would feel a tightness, a choking in my own throat, a taste of salt on my tongue.

I knew a crippled girl once who could sing like an angel. A voice so sweet and clear and pure it would break your heart, shatter it to powder, just to hear her. People used to crowd the church to hear her sing and she sang for every wedding and funeral for miles around. It is the nature of the beast to be sentimental. They listened. They had the luxury of tears. She lead them to Jesus. Look what Jesus gave that poor little old girl, they said to themselves. He's bent and twisted her body like a root in the ground, but he gave her the voice of an angel. So, you see, there is Justice.

And that girl, God knows and I know it too, had a heart as cold and hard as Italian marble and the charity of a rattlesnake. She would have clapped her hands for joy to see us all tortured, broken and twisted one at a time until we were all so mishapen, distorted, deformed that she alone was beautiful in the world. Our tongues yanked out with pliers from the roots, our eyes gouged out, so she alone could sing and we could only listen.

I stand here listening and even liking the sound of it now. I look down and see Moses plunking away at that two-bit piece of a piano just as solemn and serious as if it were a piece of real music. Moses, he can play Bach and Mozart and Debussey. Only he don't ever get the chance. I keep him playing crap.

And, you know, it tickles me – he's come to like it too. I see E. J. Cartwright, *Elijah* Cartwright In Person, absurd in his choir robe as a clown, singing away to beat the band, his eyes roaming easily like a pair of trained doves all around the tent to gently undress every half-way-decent-looking woman in the room and see what's underneath. I saw a stripper one time who used a pair of trained doves in her act. They fluttered around her and were trained to peck at and undo the knots that held her costume together. It wasn't a bad act either, except like most novelties and specialities, it was only fun once. And do you know what's underneath? Woman. That's what. If she's all together and hasn't been too much carved up by the surgeons yet, you'll find a couple of titties with nipples, a soft stomach and a fat ass and at the crotch a little patch of wiry hair camouflaging a set of lips, the portals of desire. Why do we worship that small hairy portal? God knows. Cartwright don't. In fact the truth is he don't really worship the Pussy. He does not bow before the Ideal Pussy. He dreams a heaven of women all his slaves. A harem-heaven. A vague, gauzy kind of a harem-heaven. Replete with disjointed, amputated abstractions of Woman. Filled with beautiful breasts, buttocks, thighs, hands, and feet or what have you. What do you think he would do if I could offer him a harem-heaven in abstraction all right, but all reduced to the ultimate truth? A harem-heaven of Pussies. Every kind, size, shape and form. All alive and all obedient and eager to gratify him. And all without the unnecessary encumbrage of bones and body, mind and emotions. Merely the *ding an sich*. What do you think? He'd run away and hide. He'd choose hell – even if hell meant eternal celibacy. Because for him it's an endless search, a continual undressing in search of something else. Truth? No, because when he gets there, there it is. He knows what he's going to find, but he hopes he won't find it. In which case, it's

189

the striptease, it's *the search itself* which is his idea of Truth. He doesn't really and truly expect to peel some bitch down to the basic essentials and find a beautiful Pussy waiting for him. Who ever, in human history, recorded the discovery of a *beautiful* Pussy? Good ones and bad ones, yes. Happy, sad, tight and slack, warm and wet or dry and cold but never a thing of beauty and a joy forever.

Meaning, by this analogy, the simple platitude that we keep on going back, digging, poking, searching for the *essential*, the heart of things, knowing from the minute we start that when we get there it's going to be what we knew all the time. Wanting to find this and not wanting to at the same time. Knowing as we all slide down that gleaming roller-coaster of the rainbow that there is, indeed, a pot at the end of it. It's not a pot of gold. It steams and stinks.

I keep Cartwright around to remind me of that simple fact. Call him a fool if you want to. Fool is what he is all right. But I reckon if I was (were if you insist on grammar once in a while) John Bunyan I'd call him Mr Wordly-Wise and be done with it.

Here I stand looking at this little field of folk, the same faces, always the same faces, hating and pitying them. We're getting there. Only a couple more verses to go and I'll tip old Moses a nod and away we go. Get the show on the road. Oh, they'll get their money's worth all right. More than that probably. Because I don't feel the least twinge of regret. And that's a blessing.

All day long, with the usual crap and nonsense going on all around me, I've been looking for a text to preach. I like to have thumbed that Bible to death. I've read the great and the famous ones. I've read the hard sayings. I've read the easy ones that any half-ass, half-baked, country preacher could make a four-square shouting sermon out of. And I've looked at obscure ones it would take a true poet to translate. I've meditated, memorized, contemplated. I've prayed for a sign. I've closed my eyes and pointed blindly, jabbed my finger into the middle of random verses thinking maybe, Las Vegas style, I'd hit a row of oranges and lemons, a bell would *ting*! and out pops a tinkling cascade of silver dollars. But all the words were stale and grey and finally only ink printed on a page, little squiggles like the tracks of a small lizard in the sand.

I had a fury within me all day long, a fury of frustration. I was still looking for kind of rough and ready justice. I was using my mind. I figured this: God chose me. He made me a preacher when I didn't want to be one and when I knew better. He even took all the joy out of it. Because I knew, I always knew I was just as good and just as successful, maybe even more so, when I was faking it, playing the part, being the pure con man pure and simple, as when he grabbed hold to me, as a cat grabs a mouse in its mouth, and shook and rattled my ribs and timbers until I thought every bone would snap like a match-stick and all my innards would pop out. Cat and mouse, that's us! And I never could enjoy even the relief of being free of Him because He always had His little ways of letting me know I was only on parole. He would be back to claim me again and use me again. And nothing I could do would ever set me free of Him. I couldn't do anything bad enough. Naturally I could do something bad enough in the world to get myself slapped in jail. But a cell is no place you can hide. I could get myself strapped in the electric chair and the last thing I would hear would be His voice in my ear and maybe His terrible laughter.

Well, a man can get used to almost anything and a rare wise man can even start to like it, choose to, by free choice make not only a virtue but also a pleasure out of his necessity. If that's the limit of freedom, then you can reason yourself into the simple recognition that it's still better than nothing at all. But that wise man all by himself is a fool if he forgets about God. God can take even that away from him.

Here I was, figuring it would go on the same way world without end as long as forever, and I'd just as well get used to it. Even my own rebellion, running away, drinking, and fucking, in the profound delusive hope that He would just *leave me alone*! even all that would go on just as steady and regular as clockwork, the tick and tock of an oldtime railroad conductor's well-kept gold pocket watch.

That's bad news, when you think about it, to know that even your resistance, your rebellion, your blasphemy, is part of the programme. My solace and my consolation, was the fact that after some hard times I knew. I knew the score long before the end of the game. And there was and is no way, better or worse, to change it. Even that desire was part of the plan. But, you know, I actually *thanked* God for slacking off on me that much, enough to let me figure it out on my own. I told myself, all right I can take it. Thank You, God, I said, for finally letting me know I don't need You that much. I'm at least free enough to take You or leave You.

Then this morning I woke up empty. I knew He was gone from me, maybe for good. The world looked all young and green and beautiful again. Gone for good. I'm free! I could have jumped and sung and danced for joy.

I wasn't even awake good, though, hearing them squabble among themselves (and for once to me it was music and I would have run out of the trailer and kissed all three of them for love and charity to share my joy) when a cold notion flew into my brain and squatted there in a pulpy corner like an old buzzard, patient, in a tree: *He's through with you all right, but what makes you think he's going to let you just walk away?* I mean, it's like you have been sick, weak and delirious with a high burning fever for as long as you can or care to remember. Then you wake one time and the fever is gone. You lay there weak and you want to smile. You would kiss the ass of the Head Nurse, as tough as the hide of an old alligator, just to prove you love to be alive. You raise your hand to clench a fist and you can't, and all of sudden you realize that the fever has gone, but so has your health and power.

I woke up then, sat up in the cold sweat thinking: *What if the power is gone?* I don't mean His power. I mean mine. What if He decided to let me be, but just to let me know He had been here awhile, He snatched away the only gift I've got. What if I can't preach no more? Just when I should be able to make something out of the fit He gave me for the first time, purely, without His static or interference, He took that away from me too. Wouldn't that be the last laugh?

I was afraid to stand up for fear He had left me, as He did old Samson once, as weak as a little girl or a young colt. I was afraid to look in the mirror for fear He had given me the face of a monster. I was afraid to think about anything for fear He'd snatched away my mind. Why not? Didn't He do that to Solomon, the wisest of men?

I was afraid to open my mouth and curse His name, for fear that the cackle of a goose or a grunt like a pig would be the only sound I would hear.

I would be laying there yet, I guess, paralysed, a statue, if I hadn't realized that I still had the freedom to find out. I still had that much. So I reached for the bottle and I took a drink and it felt all right. I jumped up and ran outside to give them three fools of mine a trial by ordeal, a little dose of hell. That would be a fair test. They would smell it before it was even an odour. They would sense the rot and decay within me before the least sign of it showed. And they would rise up and rebel. They would want their freedom, their simple wordly freedom from me; and if what I feared and suspected was right, they could have it too without even asking for it.

Miami would know in a flash. If I had been robbed of what had been given me. If God had decided to play Indian-Giver. Then she could have the one thing she's been patiently waiting for, the one thing she thinks she needs. She could pity me. She could comfort me. She could cuddle and pamper me like a baby or a basket case. And I thought, as I tested her, studying her for any least sign, what if God just took *one* power away from me? If He blasted and wilted my tool of sex, the one sweet solace of oblivion, the one little death I can die again and again and defeat at least the surprise if not the pain and fear of His last victory over me. I didn't dare to look. I didn't dare to know. If it were, indeed, shrivelled to cigarette size, not even king size, limp itself as a used rubber, she'd laugh and clap her hands for joy. Then for the first time in her memory she'd anyway have the excuse to be chaste. Miami should have been a nun. She missed her true vocation by a hair. But if it was unchanged, still proudly able to charm her, to daze her with dreamy hungers as a snake is charmed by an Arab's music. I'd make her blow me then and there in celebration, in sight of God and the world.

Even as I thought this, I dismissed the idea. Not because the cruelty and the humiliation of her wouldn't be more than just the pleasure that cruelty and humiliation always are and also be a medicine against my own sickness. But because it would not prove anything. Perhaps His plan for me was to deprive me of even the knowledge of and hence the solace of change. Perhaps it would be a gradual, piddling dimunition of ability and power, so slow as to be hardly noticeable, so slow and gradual as to be only another illusion, able easily enough to be construed as merely the inevitable cumulative effects of age, decay, degeneration and God's other democratic gifts to all His creatures; ending at last in trembling fingers, drooling lips, toothless gums, rheumy eyes, scaly skin, brittle bones, sagging useless muscles and senility. When the mind wanders away from itself. Where will a mind wonder when it leaves the limp tedious dying flesh? Does it soar into new heights and atmospheres? Does it turn to some ancient conventional wall to wail? Or, taking Hookworm as a model, does it toss and turn buoyed on the soft, lukewarm seas of impossible pleasures, a dream of the final and complete gratification of all our insatiable hungers? Will it, like Miami's, grovel among shameful memories; being wounded not once, but again and again by the same blows? Or maybe like the sick mind of the girl, Judith, it will writhe forever on a single bed of nails, naked, spotlighted. . . . It could as well have been a part, it seemed to me then at that moment in the morning sun, standing among my little trio, my private trinity of the utterly defeated, that it might have been part of God's final plan for me that, worst of all, I would never know for sure even that.

He had left me, but how? Was He finished with me or would He add to my natural share of woe, by adding to the needling of doubts, the decay of knowledge and awareness and at last even of memory and the desire to know?

I was lost.

One by one I tried to cut the strings that made me jerk and dance. One by one I tried to cut the strings by which I, in ironic parody of the Master, jerked and danced my little trio of lost souls. Better: as if holding a bright bouquet of gas balloons on strings, I, one by one, freed them to rise and soar away, leaving me at least with empty hands.

195

Then a sound like an insect singing. The absurd sports car and the absurd girl, flaunting her celebration of folly like the trail of exhaust and dust behind the car. I ran toward the car laughing then, wishing first of all she would run me down then and there. Then we talked and I remembered the time and the healing. A night for me terrible and magical. For truly then, as before and since, truly God had passed a portion of His power through my hands to heal. I had truly known the ineffable radiance, the terrible presence. Yet she had returned, one dark shard of that shattered night. To perplex, to baffle. Maybe to mock. I could hardly be said to have healed anything at all. For she, too, is lost, and utterly lost. And I thought to myself, this is what it comes to after all. This is all that it adds up to in the end, all that any of it means; and all my works have come to ashes and dust.

Then and there, like dawn, a new light touched me. The message of her presence was more subtle. God sent her to me, I believed then briefly, not only to mock me and my whole life, but also as a sign that I was truly free now, free even of any good works I might have wrought in His name. Free to live until I die like any other creature. Free also, like any other creature, at last to let go, to doze and dream into a peaceful madness or to destroy myself. He was restoring my simple humanity to me by taking away, now that He had wearied of me, my past life. Not *all thy sins are forgiven, go and sin no more,* but instead: *all your works of days, all your gifts, all your blessings are removed, erased, and all your sufferings amount to nothing and all your life amounts to nothing and I leave you as I found you nothing and I take from you even the desire for My love and forgiveness and I not only banish you from My sight I banish mercifully even the memory of Me and the need for Me.*

I rejoiced! My cup ran over at the brim with new wine and I raised that cup humbly in gratitude and thanksgiving for that last best blessing. Metaphorically. Literally I celebrated my independence day on the lithe, willing flesh of a girl, pinned her like a living butterfly beneath me on the sweet, dry, pine-needled floor of the woods, stabbed to the core of her being and evoked a covey of sweet four-letter words which fell on my ears more beautiful than any psalms or prayers.

Freed then, I hastened to my task. Now I could preach again. Now I could preach in High Pines and anywhere else under the sun. I could, without emotion or feeling or regret or the deep doubts of a believer, preach the gospel coldly using only my mind, my voice, my training by experience. Now I would preach better than ever before. With the Word gone for good, I could be master of little words and the letters that are said to kill. And I turned to my Bible, to the words and the letters. To find a text to preach.

The words danced and blurred and swam without any meaning at all to me. It might as well have been Chinese.

Then came Caesar to torment me. As if the panic itself were not more than torment enough. My past rose up and spat in my face. Ha! God had taken away His part, freed me from that, but returned to me my past. Returned me the world. How like you this?

Which, of course, was irony or seemed to be then above all times, to remind me in the form of a smartass country john-law what precisely my share of the world and its goods and my worldly credentials is.

Suppose He had told Peter that after the cock crowed three times he would find himself magically and untouched right back where he started, hauling in fish?

I went to the girl again. Found her pagan, Greek, a nymph of Diana, corrupted, singing and swaying in the shower. And she was beautiful to look at. This too was a sign, the last one it

197

seemed. I had only to bathe with her, to purify myself in a new baptism. I laughed for joy and, tears of relief in my eyes, I crowded into that tiny shower stall with her. Not even stopping to remove my clothes. Laughing, gritting her teeth she fought me, but I mastered her until the two of us sank, contorted, to the tin floor to finish in a unison of spontaneous animal cries long after the last of the water was gone. My clothes ripped to shreds and the soap already drying on both our bodies.

Now I am free to preach as I please. No more madness, no more frenzy. No more doubts when there is nothing left to believe in.

I look into their faces, their hopeful faces, knowing what it is exactly they want and need to hear and knowing that in perfectly calm lucidity I can preach to them exactly that. I stop singing. I nod to Moses that this will be the last verse and he signals with a slight tip of his head. I listen to them sing now. Oh, was there ever such a cackling of crows? Have a flock of starving crows staring with malicious eyes over glazed winter fields ever sung more beautifully? Long live crows! God must have loved them because He made so many of them.

The hymn is over. I bow my head as if in prayer. A hush fills the room until the loudest noise is my own steady pulse. I raise my head and toss my hair and smile my best and brightest.

"I got news for you all! I come all the way here to High Pines to bring you a message!"

I look into their faces now, studying them even as I speak. And what do I see? The old people, already sickened and weary of the bodies they have to live in, tortured by self-disgust, by the rot of regret that gnaws the vitals, regret for the inevitable things done and left undone, lonesome too and tired, tired of the world and all its insane mingling of the habitual and the marvellous. The old, they always come, partly out of memory of the tent revivals of their youth, partly out of the bitter hope of hearing something that may give them at least briefly the strength to accept their bodies. Cruel involuntary will to keep on drawing in oxygen and casting out carbon dioxide, asking not ease or even much relief, but only some words of comfort like candy they can suck or chew on in the bad times they are going through and the worse times they know are coming. Afraid too. And why not? False comfort from false comforters to tell them nothing is as bad in fact as it is imagined to be. Stupidity of that false comfort. How can the human imagination be cut off? There is no way. Oh, you can be robbed or shed of poor reason by pain, drugs, fright, or even the fierce fist of the unconscious squeezing the brain out of shape as a sculptor moulds a chunk of clay. But who can deliver us from imagination? And then what comfort from a young man to an old one who has already felt the thorn in the joint, the first pains testifying to the long slow pain of dying. The old with their hearing aids, glasses, false teeth, trusses, crutches and canes, their slowly cooling and congealing blood?

Also the young, but not many. These are the young who have already suffered in mind, body, or spirit too much to be truly young. Who see only a waste of years ahead to hobble across, but because of the limits of the human imagination, and mercifully it has limits, do not know the truth of that waste, cannot conceive the world of the old to be contended with; and if they could conceive it, would cut their throats with a razor blade and be done with the whole stupid business. And who would blame them?

A few young girls, as always, feeling the first female itch and hunger of sex, that hairy mouth, bearded, that cries in an animal voice for honey and frightens them in dreams; knowing, but not knowing truly yet, the sweat, pain and agony of childbirth.

Knowing, but not knowing, the first wincing stab of the hungry snake inside them. Wanting, but fearing the inner shudder of total release, the pleasure of abandonment, wanting that, but fearing to want too much lest, vulnerable, they be deprived of even that. Some, maybe most, ignorant, ashamed, disgusted with themselves, confused, tormented, knowing truly only the undeniable itch itself.

The halt, oppressed, crippled, lame, blind, spastic, deformed. *How many freaks do gather together in Thy name, O Lord?* Hoping without hoping to be healed and whole. Cursing the healthy and lucky, yet unable to enjoy even the purity of hate, having been *commanded* to love, having been told that Life is or can be good. Forced to curse all those for whom life seems to be good; but forced also to reproach themselves even further for the hatred and the cursing. Driven daily, even by smiles and comfort, deeper into the lonely labyrinth of themselves where they know, without knowing, that a great beast yawns and waits for them.

And the poor. Those with no more really than the apt sparrows for whom each day is an effort not only to keep alive, but to conserve, as if misers, the pittance of strength and energy they possess else they will be too weak, unable to rise up the next day and struggle to keep alive. Crushed by the world these poor whom God said He specially loved.

Few, if any, of the rich, the healthy, or even the good. For why should these whom God has so blessed need to come crawling to Him? To speak of Justice: He wraps them in the mink and fat of health, success, virtue. They do well. They live well. They do not need Him, not with the easy hunger of these whom He has selected to be His losers. Then are they damned for their involuntary good fortune? So it says. Else there would be no justice. But consider the limits again of the human imagination. How can it picture or create that which is not? The human imagination creates only from what is. God alone can create out of nothing.

So I have one shabby tentful of the world's shabby seconds and rejects. I seek out a dying town, a brackish stagnant pool with lost creatures thriving on its slime and in their own excrement, and it is my knack to try by words and images, tricks of logic and disputation, by tickling their sensitive feelings and raw emotions, to try by all the sleights of hand I can muster to delude them into believing, however briefly, that some of their intolerable burdens are, will, or may be lifted, that maybe somehow they will someday be able to live with themselves.

Is it any wonder I have to hate and despise them almost as much as I hate and despise myself?

Tonight we shall talk of pain and suffering, the grand minted coinage of the King, distributed with regal, impartial largess among His loyal subjects, the just and the unjust alike.

"Now then," I say, "a messenger comes aknocking at your door. Say a boy from Western Union. 'Got news for you,' he says. 'Got a telegram for you. Just sign right here . . .'

"Now what do you think when that happens?" I ask you. "You think: Uh-oh bad news from somewhere. A telegram means bad news most of the time. You know it's foolish to feel that way when you don't even have a clue what's inside the envelope. But maybe it isn't foolish. Experience teaches us to expect bad news from a bad world. So with trembling fingers you rip open the envelope and read . . .

Only – and here's irony to chew on, irony being the last resort and refuge of intelligence which has fed upon the bitter bones of experience – God's messages always come in code, in the Unknown Tongue. How the hell are you going to read it when you get it? God has the key to the Top Secret Code. For Your Eyes Only, all documents say. Suppose you are merely the telegrapher, the sender, as I am. The sender has no clue what the message means. Nor does he know if it is received. Nevertheless it is his duty until power and energy fail him to send forth coded gibberish, cryptograms merely decorated with stock phrases and platitudes. And it is his duty to believe that somehow, quite beyond any known power of comprehension, all this can be transformed to sense. Maybe music is the closest analogy. Made up not just of the words of our mouths and the meditations of our hearts, oh hardly ever acceptable, but also of all thoughts, all memory, all fears and wishes, more frantic than a whole sky of startled wings. And not only that, but all else we know and do not know we know, all that we suspect, all that we dream and all the stuff not even dreams can be made of because it is so secret. It is the bounden duty of the sender to believe that all this gibberish somehow becomes beautiful music. Suppose you did get a Western Union telegram. What would it say? Hey there, Belshazzar, I got a message for you. Message as follows: MENE MENE TEKEL UPHARSIN. *Got it? Want me to repeat it?*

"But it's not that kind of news I bring you tonight. I'm bringing the Gospel and the Gospel means good news. I know you people and I know your hearts . . .

(*The heart is deceitful above all things, and desperately wicked. Who can know it . . . ?*)

". . . are hungry for some good news and I know your souls are aflame and burning and thirst for it. . . .

(*It shall be even as when an hungry man dreameth and behold he eateth but he awaketh and his soul is empty or as when a thirsty man dreameth and behold he drinketh but he awaketh and behold he is faint . . .*)

"You suffer. All of you out there. I suffer, you suffer, he, she, it suffers. You suffer one way or another because we all do. And you make other people suffer. Don't dare to deny it. Not even to yourself. Because we all do. Suffering is cheap as grass and free as the rain that falls on the saint and the sinner alike. It's one thing we all got in common."

And here beginneth the first great sleight of hand, the lie, the deception, the truly false comfort, for is it true that all suffer?

(and even if I believe that I do not know it to be so so is my belief then an act a leap of faith & if so what a thing to cleave to faithfully that all creatures suffer but why not is it not written that one should choose rather to suffer affliction with the people of God than to enjoy the pleasures of sin for a season implying somewhere anyway a distinction & for some at least one season without suffering)

I think even Job never had it so rough as the typical rectal cancer case with his sewed up, sealed off asshole and a little bag attached to his side and into his guts to fill up with shit and such. There is no equality in suffering.

"But equal or not, beloved, when you suffer, you do it all alone. Oh, you can tell somebody else about it, sure! You can tell your true friends and your loved ones and they'll try, they'll do their best to sympathize with true Christian compassion. But they can't take the hurt from you. There's no way to transfer suffering. And they don't know. They don't know what it's really like and you can't tell them because there just aren't words and signs enough to tell anybody what it's like. Nobody can ever know the trouble and tribulation you have seen."

"Amen!" An old voice coughs and croaks in the back of the tent.

I see Cartwright's right on the job, beginning gradually to cut the lights off one by one. Until they are all in the dark and

I won't have to look at their faces and I'll be the only thing they can see, standing in a pool of light.

He catches my eye and winks. Hookworm, I'm warming to my subject. I'm feeling good and feeling fine and for about a nickel I'd take the risk of winking right back at you.

"I'm here! I'm here in the little town of High Pines to tell you the good news that there is Someone you can turn to in your time of trouble. Someone who is ready to listen and understand. Think of that. Just think of that . . .!

in truth do not think on that lest your mind dazed ambushed astounded in its nakedness with no covering nor least fig leaf for shame & weakness should turn spin flee like a rat in a maze to nowhere for where can you hide from the scrutiny & care of God do not think for the fragile machinery of your mind will bend & break & mad dancers fill your hollow skull with laughter & howls & your lips show forth not praise but babbling whines whimpers howls of a tortured animal & I know I know having whined & howled so for I am the man that hath seen affliction by the rod of his wrath he hath led me & brought me into darkness but not into light

"But not just always ready to listen and understand. Not just able to understand every single word in every single language known to man. Someone who can read between the lines. Someone who can even hear the words you don't say because you don't dare to or maybe you are ashamed to or maybe you don't know any words for what you feel and are trying to say. Or maybe don't even know what you feel. Someone who not only can listen and will listen but has got to listen. Because, brothers and sisters, God can't stop his ears. God can't just switch off all those voices crying out to him in a multitude of tongues like you can switch off a radio or a T.V. or just hang up a telephone. No! Night and day, day and night, He's got to listen! And that's His burden, the infinite burden of God. You can stop listening any time you want to. He can't. Praise His name!"

'Amen! Amen!' come the voices now from the dark tent. 'Amen! Glory!'

I stand in bright light looking into the dark where they sit restless watching me, having to listen to me now. I'm warming to it, sweating already, and in a while, not yet, but when it means something, when it pays, I'll throw off my coat and send it sailing.

"I'm talking about the One from whom no secrets are hid!"

'Amen!' they said. 'Glory!'

"But wait, (lowering my voice, quieting them because it's too early yet for all that) but wait a minute! Somebody will ask me: 'Big Red, how come you call that good news? I mean, it ain't hardly nobody can stand the strain, knowing that somebody, especially God, is listening, eavesdropping on them *all* the time.' And I say, oh my brother, you right! You are so right! Nobody, no living human being can stand the strain on account of every one of us has got secrets we don't want nobody to know about. We even got secrets hid from our ownself...."

(he lieth in wait secretly as a lion in his den)

"But I'm here to tell you something else. I'm here to testify that He not only listens. He cares. I mean He cares about your troubles and sorrows. And that's the true good news. What I'm trying to tell you is you got a mutual conversation going on all the time, a two-way, long distance, person to person phone call direct on a private line all the time! And if this wasn't the truth, the God's truth, why you might just as well kneel down and pour out your troubles to a tree stump or a hollow log or a rock in the field. A tree stump's gotta stay there and listen. A stump ain't fixing to pack up and pick up and go nowhere. And it ain't no doubt about it, you can get a lot of consolation out of whispering your troubles and your secrets to a tree or a rock. Cause you know you got something off your chest and you know that there tree stump ain't going to go tell on you. But I didn't come all the way to High Pines to recommend kneeling down to no tree stumps. . . ."

I pause now to mop the sweat off my face and to let them have a little nervous laugh. I'm losing it, going away from it. Right then and there I almost let it get away from me and went off on the subject of idolatry. And that's a different can of peas. . . .

To preach that one, to preach, and I've done it, how the nature of man is so contrived with cunning that he fills up with love and the need to worship something, anything, but can't love another human being for long and can't love himself at all, and so goes out and pours that love on something, anything: a rock, a tree, a bird, a dog, or on food or money or power or pride or even humility; or on sex chiefly, most often on sex, on the body of a woman, say, on her lips and eyes and breasts and thighs (*never her self because her self is a mystery*) and feet and hands and hair and ass and fall down and worship that; so that even the poor masturbator sowing his vain seed is fumbling, trying to worship, and don't know, but knows in his heart, he's worshiping nothing, knows that what he wants is only a sign or a word to say, go now and live easy with yourself, but knows too he will never get that sign or word in this world.

"I'm here to tell you there's Someone who cares. I'm making a special announcement that Someone loves you and cares about you. Oh, I can hear some of you already mumbling to yourself: 'We know that already. It don't take no evangelist preacher to come here and tell us what we already know.' That's right.

You're so right! But I'm making it my business to come here shouting good news and reminding you it's old news. I ain't no prophet and Lord knows I'm no kind of a saint, but I'm making it my business to come here with the oldest good news in the world.

"Lemme ask you a question. One question. *How* do we know? *How?*"

Now pause as if to wait for an answer. Nothing to make a crowd more uneasy, self-conscious than a rhetorical question that just might be for real. Bend over the edge of the platform to look at them. Frown, lift my chin, clench my fists. Glare out there into the dark where their eyes are and wait as if for a reply.

"We know three ways (quietly now, ticking it off on my fingers). We know in our hearts that it is the truth, we feel it there."

The heart. Call that vital organ the symbol of all that is wordless and true and escapes the fenced pasture of the mind. Call it the treasure chest of Truth. But the game is to bury the treasure and burn the map and go away, be turned away and around and around, as in a child's game of blindman's buff. Then begins the search. Somehow to find it again – "X marks the spot!" – and in a sweaty frenzy dig in the sand until the shovel strikes steel and rings. Panting and gasping and straining to manage to heave the chest out of its hole. Then to fumble with the keys of a huge key ring, all but one of them fitting locks you have long since forgotten. Finding by trial and error the right one at last, turning the lock and opening the chest, terribly anxious and fearful – for what if there are no coins or jewels? And maybe at last to stand, to grin and laugh a hoarse pirate's laugh that it is all there after all, glittering and appalling and all mine . . .

*but go another layer down peel away yet one more veil & find yourself
to be again self-deceived beyond measure for there is not never no
never was any treasure whatsoever only maybe a broken doll some
marbles won on the immemorial schoolyard a baby tooth still waiting
for fairies to come in the night like thieves & replace it with a dime
some string maybe too & a faded ribbon which once wrapped a forgotten gift from someone forgotten*

    *this is all that's all there is except for of course an host a multitude
of winged things like bats & moths & wasps & flies which fly up
each time & free do freely torment the world like those which arose
oh marvellous flapping from Pandora's mythic box*

    *which myth which box tells precisely the truth beyond words I
grope for in form beyond words yet by means of*

    *grope for in form of the pirate chief with beard patch over one eye
ring in one ear*

    *truth being that she Pandora saw not saw nothing the things she set
free to swarm & go forth & multiply & possess the whole world no
saw not that but only that the famous box was empty was only really
empty after all empty of anything*

    *for even the poor shabby shards in the pirate chest which of course he
sees as money & jewels taken away from & off of fine ladies while
his crew of gorillas & baboons & goats & monkeys jeer & leer while
he sizing her up fore & aft & stem & stern must decide with a yawn
to toss her a reject to them or lay her there on the poop deck or maybe
tie her a figurehead on the bow of his vessel & let her cries be softened
& sweetened by salt seabreeze to sounds less keen than cries of gulls
while we pitch & roll she breasts waves with her breasts & gradually
cries of anguish become sweet music to ears*

    *as once that Greek bull they roasted victims in & groans made
sounds like Caruso no doubt singing o sole mio*

    *her cries also serving as foghorn & whistle till she is mere bone
picked clean & silver as driftwood*

all this merely dream & delusion a mask a gauze veil of truth for-
ever clad in swaddling of disguises
   the box is empty after all
   Pandora is no pirate chief only a slim thing a young moon with
wide bright eyes fresh lit & young flesh & shining hair & one hand
ah so delicately shielding the slight oh soft & downy bulge of yes sex
from eyes of even lazy gods who have anyway seen everything any-
way & are not impressed anymore by natural habits of natural inno-
cence & trust without thought plan premeditation permits her the girl
to cover the gateway to her treasure with one hand while she peeks
first then stares astounded & feels cold chill in her bones sees the box
is empty after all & then begins to cry bitter tears in honour of bitter
fact that the heart of the world has a bitter taste
   there's the truth of the heart

"And we know the truth from the World, the book of the world, the world which God created in all its glory and infinite variety!"

From the book of the world I have read confusion only and mystery. I read that everything lives and dies. I read the un-alterable and inexorable law of appetite, laws of infinite hunger and desire. In science I read the same laws, laws so fine that they can only be hinted at in delicate and subtle equations. In these laws I never read answers but only questions, riddles. So we are to be judged by a Question like the Sphinx. I can prove anything and its opposite from what I know of the book of the world, yet I know the book of the world is written in the Unknown Tongue.

At this point, if I had courage to tell them, I would bring together the truth of the heart and the truth of the book of the world. Say first the man divided. Divided within himself at whatever depth and at the same time divided against the world. Divided from nature and from his own nature, yet forever indissoluably bonded to both. For all his fist shaking and roaring, for all his prayers and sweet resignation, he is as helpless and hopeful as a blade of grass.

Divided most deeply and at his deepest places against God. No, not so much divided as broken. Broken to pieces. Made in His image then shattered, broken like a mirror into glittering slivers and fragments, each with its own distortions.

Picture each fragment as painfully alive, knowing by guess and by nature that it is what it is, merely a broken fragment, a suffering sliver. And desiring most of all wholeness. Hungry, thirsty, desperately, urgently anxious to be together again. Given therefore (call that a blessing?) an insatiable appetite for something he can name but cannot imagine. And given knowledge. Knowledge that the only certainty is perpetual uncertainty. Knowledge that the only thing unchanging, changeless, is change itself.

Now place this creature in the world. Picture it as a battlefield, but not as a battle. For no matter what, in the image of battle there is still the lingering ghost of flags fluttering, glittering gear, shining armour, proud steeds and fair ladies, drums and flutes, and from far, far, far away the lonely, lovely echoing resonance of the dying trumpet call.

Thus it is better to picture the state of man in the world as *after* the battle.

Pick the First World War for the proper mood. The mud and the stink of trenches, rusty hedges of barbwire from which hangs screaming fruit, mud and gas and blind, stupid attacks and counter-attacks over utterly worthless and denuded ground. After the battle bored medics go forth to stifle the chorus of screams. Grave-diggers wearily go to loot and to bury the dead. . . .

After that time even, picture a vast landscape cratered and lifeless as the moon and perfectly still. Now listen. There is a stirring, a long tired sigh which could be wind but there is no wind. Come closer to see. See how all the shattered and remaining parts, each so hoarse from screaming the truth of pain, that only a sigh, not enough to blow out a match is left. Each separate part, large or small. Here a leg, there a hand. Here a bloodshot eyeball. There a mere squirming string of nerves. And, look there! a piece of gut like an eel. Each separate part slithering in the filth. And in all of that crawling, slithering, writhing, slimy chaos, not one part knows the name of the body it came from, nor, in fact can picture a body since it knows only that itself is nothing and knows only that it suffers and is lost.

Now let us suppose. Suppose now that by accident, by odds, by statistics, by what-have-you, out of all those maimed, disjointed parts somehow one came together and became a thing with two legs like a man. Able to think, feel, dream, remember imagine . . . Able to suffer and rejoice. And that this thing, the sole survivor of all those miscellaneous fragments, staggers away proudly toward home and peace.

Who could bear to look at it?

Yet this creature has pride. Yet this creature yearns to love, to be able to love itself and to be loved. Hand it an honest mirror and watch what happens.

"And third and last we know from this."

I hold up the Bible and wave it with a flash of pages, holding it flashing and rustling as though it were a wild thing, a falcon, unhooded, straining to soar off into the sky and circle light as a kite on the air, eyes aglint in search of prey.

"The Holy Scripture where it tells me about Jesus Christ who came down and was man and died for me. For you and me . . . And that should be enough. He died for me. He took my suffer-

211

ing and my trouble in his arms and he carried the cross up a hill and let them nail him to it. And they raised that cross off the ground and he hung there, hanging, heaving in pain for each breath until his muscles failed, dying a long slow painful death. A death for you and me for once and for all. . . ."

Why now, even as I am speaking and not trying to picture it, do I feel the muscles of my chest constrict? As if I were myself hanging there, groping for breath and unable to prevent the involuntary spasm of my muscles in their simple and insatiable hunger for oxygen. Heaving up and down with Him. Not able to die until my muscles give out of their own accord. What a way to die! At the mercy of muscles!

Lord you gave me a bad, black heart and the mind of a sceptic. You gave me the guts to try anything once and maybe twice. And you gave me a fairsize pecker too, a weathervane, a rooster between my thighs, a stovepipe in my hips. But Lord, Lord, Lord, you gave me a set of muscles too. The big simple crude muscles of a farmboy. Made for ploughing, cutting, toting, fetching, hauling, pulling, lifting, heaving. And Lord, when my heart goes as sour as a swamp orange, bitter as a green persimmon, and my head is awhirl with doubts like a sky full of starlings, still, Lord, my muscles are built to feel the strain of Your dying whether I will it so or not. Try as I will to rule with my head and my heart, I cannot. My lips say the words, the lifeless words only, of Your dying and there I hang high on each side of You, both sides, split in half and two kinds of a thief. One sneers at You and curses You out of the red fog and pain of his own slow dying. The other, seeing Your nakedness and suffering, seeing the Truth naked for the first time, grieves even as he is hanging and killing himself in spite of himself. In the pain of his slow dying he grieves and thinks this world, so terrible, so frightful always that it will always strip and scourge any servant of Truth, crown Truth with a crown of thorns and hoist it high; knowing this and also knowing once and

212

for all that God is too good for the world He made. Too good for the the monsters He created. And it is then always that this thief feels, most marvellous and strange, a deep pity for God Himself.

But not to Paradise is that part, that half of me ever to be lifted with Thee. But always forever, so split and tormented and suffering, I must hang twice crucified on each side of You, cursing and praising Your holy name.

Now off comes the coat and I throw it back across the platform feeling a sudden cooling of my sweat-stained shirt. I raise my arms high. I unclench my fists and open my palms and let my wrists go slack.

"And on the third day He rose again from the dead and ascended into Heaven and sitteth on the right hand of God the Father Almighty. And that's what we know and how we know and all we need to know. Rejoice! Say hallelujah!"

I accept their chorus in reply. Now I ought to be happy. I got them just where I want and I haven't even started on them good, and before I'm done I can tell them black is white and night is day and they'll believe me and holler their hallelujahs and their amens. Sometimes at this moment I hear a Voice, and all my triumph and all my strength is gone like a puff of smoke. And I'm carried on the edge of an explosion like a dead leaf in the wind, head over heels, gone with the Gospel like a man possessed. Not now. Yet now I hunger for it. Lord, you left me. You will not speak to me again. But I'm going to fool You now. I'm going to spite You by preaching the Gospel just like You did, indeed, have possession of me, like it was Your voice speaking through mine. Because I know I am free to do even that. I am free whether You help me or not. Because I have heard You before and known You, and, though You leave me to die, to stew in my own juice, still this once I have memory and I have my text for I know Your book still as I know the beating of my own heart.

Peter was grieved because you said unto him the third time, Lovest thou me? And he said unto you, Lord, thou knowest all things; thou knowest that I love thee. Jesus saith unto him, Feed my sheep.

"I stand up here to tell you I am a damn fool. Yes! A damn fool. I been preaching at you about your own suffering like you mattered. Like I mattered. I confess to you, brothers and sisters, confess I was hoping to cheer you up, to send you out of here with a smile on your face and a lightness around your heart. Oh you'd get your money's worth, but you know and I know it wouldn't even last till morning. Time the first rooster crows you'd be back in the arms of your troubles, and your heart would be as heavy and cold to you as iron shackles and a ball and chain. I know. Yes I know. I've had iron shackles on my legs and I know what I'm talking about.

"I been standing up here talking to you and commiserating, feeling sympathy for your sufferings. But truly I don't feel a sympathy for you. And, look in your heart of hearts, and ask yourself can you really and truly feel a sympathy for me or anybody else. The answer is no. I was trying to fool you and make you happy because only a fool can be happy. Well, I ain't going to try to fool you no more. I'm going to lay it out for you straight and simple. I'm going to take every stitch off the truth and lay her out like a corpse for you to look at. Behold! You can leave now if you want to. You can go home while you're ahead. Or you can spend this hour with me at your own risk. Proceed with caution at your own risk. Danger ahead! Go home! Go home all of you if you don't want to hear the God's truth!"

Now it is quiet. So quiet I hear my own deep breathing. Yes, I'm breathing free again and I know I could suck in a deep breath and blow it out and blow the tent away. And nobody's leaving.

"Let me tell you what I see. I look out in your faces and, sure, I see suffering and tribulation in everyone. What else? You ain't special. You can't hide it. Wherever I go, towns I forget the name of, I see the same thing. I see people suffering. And I see the same people making other people suffer. I see the tyranny of strength and the tyranny of weakness. I see pain and injustice, I see poverty and ignorance, I see disease. Everywhere I look I see evil and corruption. I see death in everyone of your faces. Ugly or beautiful, proud or plain, it's all the same. I see a naked skull grinning behind those rosy cheeks and red lips. I see black hollow holes and emptiness behind the sparkle of those blue eyes. And, oh yes, I see the same thing in my own mirror. I see death. Every time I look in a mirror – and I look every time I get a chance because I'm a vain man like anyone else – every time I look in the mirror I greet death. I smell death. I taste death on my tongue. I feel the shiver of death deep down in the marrow of my bones . . .

"I see the same thing when I look at the world. When I read the book of the world I don't feel no sense of joy. I feel death. I see the needy and the humble and the down-trodden. I see the ways of the sinner prosper. I see the tall grow taller and the fair grow fairer and the mighty become mightier. I see the rich get richer and the fat get fatter. And all the time I see the ways of the wicked prosper, I see the good man, the few good men you see in a lifetime, I see them licking and swallowing dust. Brothers and sisters, everywhere I look I see old men hoard the sweet fruits of the earth until they rot. And all the while the little children starve.

215

"I turn to myself and deep in myself I feel two dark angels wrestling. Fighting for my soul . . . And most of the time I know the angel of Satan is getting the best of it, choking the last life out of all that's good in me. And I despair. Oh yes, I despair! Look down, Lord, I say. Look down at this mess. Look at this stinking and corruption. Would you just look and see what has become of what you made? Look what has happened to your creation. Come down! Come down, Lord! Come on down with the noise of strangers like the heat in a dry place. Come fire and flood. Come bombs and plagues. Take it away. Purge everything. Destroy everything. You're having a bad dream, Lord. Wake up and let it vanish away.

"Oh yes, I despair. And how about that? A preacher. A man with a call to preach the Word. I squat down on my shanks like old Job himself and I gnaw on the bitter bones of despair. Now, that sounds like the worst, don't it? But it ain't. Not by a long shot. It's only the beginning . . .

"I despair of the world and I despair of myself. I despair of God and of all the suffering and evil He permits. And then I hear a voice. A still small voice whispers inside of me. A soft dry voice like the voice of the serpent in the garden. "Curse the Lord,' it says. 'I dare you. Curse the Lord and die.' Brothers and sisters, I'm not Job. I *do* it. I grit my teeth and I curse God. But I don't die. He won't let me just lay down and die. Because He has chosen me. Because He has called me to rise up and stand tall and preach His Word whether I like it or not...

"The first time I got the call it was in a filthy, stinking jail cell. Oh, I tell you I've been a bad man in my time. I have done terrible things. And I have left undone most of the things I ought to have done. And there is no health in me. Still I got a call . . .

"One night I was lying on my hard cot in the cell, not thinking anything, just wishing I was anywhere but there, when the call of the Lord came down and hit me like a lightning bolt. Sprung on me like a roaring lion. I was commanded – because God don't ask a favour – I was ordered to go forth and preach the Word. 'Don't pick on me,' I said. 'Please don't pick on me. I got troubles enough already of my own. Let me alone. Please just let me be.' And you know what the answer was? All the answer I ever got was a sound like laughter in my heart. I heard the laughter of God in my heart. Pray, pray God, brothers and sisters, that you don't ever have to hear it . . .

"I have done terrible things in my time. My share and more than my share. I confess to you I have sinned in the past and no doubt shall sin again. Some of the things I have done would give you bad dreams if I was to tell you. I am not worthy. I am not worthy of the crumbs under the table. I doubt and I suffer and I despair. I cry out, Lord, I believe. Help thou mine unbelief.

"But I have been called to go forth and preach the Word and by God I will preach it. Amen!

"Isaiah, Jeremiah, Ezekiel, Solomon, Saul and David, they preached the Word of God and praised His name. The God of Abraham and Isaac and Jacob. The God of justice and a terrible swift sword. And I preach Him too. But I bring you good news along with the bad. I come with the Gospel of Jesus Christ . . .

"The Lord God Himself came down and walked among us as a man. In the form of a Jew, a poor Jew and a bastard. I say bastard because in the eyes of the world that's all He was. He lived a while in the eyes of the world and he preached the new Word. God couldn't trust the message to a prophet. Even John the Baptist wasn't a good enough man to deliver the news of the New Law. Jesus walked the earth for a while. And He healed the lame and the blind and the deaf and the lepers and He spread the news of the mercy of God. Amen!

"What good did it do Him? Well, they grabbed hold of Him and they whipped Him like a dog and they jammed a crown of thorns on His head. 'So, you're a king, huh?' they said. 'Well, now, if you're a king, you better have yourself a crown.' They jammed that crown of thorns on His head and the blood ran down His face. Then they dragged Him up to the place of the skull and hung Him up on a cross between a couple of thieves. There He was, the Lord God Almighty, Himself, hanging between heaven and earth dying. And they laughed at Him. And that's where He is to this day, every day, hanging between heaven and earth with a thief on each side of Him, listening to the laughter of the world.

"But the joke is on us. The laugh is on us. He was the biggest thief of all. He stole death. He stole death away. When they killed Him, He killed death.

"That's the call I got. That's all the good news I got to tell you. We are saved. *We are saved*! Yea though I walk through the valley of the shadow! Yea though my flesh rots and shreds away and in the end there's nothing left of me but dry bones, a set of bones rattling like dice in the valley itself of dry bones, yet I shall rise up again all whole and clean and shining. Yet we shall all rise up and we shall see God. Amen!

"Though my sins be as scarlet, yet shall I be white as the lamb. *I am saved*! *We are saved*! We are saved and forgiven before we squawl and draw our first breath in the world. We are saved and forgiven whether we like it or not. We can curse God every step of the way. We can heap sins on our heads like confetti. No matter what I am saved. You are saved. We are saved. Amen!"

so there it is for what it's worth my belief not ever shared by many but always by some & how anyway can many share in fellowship such a belief as if in organized anarchy

belief in yet election & damnation maybe but surely election for some & maybe for all at the whim of God So are we all saved then in spite of ourselves yes Hookworm & his harem of mindless soul-less female bodies all shining all arched in taut soft pelvic answer to every question & Miami forever bathing in the excremental cesspool spring of her memories a smeared befouled Diana running wild & mad in a forest of pubic hair where all plants are boils & a garden shines with scabs a Circe whose wand reveals the pig beneath the skin grunting avaricious lustful slothful gluttonous proud wrathful envious at her touch the man falls apart like old humpty dumpty dividing into 7 ugly dwarfs each screaming for love & attention yet she still besmeared & befouled in filth of the world is unflinching unblinking unwinking unbelieving unbroken yet anyway still dreaming her dream of purity still forever dreaming a perfect urn of unravished quiet & calm herself a chaste bride diaphonous & trembling & innocent moving to melodies never heard solemn & beautiful under a sky the blue eye of a god she could believe in under a bright sun the bright smile of a god she could smile at offering her shining unsmudged untouched body as his bride dreaming him a shower of gold a white bull a blazing tower an archer with no not one limp arrow in quiver Miami the old whore who lives one dream a nightmare & dreams another & never ever heard of C. J. Jung or John Keats & wouldn't know a real grecian urn from a chamberpot

God bless her

God bless Hookworm

whose fear takes the form of a round perfumed powdered tough pig blond called Dreama the Denver Bombshell who flees from her always dreaming his total domination of all the rich strange mysterious world of the female she to whom serpents can speak without inter-

219

preter or translation dreaming that false dream but knowing in his heart of hearts it is Dreama he worships & fears knowing truly that heaven would be to lie prostrate at her feet & kiss the cracks between her toes while she idly whipped him with a leather thong knowing he'd rejoice to fan her with a palm leaf while she took a lover knowing her laughter cruel as barbwire would be music to him knowing too her forgiveness would be the utmost shudder of catharsis uprooting his soul beyond his most extravagant imagined orgasm leaving him limp empty & at last alive he who never heard of the magna mater of many breasts or bloodcult of bull nor Mithra either he who flees in the maze toward the jaws of the monster & will die without knowing where he has been astounded & cheated some final foolish four letter word on his lips for unction

God loves him too died for him too he is saved

forget not Moses of the chosen people chosen for what God knows yes chosen to be the vessel of the law His holy vessel also of suffering trial & tribulation ordeal unequalled chosen also as form for Himself in flesh in which to sweat bleed suffer & die Moses who might save for whatever set of circumstances he was dealt have been an artist a musician maybe but instead finds himself in loveless middleage plunking hymns on a portable piano surrounded by strangers & enemies for whom he has so much affection which is so deep it borders on compassion in turn a cousin of charity

God loves him too

God bless him too

the girl called Judith lean-legged keen-legged bearing between those scissors & matted with so soft curly hair her own cup of wormwood grail of tribulation a tight little hot little pussy with hungers beyond satisfaction with malice toward all because she was not born with two grapes & a dangling ripe banana of flesh a man so filled with destruction she will settle for nothing less than castrating every male animal in creation yet sick with guilt for this desire she

*offers herself her unholy grail to any & all comers in self-abnegation
& still finds no peace but once at the touch of my hands it seems
was given not peace that passeth understanding but instead a brief
taste of the wine of joy & gladness only a sip but enough to torment
her forever*

*all three each in his-her own way ridiculous fools in the world
fools of God who must love them much to chastise & torment them
so*

*is it not written my son despise thou not the chastening of the
Lord nor faint when thou art rebuked of him whom the Lord loveth
he chasteneth & scourgeth every son whom he receiveth*

*I now witness to the power & love the strange love of God for
the least of His creatures ask nothing for myself not power not
wisdom not peace not anything but for these I love too in my own
way & these in my tent Your tent I know not & love not at all
being no more than comical & pathetic cardboard to me for these I
ask Your blessing & love knowing without doubt it is in Your
power to give should You incline Your ear & be so inclined*

*my flesh my spirit I cast like a shadow between You & them
promising nothing asking everything*

if I am damned for that then damned I am & will be

*I have heard Your voice have known the beauty of ashes & oil of
joy of mourning & here & now I mourn these the least & most
foolish servants saying only from the psalms of David also broken
thou shalt make me hear of joy & gladness that the bones which thou
hast broken may rejoice*

"There's a day coming, brothers and sisters, a great day I
believe it. Without no *reason* to believe I bet my life and my
soul – and that's all I got to bet – on that great day. What a day
that will be! Then shall all the crippled join hands and dance
together. Then shall the blind see light and the deaf shall listen

221

to the music of the stars. The old shall be young and the weak shall be strong. The least shall be most and mighty. The last shall be first and the meek shall inherit the earth. Amen! Oh now, what a great and glorious day that will be when all of us rise up once more naked and clean to stand in the sun as God wants us to. For the sun is the unblinking eye of God. And then shall the moon fade away. And death shall be no more. Pain shall be no more. Amen! And all our despair, our anguish, our weeping, and wailing and gnashing of teeth shall vanish away like the ghost of breath on a cold winter day. No! It will not vanish. First we shall hear, our ears shall hear all these howls and wails and moans and groans in one great sound, a symphony of agony, a great orchestra tuning and God shall raise his hands to conduct and our ears shall hear how easy it is for Him to transform all that to beautiful music. He will turn our very groans into an anthem of everlasting praise. And the music will rise up brighter than the stars and be transformed into light in a place where light is music. Amen!

(come down now Red to earth to simple words & simple things lest you lose them all for a firework display is not the only way to celebrate your independence day come down boy down)

"High Pines is just a little town. It's far, far from the great and beautiful cities of the world. It's a place to grow old in and die in. But I'm here to tell you God has not forgotten you. He looks down upon you. His eye, which sees the fall of every sparrow, sees also your open and secret suffering. And it is all of it remembered. Who can even begin to imagine the memory of God? It is remembered and it is written down, all of it, in a great book of seven seals, written in blood, the infinitely precious blood of the lamb. Rejoice then. Rejoice! Rejoice in the precious blood of the lamb! Then shall the lamb and the lion lie down together. And then shall all men – the white man and black man, yellow man, brown man, red man, the Jew and the Gentile, Mohammedan and Hindu, then shall all men be brothers again. And Cain shall kneel down again by Abel. And Abel shall rise up as if from a sleep, a dream, and kiss away the tears of Cain and forgive him with a smile. Amen!"

I'm through. I'm finished. There's nothing more to say. I have said nothing but said it all in spite of myself. I have never been so tired, so empty. Is this Your plan then? To crush me with hammer blows, to drive me one blow at a time, babbling words the whole time, into the ground, one ringing blow at a time, like a poor tent peg? *Eli, Eli, lama sabachthani* . . . ?

"I don't know what you good people have been expecting." (softly now, make them strain and listen) – "Maybe some of you come here tonight to see me do things with snakes. I'm bound to disappoint you. Not just because it's against the law. I've never been what you'd call careful about the law. But because it don't prove nothing. It's only a kind of a trick . . . And maybe some of you come here hoping to be healed, hoping to try my healing touch. I don't have any healing touch. Only God can heal you. I can't. I'm only here a little while to preach at you and pray with you and ask you to pray for me.

"I know there's a lot of stories running around about me. Some of them are true and some are false. They'll tell you I bug my eyes and try to hypnotize you and take your money away. I wish I had that power but I don't. And what do I need your money for? Why do I want money? I'm going to prove to you how much I care about money. I'm going to prove it to you right here and now . . . !"

Lord now lettest thy servant depart in peace

223

6

For I know this, that after my
departing shall grievous wolves
enter in among you, not sparing
the flock. Also of your own selves
shall men arise, speaking perverse
things, to draw away disciples after
them.   ACTS XX, 29–30

I'm standing here, kind of off to the side near the front row, while he's preaching, feeling good, feeling fine. Thinking:

Red, you old son of a bitch you, you can always pull rabbits out of a hat. I mean it takes a freaking professional to get his ass up there when he don't even feel like it, and then preach like he means it. Keep rolling, Red! Pour it on 'em baby! I wish to hell Red would give this up and go into something solid like Real Estate. With all his bullshit he could sell folks plots of sand in Death Valley and 100 foot sections of the Everglades. Maybe he ought to go into Politics. He could have a freaking future. Governor Big Red Smalley and his entourage! Smiling on left stands Lieutenant Governor Cartwright in full military dress uniform with about five pounds of medals; He is reported to be the biggest Playboy since Baby Pignatelli. End quote.

It looks like everything is going to end up okay after all. Looked kind of gloomy all day, though, and even this evening started off on the wrong foot. Quick as the first truck come and the rednecks hopped out and squatted down around it to wait, Moses give the word. I come out from underneath the truck – I was resting my eyes a little, that's all – and seen him walk right over and cut on the generator and turn on the lights by himself. No trouble at all. He knowed how all the time. Didn't even have to kick it to get it started. Which naturally reminded me of my poor swole up foot and that girl's car. Nobody saw me do it. In the morning I can lay the blame on juvenile delinquents.

We all went in the trailer to see what was going to happen. I see the Redheaded Bitch is sitting on a bunk flipping through the pages of *Male Action* magazine. *My Male Action* magazine that I bought and paid for and it was sitting at the bottom of my footlocker too.

Red told us how it was going to be and he was looking fine, ten years younger than this morning. He said we was going to do it right. Me and Moses to put on our choir robes and even help out with the singing.

"I can't sing for shit," I told him, but he didn't pay any mind. He seemed real happy planning the whole thing.

"On the offering we are going to milk them dry, *dry*!" Red said. "The two girls can work the centre aisle and you two take the sides."

About that time we started to hear the sound of more cars coming.

"I better get out and sell tickets," Moses said.

"Don't forget your choir robe," Red said.

Moses nodded and took off. When it comes to selling tickets he can forget all about being lazy. All of a sudden he is a freaking ball of fire.

"I'll take my magazine back now," I told Miss Bitch.

"Do you really read this stuff or do you just look at the pictures?"

"For your information, I try to keep up on current events."

"How about all those nudist magazines?"

That meant she'd been through everything in the entire foot-locker. Because I had them really *hidden*.

"They're all in Swedish."

Everybody seemed to think that was very funny.

"Hookworm is a student," Red said. "He studies foreign languages."

"Forget Swahili," Miami said. "You stick to Swedish."

"Some of the pages are all stuck together," Miss Bitch said.

"You got hair on your palms?" Red said.

I have heard that dumb joke a million times I guess, but when they pull it on you, it's only human to sneak a quick look at the palms of your hands. I mean, you never can tell.

So, naturally, that gave them all something else to laugh at.

Right now, though, I'm feeling great. I can tell Red is about to wrap it all up and put a big bow knot on it. It's getting to sound like the end, like any minute he'll be saying "Let your light so shine forth among men" and all that jazz. So I turn my back to reach for my offering plate.

He stops talking. But instead of saying anything, he starts breathing hard like he is carrying a real heavy sack of flour. I look around and sure enough he has got a armload. He's got that safe in his arms. It ain't that heavy, but it sure took the two of us, me and Moses, all the strength we've got to tote it out here and hide it in back of the tent. Red told us somebody might try and steal it while we was all performing.

"Come here, Moses," he says, setting the safe down.

Moses gets up. He looks at Red and nods and then kneels down in front of the safe and starts dialing the combination. I wisht I was close enough to read the numbers and had a piece of paper and a pencil to write them down with.

Now I got it! Red's going to show them how *safe* their money is with him. Just like in the Bank, only it's loaned out to God to do God's work and drawing interest and dividends in heaven. You can cash in on the principal and accumulated interest, compounded quarterly, there.

"Folks," Red says. "This is the time in the service where we usually have our offering. But tonight we've got a different kind."

This is going to be a good one, a stroke of genius. He just stands there looking at them with that wild, crazy, bright look in his eyes and they don't have a clue.

"We're not going to take anything away from you, not a red cent of your hard earned money. It is more blessed to give than to receive and tonight we're giving!"

He grabs two big fistfuls of bills and jumps down off the platform and runs halfway up the aisle.

I am just about to figure this must be the slickest trick since P. T. Barnum when I see him start throwing money up in the air over their heads, laughing like a lunatic. I sail my collection plate away like one of these here *Frisbees* and don't even wait to see who it's going to hit, if it hits anybody. I run up to the platform waving my arms to get everybody's attention. Which isn't easy because all around Red people are scrambling for the bills as they float down.

"Take it!" he's saying. "It's all yours."

"Folks!" I yell. "Hey, everybody! Don't fall for that. He's just trying to tempt you. Lay not up for yourself treasures on earth! Give it back before you all go straight to hell! Don't pay him no mind! Come on everybody, let's sing. Let's sing one of the good old gospel tunes. Let's all raise our voices together and join in singing . . ."

Right here I draw a blank, a complete blank. You know how it happens. I can't even think of one hymn, not even the *name* of one. And the only tune that pops into my head (it's one of the mysteries of Life how a tune will suddenly sprout in your head and you can't think of another one to save your fool soul) is that old Elvis Presley hit "Love Me Tender." Never say die is my motto and I'm ready to sing that if I got to, anything, only Red has already got rid of all the money in his hands and is running back for more.

"Get out of my way, you damn fool!" he says.

Laying here flat on my back near the back of the tent, I think that suits me just fine. I may be groggy, but I can damn well see Moses is helping him throw away money too. And Red is hollering for the two bitches to come and help him get rid of it quicker. People are scrambling for it, crawling for it, pushing and shoving. Some of them stand up on top of their chairs and jump so they can catch it floating in the air. A couple of guys in the back are fighting. It's going to be a riot.

I roll over easy and kind of shimmy under the edge of the tent the way I use to when I was a kid and wanted to get in the circus. Out in the dark the air is cool and there must be a million million stars in the sky. It's pretty, but I ain't got no time to study about stars. I mean, there may be little green men, with two heads and a T.V. aerial on both of them, looking right at me, but I don't give a shit. They can't do me no good now. And if they want to stop me they better get their freaking flying saucer into high gear and roll. Cause I got important business to take care of.

MOSES

I knew what had happened as soon as we all went in the trailer. Red was exhausted, pale. But still brighteyed, full of quick smiles like somebody with a fever. And behind the bright and shifty delirium of his eyes was an emptiness so vast it yawned like a pit of hell.

Well, I thought, he's going down there again. He's been, but he must go again and try to claw, clutch, scramble his way back to light and air again. Of course, I know nothing of these things. I have never been to that deep hell. My own was and is fairly simple. But I do not doubt his for a minute anymore than I doubt the hell of Orpheus, the one Odysseus saw, the hells of Aeneas, Jesus of Nazareth, Dante. They are all true, I believe. There are more hells than any of us ever dream of.

I saw the eyes and lips speaking, and behind that, as if superimposed in a photograph, I saw a second face, a second pair of eyes, and a third. The second, sly, wanted desperately to believe that it had escaped, outfoxed, gone to ground, and eluded his God. The third was a mask of terror, pure and simple. There was no process of thought in this vague, floating head. Only an enormous sensitivity, terrifying in itself to me, more ineffable than the cries of the Delphic Oracle. It was this head, this pair of frightened eyes which had looked down and seen hell again. This pair of eyes was pleading. It is amazing and marvellous to find one human soul on the battered, scarred face of the earth (O *earth of cauliflower ears thick lips flat broken nose & scar tissue rising ever again head shaking ears ringing sight vague & dimmed like Anteas the sure-to-be-defeated undefeated*) to whom one's strength, small, fitful as it is, can mean something. Even I suppose to some *thing*: a cared-for rose bush, a tree, a postage stamp of lawn, a well-made piece of cabinet work, even, by God, a hole in the ground, a grave dug right with honour and respect for the earth, the shovel and the occasion – can be an act of love. For that's what it is, after all the bullshit, philosophy, psychology (fooey on Freud! you bearded Viennese Kike!), theology, astrology, the whole kit and kaboodle of names and labels blows away like a deck of cards in a hurricane. You're left alone in the vast desert of yourself with rocks and stones for loaves of bread. And all you have left is the sure knowledge and rememberance of that. Not sex, for God's sake, though I can imagine that there is some Ideal Copulation, a wedding and multiplication of spirit and flesh in flesh which, in that Ideal, never to be attained, is indeed the perfect parable of love. The sign and the symbol of it anyway. Not the giving itself, for then it would be a measurable thing and he who had most to give would be the truest lover. Not quantity, or any statistical frequency, for once only (or a thousand thousand times) is more than enough and always never enough. Not even the joy that comes from giving. But instead that joy, which strikes with a flash, a wince, an inner shudder like thunder, coming from the sudden knowledge that you can, are able, for no reason worth mentioning, to give, to make an offering unto some other. All is dangerous, corruptible and corrupting, weak and defenceless to the cruel torments of pride and vanity, so that even the best of us Saul, David, Solomon suffered. Yet (once only or a thousand thousand times) once performed and once known, never to be denied though every rooster in Creation crow. Though every jackass bray his bray. Though lion roar and buzzard mark you with his beady eye, it is still there, itself unchanging in a creation which is only change. But always, as long as always is or may be, perfect, flawless, beautiful like the finest pearl. Oh, you can lose it, let it roll away and spend the rest of your life on all fours like a starved dog. You *will* lose it, no doubt about that. But you have (once only or a thousand thousand times) held in the palm of your hand perfection. The light that glitters then, brimming from some infinite, invisible fire, a current more shocking, burning and even paralyzing than all lightning (that simple moment when all words and all images fail and fall short, oh far short of the target's eye), that joy and that knowledge have shattered all mirrors of myself, made even the thin pride of endurance and toughness forever shabby, stale and cheap as a second hand garment, ill-fitting, stained, worn, foul-smelling, myself becoming nothing or rather something not my own, and the

233

only truth and only self for a wink of time, like the brush and squeak and flap of a bat in the dark, my self being only the illumination and the joy.

We have been shipwrecked together before. I cling to his wrists as long as I can before the waves part us and he drowns. Then I swim clumsy to shore and lie there like a soft, white stranded whale waiting for his limp body to be tossed up on the sand, waiting then for my next duty – out goes the bad air in comes the good air – to lift him living and breathing again to his feet. Tall above me, breathing deeply, he shakes the water from his curls like a dog, grins down at me and kicks a cloud of sand.

"Godamn your eyes. Why didn't you just let me lay there and die?"

Hand in hand we walk together as far as we can go to the lip and rim of his hell. There I must fail, unable even to go close enough to find the barbwire and the paint-frayed sign reading: "TURN BACK/KEEP OUT ALL/JEWS/HINDUS/MOS-LEMS/BUDDHISTS/SHINTO/LEOPARD MEN/PAGANS IN GENERAL /NIGGERS MAY ADVANCE BUT AT THEIR OWN PERIL/PAP-ISTS AND ROMAN CATHOLICS TAKE THE EXPRESS WAY EXPRESSLY VERBOTEN TO ALL OTHER SECTS & HERETICS/ ACHTUNG!"

I have never even seen the sign nor seen him, despairing, take the rough, twisty, rock-strewn path for the heretical, moving like a serpent towards the pit from whence an odour, to which excrement is roses, rises. I do not want to see it, even if I could. I have seen enough of the captured, leftover, fading light of that hateful place in his eyes.

I let go, withdraw, and hasten to my own place, not hell by any means, but a place of retreat and lamentation. Where old men with long beards and the sad luminous eyes of my

grandfather stand gravely waiting to greet me in a language I
have forgotten. They nod, I nod, and enter. I don sackcloth
and sprinkle myself with ashes. I go to a place in burning sand
and kneel by the others before a ruined wall, bathing it with
my tears. I open my mouth and hear my voice lament in the
language of Isaiah and Jeremiah. Somewhere I hear the voice
of my mother, my fat (I have inherited your body, Mama,
alas) Mama who does not understand this any more than I
understand Hell, but who reaches across time and space to
give, too, her kind of love: "Moses, would you like a nice
glass of tea? Sit down. Eat, eat, and you will feel better . . ."

The others?

Poor Cartwright who has wandered in hell most of his life
under the mistaken impression that it is an Amusement Park
and he ought to be having a good time. How can Red ever
tell him? He can't. He must, as you chase a dog back home to
safety, throw rocks at him, kick and curse him, and in so
doing endure the last, sad stupid, wounded glance.

Miami . . .

She will survive, live until she dies. You could drop Miami
in a parachute into the jungle and I believe she would manage
even among baboons or among the bull gorillas. Nothing
animal or living is alien to her. All are equal by now. Among the
baboons, barking and fierce, or the envied jet-set basking in the
expensive sun of the tepid Mediterranean, she would be equally
at home. Miami knows his hell like her back yard and to her it
is as tame. Strange Beatrice, she could lead him not through
Purgatory, but through the purgative tour of the Inferno
instead, pointing out the sites and sights in the matter-of-fact
monotone of a museum guide. If she would. I think she won't.
I think, without realizing it, she fears that she may be just
beginning to care too much (for her even a little is too much)

and thus stripped, she's as vulnerable as a snail without its castle.

I left to take care of the tickets, stopping at the truck to slip on the black choir robe. Hastily buttoning it up, moved to take my place in a chair behind the card table with the battered tin tackle box holding the tickets. Three people were standing there waiting for me. A tall thin farmer in freshly laundered overalls and a white, starched shirt, his face screwed into bitter lines, his mouth clamped tight on a kitchen matchstick. His wife, in a shapeless cotton dress, equally thin, wind-and-sun-burned, with gnarled hands. Her eyes were frightened as if she expected any moment the stunning blow of a fist. Her lips, too, were tight, but what she seemed so anxious to contain was a wild animal cry of pain. A high, long piercing, terrible scream in the night limited only by the breath her body held. With them, but a little to one side, was the boy, soft and fat of face, pimpled. Heavy braces gripped limp twigs of legs like bright shackles. He leaned at ease on two metal canes. Petulant, perhaps spoiled, he smiled tolerantly on them and me.

"How much?" the farmer said.

"Most people give a dollar."

"What about a cripple?" the farmer said. "Do it cost a whole dollar for a cripple too?"

Before I could answer her mouth opened. Her voice, surprising, was delicate, hardly more than an eggshell whisper, prim, precise, vaguely lady-like and not in the accent of this place.

"What he, my husband, is trying to say, to ask you, is that we heard from someone that there is a special reduced rate for the handicapped."

"Half price, madame," I said.

The farmer grunted and slapped two crumpled bills and some loose change on the table. The boy laughed to himself. Her hands clasped tightly in front of her, like a singer, the woman looked straight ahead past me, past the lit tent, blindly. I looked past her, looked up, and saw that there was a full moon. White and remote, a grinning skull set among jewels on cloth of black velvet.

"Is that all?" the farmer said. "What're we supposed to do – just keep standing here?"

"I believe," she said, her gaze never wavering back to me. "I believe he means the tickets."

"Make him give you a ticket," the boy said.

"Excuse me, I'm sorry," I said, handing the farmer three tickets.

The boy laughed. They moved past me, toward the tent, walking slow and stiff so as not to leave the boy, who was heaving himself forward in lurches and twists, one cane at a time.

He has finished preaching. His words die in the dark outside the tent. There is a breathless, silent moment so quiet you can hear the moths, beating against the naked light bulbs, hear also the strain of his deep breathing; he pants like a runner after a long, gruelling race. He stands there on the platform looking small, almost frail, utterly defeated. His knees are bent a little, his arms hanging simian and limp, the great hands as loose as if they floated in water, his head hanging down and a little to one side, almost as if broken, surely as if his neck no longer had the strength to support his head. His sweat-soaked shirt clings to him as if pasted on and there are rips on each side where a sudden twist of the arms tore the shirt with a sound like ripping adhesive tape. His eyes are closed and on his brow and face great drops of sweat, thick as rain on a window pane, run streaking, then fall slowly in small single splashes at his feet. His chest heaves with the effort of breathing. His lips are moving quickly, but whether in prayer, pleading, or a string of curses I cannot tell.

Only seconds of time, that kind caught, caged, tamed, and taught to perform a steady goosestep to the intricate tick and tock of clocks, only seconds, are passing. I glance over my shoulder at the crowd. They sit silent and still as if they were in a photograph, slightly out of focus. Farther a motion across the tent startles me. It is only a wink. The emphatic wink of Cartwright to me. Even he will not risk a grin now, but he is sure, as sure as he can be of anything from the depths and within the given limits of his experience, his mind and soul, certain beyond reasonable doubt that this is a planned, staged, wonderfully "Dramatic" moment, all somehow part of a plan, part of the Big Picture, designed, he can only surmise, to lift from the hidden corners of pockets purses and wallets the last coin of this crowd as surely as if drawn by a monstrous magnet, or as if one by one each one of them were hoisted upside down to the top of the ridgepole and shaken like a dying mouse in the jaws of a cat. Cartwright is, even as he winks, already spending the money.

I turn back. Still only seconds of time pass or have passed. I see the hands clench into hammer-head fists. My own still rest, poised over the keys of the little piano, ready in a reflexive instant to make music, any kind of music to fit whatever action will come now, to thunder enormous chords of confusion, if some distraction is required, or to tinkle as sweetly, softly, discreetly as tiny bells in a gentle breeze.

He has stopped panting. His bent legs begin to straighten. I see the shoulders slipping back into proud width. He stands up, shakes his head with a shower of sweat and smiles at his flock. I begin to play sweet tinkly, rippling hords as he starts to speak.

"Ladies and gentlemen, brothers and sisters in Jesus," he says quietly, falling in with the beat and the mood of the music. "It is at this stage of our service that we usually take up the offering, hoping that some of you will be so kind as to give a little something so that we can go ahead a little farther, carrying the good news to still another town in another place. I usually stand up and ask you to help us go on, each according to his own ability. But tonight I intend to make an offering to *you* . . ."

A kind of a wild dissonant chord, as if somebody stepped on a cat, slips in without any help or intention from me. It's just a reaction of surprise. I'm not trying to say anything. But he glares down at me quickly and I stroke the keys and make sounds more tinkly than ever with my right hand.

"Tonight," he goes on, "the time has come for a surprise."

With that he spins around and moves to where we put the safe. He lifts it high and carries it up into the middle of the platform so that everyone in the tent can see it. He sets it down and points a finger right at me.

"Come here and open the safe for me."

I stop playing and come up on the platform and bend down in front of the safe, working the combination.

"Wait till you see what's going to happen next."

I finish, give the door a pull and it opens. He kicks it wider and, bending, scoops up two handfuls of bills. He whirls around to face them, grinning, holding the bills high in the air.

"Glory!" he shouts. "Glory Hallelujah!"

He leaps off the platform and runs up the aisle. He leans back like a pitcher, and then he begins throwing the bills in bunches high in the tent. The air explodes with floating green.

"Get it!" he cries. "Take it! It's all yours!"

Meanwhile here comes Cartwright. If Dreama was right behind him waving a summons, he wouldn't be moving any faster. He jumps up on the platform waving both arms, flapping them as if he is trying his damndest to take off into the air. He is waving his arms like a deranged pelican and shouting incoherently at the top of his voice. I am right beside him, slightly crouched so as to avoid his flailing, and I can't understand one single word. Maybe it's Swahili. Maybe the spirit has at last reached him and he is shouting the good news of his salvation in the Unknown Tongue. He stops, his arms rest, and he turns to me.

"Would you mind playing so that I can lead them in song?"

"What do you want me to play?"

He furrows his brow in intense concentration. He scratches his head. Then smiles with decision.

" 'Love Me Tender'," he says.

He has gone mad. The sight of all that money being thrown away, all that lovely money which he has imagined spending a thousand times over. When he saw it floating slowly down, something happened to his current. The switch of his 40 watt lucidity was thrown. Darkness followed. In that darkness he spilled and lost every marble he ever owned.

"Yeah," he is saying. "You know how it goes."

He begins to whistle "Love Me Tender" softly and has only just begun when Red is back on the platform knocking poor Cartwright flat on his back. Red scoops up more bills.

"Come on, Moze," he says. "Help me."

I bend to the safe to gather some bills. Over the top I watch Cartwright crawl to the back of the tent and wriggle under a spot where, if I had driven the stakes in the way he wanted, he

240

would be trapped. He goes under and out on his belly, I expect him to re-enter at any moment from the front disguised (perhaps in dark glasses and one of those long fake beards I used to wear when Red wanted me to play the part of an Old Testament Patriarch; it didn't work; I'm basically not the patriarchal type) and rush forward into the fray, leaping high in the air to catch the floating bills, snatching them away from old women, children and cripples. If he did that, it would be worth the price. Hang the cost!

MIAMI

All day he's been running, trying to hide from God or whatever it is, some kind of demon maybe, that pursues him. I know what that must be like. Like a woman waiting for her man to come home, knowing he's going to be drunk and mean, going to whip her and beat her up and screw the hell out of her right on the floor (and she can't holler on account of waking the kids). He may even kill her. Only she can't run away because he knows every hiding place in the house and if she locks a door he'll just kick it in hard and be even madder. So she waits, knowing what's coming and hoping it won't. They say you can't remember a pain after it's gone the way you can remember a taste or a feeling or a smell. You can remember you were hurt but you can't remember how it really was. The thing they don't tell you, though, is you can *anticipate* a pain. If you know you're going to be hurt, you can imagine all kinds of terrible things and suffer too. The only good I can see that comes from that is sometimes the real pain comes along and just can't live up to advance billing. That's a relief, but it isn't a whole lot of help.

With Red it's like he is raped. Which is bad enough for a

woman in real life or in her mind, but at least she's equipped for it. She's built to get raped one way or the other anyway.

"I'm one of God's whores," Red used to say. "He comes and He takes me whenever he feels like it. He'll let me go awhile and I'll think He isn't coming back ever. I'll be glad. But I know I'm ruined and spoiled forever. I know that nothing else will ever equal that, the terrible, blinding, shining time when He takes me. 'It is a fearful thing to fall into the hands of the living God,' Paul says. Do you understand how it is?"

I can believe it. Not what he preaches, but what happens to him. Not only understand as a whore understands, but see and believe. I stand in the rear of the tent watching him preach, listening too, but without paying much attention. He has preached better and he has preached worse. I've heard it all before anyway. But this time I see it happening. I see him start, a free man and a clever one, doing his act. Then I see close up another face, his face, but the face behind the mask he wears for the crowd. I see him as if I were suddenly knocked cross-eyed or else stone drunk and seeing double. The figure in the white shirt, the man on the platform preaching, using the studied gestures, waving his arms, using his hands like a sculptor to shape the words he throws out, he recedes, grows tiny, smaller and smaller, and the sound of his voice becomes faint. Nearer and nearer to me a second face swims, ever more clearly in focus, bodiless, such a naked and vulnerable face. I see that face change as the experience changes for him.

It reminds me right away, so I almost laugh, of that famous scene in that famous pseudo-Blue Movie, *Ecstasy*. I see first indolence and confidence. He might be Hedy Lamar, lying among wild-flowers, contented, dozing in the sunlight. A faint, vague apprehension stirs him. Does he hear something? Is it God on horseback in high boots riding towards him? Does he hear the sound of distant hooves? He seems to listen anxiously. Now his expression shows fear. He shakes his head, silent but the lips pleading *no, no, please no* . . . Does God stand over him smiling, looking down over the points of his shiny boots at a pale, frightened form? Now the face is frantic, now, oh! hurt, wounded, stabbed! Now in anguish, in rebellion. Now in tears, but ever so slowly changing, dissolving, melting into a new expression, growing ever so slowly, gradually frantic in a new way, becoming bright-eyed, wild, ecstatic, choking on silent screams of joy, sweat-bathed, biting his lips, his tongue, a face so animal that his hair now seems fur, and in a moment his whole face will be furry, the face of a beast. But no, as the face changes, the hair grows long and silky, and it is the face of a young girl, truly ecstatic, screaming for more, more, *don't stop ever, oh! ah!;* then a second utterly calm, utterly tranquil, at peace, filled with joy, simple as the wildflowers around her. Such a pretty girl. Completely contented. A cat full of cream stretching by the fire, purring . . . Then anxious, pleading again, *don't leave me, please don't go, please!* Now bereft. Now blank. Now lost. Hearing the hoof beats dwindle away in the distance. Now come bitter tears. The face melts away like candle wax from the scalding tears. It is gone. He has finished preaching. He stands bent over, head bowed on the platform. But the man in the white shirt has vanished. What stands there is a naked woman, grey hair wild and awry, fat, huge-bellied, sagging and jiggling. Great, soft ugly, brown-nippled breasts. From thigh to toe a varicose horror. Her feet horny, calloused, filthy. In a moment I expect to see her drop to her knees and, mercifully transformed into a pregnant sow, drag herself out of the tent.

Oh, Red, I know what happens to you without understanding. And you are wrong. You are not a whore. A whore becomes accustomed to her bed and her faceless, nameless lovers. No, it is worse. You become a whore, but each time you must begin again as a virgin, a young and innocent girl, and each time end as a bag of flesh and bones with nothing but senile memories for solace.

He leaps off the platform strewing money like rose petals in the crowd. Now he's Red again! Wild, with a lunatic smile. He peels off bills and throws them high, laughing and shouting. They scramble for them, shouting too.

You fed them their loaves and fishes. Now let them eat cake and be damned!

Moses is helping too. They're having a ball throwing money!

He sees me and waves for me to come. I run up the aisle toward him thinking: *Yes, now, yes, at least I can do this . . .*

JUDITH

What a way to end, running up and down the aisles of the tent, throwing money! People scramble for it, knock over chairs and each other. They're all screaming and yelling. I see one middle aged woman, grimly determined, crawling slowly up and down the aisles among the leaping, flailing nest of legs, hat on her head, pocketbook in her hand, crawling slowly and methodically up one aisle then down the next, eyes on the earth, searching for a dollar bill that may have slipped through the confusion. I wish her luck.

Behind me angry voices, then a slapping sound and another. I turn. Two young men are fighting. Each has one hand free to hit the other one. The other hand of each grips the end of a single bill, tugging. They spin round the axis of that taut bill, lashing out furiously at each other with their free fists, cursing, bleeding. Strangely nobody seems to mind or care. They might be completely alone.

I go to them.

"Let me hold it for you," I say. "You can fight better with both hands."

They stop, look at each other dazed, blinking, and bloody, like a couple of bookends, react, then simultaneously and slowly turn their heads to look at me, first with curiosity, then the slow dawning of a polite smile. Still they cling tensely to the bill which, now that I am close enough, I see is a rather dirty, rather crumpled five.

"Give me the bill to hold and then you can fight to your heart's content."

They nod simultaneously, vigorously, smiling more brightly than ever. I am aware now that these two are more than brothers. They are identical twins. Together they hand me the bill. I fold it while they turn back to each other again, furious. I fold it into a neat small square as they fall into the classic, old-fashioned fighter's stance, beginning another circle as tense as the other, wheeling now about me, though. I am the hub.

"Boys?" I say sweetly, ready to duck.

They halt, lean to one side of me to see each other clearly and exchange their bafflement. Slowly their hands return to their sides as they turn slightly to face me, and I step back far enough so that they have to move in a little. Now they are side by side, practically touching each other, giving me the benefit of full, polite curiosity and attention. The damage is about equal. Each has a bloody nose and miscellaneous bruises.

Each has a speechless reaction of shock and horror as I drop the folded bill down the front of my white gown.

"Oh," I say. "I seem to have dropped it."

Each smiles. Each nods.

"What are we going to do now?"

They shrug eloquently. We stand, giving the problem consideration.

"I'll tell you what," I say. "It just doesn't look right for a lady to be rummaging down the front of her own dress. I'll stand perfectly still with my arms at my sides and my eyes closed so I won't see it happening. And you can get it yourselves."

Bright, appreciative grins, quick nods, a step forward.

"One at a time," I say. "Not both at once."

They glare at each other. The fists double up and their arms slowly begin to come up to action stations again.

"Wait a minute!" I say. "Don't you think we could find a nice, peaceful way to settle this?"

They lower their arms long enough to shrug.

"Well," I say. "You work it out among yourselves. I'll just leave the money where it is. But – and I mean this . . ." (wagging my finger at them) ". . . if there is any violence whatsoever, I will keep the five dollars and give it to charity."

I turn away quickly and walk up the aisle towards the front, pausing once to sneak a look back over my shoulder. Arm in arm with their backs to me, they are engaged in quiet, intense conversation.

I feel like singing, dancing. I want to climb to the top of the tent pole, grab a rope and come swinging down, a blaze and blur of shouting white in my gown!

"Silver!" a voice cries out. "He's throwing silver!"

Red has two fistfuls of change – quarters, fifty cent pieces dimes and nickels. He throws them high in the air, a beautiful silver fountain in the light. An explosion of coins. They all gasp. Then the last order is gone. They surge out into the middle and side aisles as the coins keep rising and falling, each explosion followed, underlined by a hissing gasp from the crowd, a long hiss like a skyrocket rising, then a moment, a muted *oh* . . . ! at the peak as the coins burst apart, a long exhaling sigh as they fall . . .

I try to push and fight my way forward to the platform. I must get there before the last of the change is gone. I, too, must stand on the platform and hurl coins to the crowd.

I see a cripple knocked from his crutches. He sprawls, grins weakly, then begins to drag himself, limp-legged, like a seal, scrabbling, scuttling crabwise for coins in the dirt. I see one man in a speechless fury of frustration snatch off his own glasses and jump up and down on them until they are nothing but powder. A woman passes by me, wearing a large piece of tape where her nose ought to be, holding her two hands high of her as if she bore a chalice. Her hands are full of change, some of it spills over the edges of her palms, falls unnoticed by her. She blunders past me, not seeing me, not seeing any-thing, her eyes brightly focused at infinity.

Chairs fall and crack around me. A woman rolls back and forth in the dirt, shouting, clawing at herself, tearing and ripping at her clothes.

Something touches my shoulder, not flesh but metal. I turn. One of the battlers, the twins, holding a quarter between his thumb and forefinger. Smiling now with triumph. I see the other standing at the rear of the tent, kicking at clods of earth, ignoring us.

"Yes?"

I offer a cool, impersonal mask as if I were seeing him for the first time in my life. His smile blinks, diminishes.

"Me and my brother was fighting over that five dollar bill. Remember us?"

247

"Oh, yes," I say. "Did you decide?"

"Yes, ma'm. We flipped a coin."

"Don't you know better than to gamble in *church*?" I say, snatching the quarter away from him. "Aren't you ashamed of yourself?"

"Yes, ma'm."

"QUIET! EVERYBODY BE QUIET!"

Red's voice booms out deep and enormously loud behind me. I turn to see them hushed now, standing perfectly still, all eyes on him. He waits until a few who are on the ground manage to stand up or are helped to their feet. He lets them stand and wait patiently for him. It is very hot in the tent now and I feel a little faint.

"Looka here," he says, holding up a roll of pink paper. "This is it. It's all gone, all gone, and you've got it. All except this. This here is a roll of pennies."

He lowers his hand and looks a little sad. They know he has not finished. They wait, patient and silent, for him to continue. When he speaks again, it is in a husky voice, hardly more than a whisper, as though choked, stifled with emotion.

"Now I have to say farewell to High Pines," he says. "I always hate to say goodbye. Sometimes it seems to me like man's life ain't nothing but a long, lonesome series of farewells. And I hate to say it. You are good people and you've got a beautiful place here, all ringed by the mountains . . ."

He raises his eyes to heaven.

" 'I will lift up mine eyes unto the hills from whence cometh my help . . .' God knows, God *knows*, how much I want to stop right here and rest in peace, to let my roots go down deep in the earth like a tall tree. He knows it, but He won't allow it. He ain't going to let me quit now . . ."

Now a grin, sardonic, cruel. He bends at the waist, bows

his powerful neck forward and makes a wide, sweeping, scything gesture with the flat edge of his hand. His voice booms out again.

"Because it ain't over. The fight ain't won yet. The Devil is loose in the land of the living. He moves by day and by night, stealthy he moves across the land on tiptoes. Oh, he's quiet and smiley and polite, just like a travelling salesman. But he's selling a one-way ticket to hell. And in his sample case he carries a packet of seeds, just to drop them by the roadside as he goes by. The Devil ain't no Johnny Appleseed, no sir! Where he drops his seeds comes forth strange and thorny plants bearing strange fruit. He is sowing a crop of hate, disease, anguish and tribulation! If that crop grows, if that crop thrives, it's going to blot out the sun which is the eye of God. We don't want that to happen, do we?"

One voice: "No!"

"We ain't going to let that happen, are we?"

Several voices: "No!"

"Is that the best you can do? The rest of you people, when the Devil comes round aknocking on your front door, what are you going to do? You going to let him right in and give him the best seat in the parlour, is that what you going to do?"

Chaos of shouting: "*No! No! No!*"

He raises both arms in a V. He smiles and waits for quiet again.

"I know I can count on you," he says. "And so I'm going on. I will pursue him to the ends of the earth!"

One voice: "*Amen!*"

"If he dives into the sea I'll drop a line with a hook as big as a scythe blade on it. I'll hook him and haul him in with my bare hands. You better believe it!"

Many voices: *"Amen! Amen!"*

"And if he stops running and will stand and fight like a man, I will pit my strength against his and pin him to the ground. Because my strength comes from the Lord!"

"Amen! Amen! Joy to the World!"

"I'm fixing to leave you," he says. "We're going on our way rejoicing. Lemme hear you say *glory!* before we go."

"Glory!"

"Lemme hear it so I'll remember it. Lemme hear it so the Devil out there beyond the County line – cause we done run him that far tonight . . . Let the Devil himself hear it and take notice."

"GLORY!"

"Goodbye," he says, dropping his voice to the edge of a whisper again and to the husky edge of tears. "Goodbye and God bless you each and every one."

Then as if in sudden afterthought, as though he had forgotten all about it, he raises the roll of pennies. He grins, whirls on the tips of his toes and brings it down full force on the edge of the safe, splitting the roll. He hurls the pennies high and the whole length of the tent, then turns his back on them. Moses begins to play a marching kind of a tune and they file out quickly and quietly past me as I move forward towards the platform. Some of them, men and women alike, are crying. By the time I reach the platform the last of them are leaving the tent and from outside I hear the sound of starting engines.

He sees me, smiles, and comes forward, arms outstretched, taking my hands in his.

"Judith," he says. "Little Judith. Well, you saw it all tonight, first and last, all there is. There ain't no more."

Then he seizes me in his arms and lifts me high in the air like a dancer. He spins me across the platform to the tune and rhythm of his laughter and sets me down so lightly I feel for an instant as if I still were in the air. The other two stand, unsmiling, watching. He looks at me. Then something, a kind of a tic or tremor, troubles his face. The light goes out of his eyes.

"Get me a chair!" he shouts at Moses. "Get me a chair!"

To me more softly: "Don't they know I'm tired to death?"

He looks up at the empty tent, the confusion of fallen chairs.

"Did you see what I did?" he says. "I threw it all away."

He covers his face with his hands. He hangs his head, racked with spasms of sobbing. I stand awkwardly nearby. The other two move nearer.

"Don't touch me!" he says. "Don't anybody touch me! Leave me alone!"

Still sobbing, still hiding his face, he runs up the aisle and out into the dark. We stand a moment. The others leave too.

I look into the empty tent, trying to see what he saw, as he saw it. I'm very tired. I start walking up the centre aisle looking down. Here and there a penny glints. Then I hear something, a kind of thrashing among the chairs. Startled, catching my breath, I stop.

From a tangle of fallen chairs emerges, dirty, filthy with dirt and sweat, her hair mattered, her face streaked, a wild creature fierce with triumph, the woman I had seen crawling up and down the aisles.

"Look!" she says. "See what I got. Look what I found!"

She hurries past me, smiling, clutching a wrinkled dollar bill in her fist.

7

And God shall wipe away the tears from their eyes; and there shall be no more death, neither sorrow, nor crying, neither shall there be any more pain: for the former things are passed away.

REVELATION XXI, 4

I.

In less than an hour the field was quiet and still again. The last of the cars and trucks were gone, a procession of dwindling, red-eyed monsters headed home for town, where most of the lights had long since winked off, or going out the highway in the other direction to lonely farmhouses in the valley or, farther still, among the steep, wooded foothills beneath the dark mountains. The cars and trucks had gone, carrying their cargo, a mixed cargo of insignificant, nameless, long-suffering bodies and vexed souls. More like salvage, really; more like the flotsam and jetsam of some shipwreck or disaster; a pirate's haul; the survivors perhaps retaining some broken fragments, images of those last riotous moments when whatever healing, whatever words of comfort and solace they may have come for, were all lost, tossed high and scattered in a shining explosion of small change, lost in the green fluttering and blowing of dollar bills like dead leaves in the wind. They would go home, tired now, stunned to the edge of silence, and soon they would sleep and dream. And in that dream, for in the dark time of dreaming all dreams are one, would come all the shapes of the dark, monsters and dwarfs, beasts and dragons, like paper dolls cut by a lunatic out of the very texture of the night itself, each snarling, growling, whining or howling its desperate hunger. And in that same dream would be proud dancers, hale and beautiful, perfectly proportioned, clad in sunlight only and in the sweetness of the breeze, each with the face of a dreamer, moving graceful to the music of the spheres, while the just and the unjust lay deep in the same sleep, captives of the same dream.

In less than an hour they were all gone. Slowly into the space of silence in the field came the sounds of the world – faint insect noises, the croaking and drumming of frogs from low, damp places, the cry and leathery flutter of an invisible night bird, and, at last, the sigh of a slight, warm, rising breeze among the pines.

Moses planned to pick up the pieces and move on. They could not stay. There was no place for them here, and with the money gone for good there was no other rational alternative. They must collect whatever coins and bills had escaped clutching fingers, they must all give up anything that they had long since set aside against the possibility of just such a disaster as this. There would not be much, but with luck there would be enough to gas up the truck and the car and to move on in the night to another town.

So in the morning there would be no sign that they had ever been here. Except of course for the space of crushed and stained grass, salted by sweat and tears, where the tent had been, a space they always left behind them in each place to prove that someone had raised a shout to heaven and harvested a crop of hell and gone on. A space left behind them always, like the huge footprint of a giant.

Cartwright had disappeared somewhere, up to no good wherever he was, but Moses did not have time now to worry about him. He took the lanterns out of the truck, lit them, the cut off the generator. In the tent by the yellow light of then lanterns Miami set up the little camp stove and started a pot of coffee. That would help. Then she and the girl began folding and stacking the chairs.

Moses left them, taking a lantern to the dark trailer. He found Red in his underpants, stretched out on a bunk, his eyes closed, his lined, hard face curiously peaceful. He was not sleeping.

"Can I get you anything?" Moses asked.

"See if you can find me a drink."

Moses turned to look. The trailer was a complete mess. It looked like a bomb had gone off, scattering bits of clothing and odds and ends in every-which direction. Someone (guess who? he thought) had turned the place inside out in a hurried frenzy, ripping, pulling, emptying out everything, searching for something (guess what? he thought). Not whiskey. Because there amid the debris was a full bottle with a seal unbroken.

"The son of a bitch really tore the place apart," Red said, twisting the top off the bottle, gulping, "When I get my hands on him, I'll tear the meat off his bones."

He offered the bottle to Moses, but Moses shook his head.

"It's all over," Red said. "Go ahead and get drunk."

"We'll talk about it in the morning."

Red sat up on the edge of the bunk, patted a pillow in place, then leaned back against it. Propped there, he looked at Moses and smiled.

"Don't you know when it's time to quit?"

"We'll work out something."

"Okay," Red said. "You do that."

"What are we going to do about the girl?"

"Send her in here," Red said. "I'll get rid of her."

Moses nodded and turned away, not wanting now to look at the cracked, scarred mask or into those eyes drained of all brightness.

Miami helped him load the chairs onto the truck. They worked along quickly, without a word, until the job was done.

"Got a cigarette?" she asked.

He gave her one and held a match for her. She puffed, inhaling deeply.

"I'm not going to be able to sleep," she said.

"You want a pill?"

"You're way ahead of me."

He offered her the small prescription bottle. She said thanks and kept it. He looked at her, questioning.

"Don't you trust me?"

"Do I have to?"

"I guess you will," she said. "What are you worried about?"

"I'm not worried about myself."

"That's the whole trouble with you," she said. "You never learned how to look after number one."

"Maybe so."

"Trust me."

He shrugged. "If I had the choice I would. You know that."

"So?"

"So . . .," he said, feeling suddenly very tired, feeling the full weariness of old bones and sagging flesh, feeling a heaviness in the eyelids. "Be careful."

He turned toward the truck. It was time to take the chairs back to the undertaker and to get the gas.

"Don't you want some hot coffee?"

"I'll wait till I get back," he said.

"Suit yourself."

* * *

Crawling, fumbling in the dark trailer, searching frantically for the money he *knew* was somewhere – in a cigar box, maybe between the pages of a book or folded in clothing, his fury mounting in direct and simple proportion to his frustration, Cartwright had almost been caught at it when Red came in. Lucky for him, Red stumbled on the steps. He just had time enough to hide in the shower stall. He stayed there, sweating, breathing carefully, gripping the pistol in his pocket, waiting to be discovered. So he heard Moses come in. And when they didn't even *discuss* the money, he knew for sure they had some hidden somewhere. Well, he would find it, if he could just get out of the trailer in one piece. He thought of flashing the gun and just walking out. Decided against it. Maybe Red would get drunk and pass out. Anyway if he just dozed off Cartwright could tiptoe out and finish his search.

Then the girl came in and that made things complicated. He would have groaned out loud if he dared. To have to be there, not standing upright, not able to move, squnched down in a kind of a half kneebend, trapped and sweating bullets in that little sweatbox of a shower stall, to have to listen to them! They talked and talked and it looked like they would just go on talking all night long. About that time he made the noise and Red found him hiding there.

That was a bad minute or two after Red jerked back the shower curtain and there he was with his bare face hanging out. But he still had his pistol and good sense and he put both of them to work for him, cleverly outfoxing Red and getting safely out of the trailer with no more to show for it than one ear-ringing, knot-raising blow to the side of his head and then a free ride in the dark, empty air when Red, probably trying to show off in front of Miss Bitch, heaved him out of the trailer the way they toss a U.S. Mail sack off of a fast moving express train. It could have been a whole lot worse, and, so, philosophically, he dusted himself off and went towards the tent where there was some light and the smell of fresh coffee.

"Where's Moses?"

Miami just looked at him and laughed in his face.

"What happened to *you*, Hookworm?"

"Never mind about me. Where the hell is that fat Jew?"

Thinking suddenly: *That's it! Moses has it! He's got it all! Had it all the time in a money belt. He's got the money and he's long gone!* Thinking sadly: *I should have known! Oh, sweet Jesus, how dumb can one guy get? He was the one that knew the combination. It didn't bug him a bit to throw all that money away. Mighty suspicious. And you missed it. Whoever heard of a Jew giving money away?*

"He went with the truck."

"Where?"

"To take back the chairs and get gassed up."

"You mean to stand there and tell me you just let him drive off?"

"He'll be back," she said. "Anyway I'm glad he's not here right now."

Eyeing her suspiciously: "How come?"

"Mainly on account of," Miami said, coming close to him and speaking in a low voice, "I want to talk to you alone."

"What about?"

Then she started telling him. And, whether he could believe a word of it or not, he let himself be persuaded, not so much by her words and plans and schemes as by the Weakness itself which naturally took command of him the minute she was standing next to him and he could sniff the sweetness of her perfume. The Weakness not only took command, but complete possession, leaving him weak-kneed and helpless as she stood so close to him, her body brushing lightly against his, her careless hands actually touching him for emphasis while she whispered warmly into the shell of his astonished ear.

It was a beautiful scheme. In just a little while Red would be through with the Bitch in the Black Raincoat. He would probably throw her out on her ass. Then Red would go to sleep. With Moses gone that left only Judith to worry about.

"Let's knock her in the head."

No, no, no, she explained to him. That wouldn't do at all. She had a better idea. Did he remember that powder, the stuff he used to feed the snakes to keep them all sluggish? What would that stuff do to somebody?

"Make them groggy and maybe sick to their stomach, that's all," he said. "The fella that sold it to me said it wasn't poison."

That was just fine and dandy because they didn't really want to hurt anybody, did they? Even if they did want to, it might not be the best thing. No use inviting trouble, taking a chance on trouble with the law. So Cartwright would get the snake powder. She would put some in the girl's coffee, then she would be easy to handle.

"What do you plan to do to her?" he asked.

"Not what you're thinking," she said. "We just have to get her away from the trailer, some place where she won't be able to wake up Red until we've got a good start."

Sure, but where would that be? Well, she had been thinking. . . . What about those cages? Of course, the old zoo cages! A piece of chain and a good stout lock and she would be out of action at least until daylight when somebody driving by would hear her hollering and let her out. What about Moses? Well, if he got back in time, and he probably would, he would have to spend the night in a cage too.

By morning Miami and Cartwright would be long gone in her car. Cartwright liked the idea fine. Except for one thing. He wanted to wait for Moses to come back. He wanted to see the look on his fat, old, ugly face when he locked him in. He wanted Moses to know how he had been faked right out of his shoes.

"If you think you can handle him," Miami said.

"I can handle him easy. Don't you worry about that."

261

And here, inadvertently, he almost revealed his one ace in the hole – the pistol. He almost pulled it out and showed it to her right then and there. Like a damn fool! And he knew he couldn't trust her, not a woman like Miami with a long full career behind her, professional career based on exploiting the natural Weakness of men. Just as long as he had the pistol and she didn't even know it, just as long as he stayed wide awake and kept his head, he would be all right. Just let her try to pull something on him! He was ready. She better be ready too. Ready for some real high-class, all night, mattress-busting, bed-spring-breaking Action of all kinds and types known and devised by Man. He had that book in his footlocker with thirty basic positions not counting the variations. And before he finished with old Miami he would try them all too, every one of them, and the good ones a couple of times and once to grow on. Even if he didn't get a chance to go back and get the book it didn't matter because he was sure he could remember them once he put his mind to it, having once, just to train his memory, learned the whole book by heart.

Still, there were problems like –

"What are we going to do for money?"

"Don't be silly."

"I'm serious."

"I thought you knew," she said.

She fumbled in the edge of her bra and produced a fifty dollar bill to wave it briefly, crisp as fresh lettuce, then restore it safely to its sweet, soft resting place. And she calmed him with the promise that there was plenty more, not only where that came from specifically, but also elsewhere on her person and among her things and, best of all, more yet in a Bank, far off and as safe as Fort Knox. He didn't think she was stupid, did he? And he allowed as how he didn't. He didn't think for a minute, did he, that she had lived all her life with such reckless, careless abandon that she had never even once had one little thought of the future when the best merchandise she had to offer would be gone and she could either sit on her ass in a rocking chair on the front porch of the Poorhouse or else settle down somewhere in comfort and peace and quiet with plenty of sweet, happy memories?

The prospect of the future, *that much* future, worried him. Where would he fit in? He couldn't marry her, even if he had to, to get his share of the loot. Not at least until he got a legal divorce from Dreama. And in order to get that heretofore, aforesaid and above mentioned same and said legal divorce, he would have to notify Dreama and she would have her day in Court. She would put on some good clothes and bat her baby blue eyes and some dirty old man of an heretoafter and below mentioned party to be called the Judge would take everything including the gold fillings in his teeth. He would sock him below the belt for retroactive desertion and non-support.

The worst thing was that Miami probably knew that. She knew she was safe. Any time she wanted to she could leave him penniless and all alone out there in the cruel world and, if worse came to worse, he might have to go to work for a living. It made Cartwright profoundly sad to picture it. It was pitiful. But he knew how to restore his confidence and courage, how to think positively and get rid of that gloomy picture.

"Just one thing," he said. "Why me?"

He knew even as she came closer to him, kissed him full and sweet on the mouth with just a hint of her tongue in the lively, friendly French style, even as she kissed him and her hands like a pair of trained and leashed pets roamed in exploration of bone and muscle, knew as she pressed tight against him, leaning her smooth cheek against his so he could smell the sweet, mysterious

263

roots of her hair, while she first tongued then talked into his ear with a throaty whisper that made him shiver and feel goose bumps, telling him of the wonders of himself that she had often imagined and even sometimes dreamed about but never once dared to speak of, telling him how she of all women surely ought to be able to tell a real man when she saw one, and then in a rush of old explicit words that somehow this once, coming from her lips into his eager ear seemed new and mysterious, all velvety and delicately intimate as fine, filmy silk, as if alchemically transmuted from dross to pure gold by the magic of her tongue, words which abstracted would have made him blush but whose texture and meaning sent signals of delight along the circuits of blood, nerves, and bone as she conjured up the pleasures she intended to lay at his feet like a dutiful slave serving her king, and, moreover, also stirring him to the dark, clutching roots of his being as she described, not implied, and without a wince of shame, the pleasures she knew would be hers in the perfect service of his youth and manhood, he knew as he stood there now like a soldier and her words became music, the national anthem, and he the good trooper did proudly come to present arms, he knew all the time from beginning to end that it was only Weakness, his Weakness listening and reacting while his Weakness, using the voice and the form of the woman, spoke to itself.

He knew it was dangerous folly to pack up his doubts and send them into exile to the farthest and coldest Siberia of his brain; but, folly or not, he couldn't care less. He waved good-bye to doubt and suspicion and agreed in groaning assent that love conquers all.

He reached for her, his hands a pair of starving lions, but she deftly avoided their lunge and, frowning, glanced at her watch. They would have to hurry.

Reluctantly, he nodded and then scooted away into the dark on his errands, swaying inside like a cobra to the charming music of his future joy.

*　　*　　*

When Judith saw the look on his face, lit theatrically by the yellow-orange flicker of the lantern flame, she felt suddenly afraid. She wanted to turn, to run out of the trailer and across the field to the speed and safety of her car. But she mastered that impulse and came slowly toward him, knelt by the bunk and bowed her head. She uttered no protest when he seized her hair and lifted her head and forced her to. look in his eyes. His eyes, catching the light of the lantern, danced with little flames. Now he was neither healer nor preacher. He was not her lover. Now he was, perhaps justly, she surmised, her cruel inquisitor. Holding her hair so tightly she had to struggle to keep from screaming, he began to ask her questions about herself, questions she had never dared to ask herself out of fear and shame. And instead of the sound of a scream she heard herself answering him, heard herself speaking in a flat, soft, toneless, mechanical voice. She was speaking clearly and audibly, even savouring the speaking of each word, and calmly she allowed him entrance to the most private precincts of her mind. She guided him on a tour of chaotic secret places of voluptuous luxury and credible squalor and filth, of fact and fancy, history and dream, so locked together as to be inseparable, as if these things were naked sweaty lovers joined like dogs in heat, wallowing to a chorus of barks and snarls. Not shameless, but anyway no longer ashamed, she did not try to hide anything from him. Her confession was not spewed forth nor blurted or scrawled, but instead, careful as a calligrapher, one word at a time, she spelled out her history to him in truth and fantasy. She spared him nothing in spite of the pursed contempt of his lips.

Looking into his eyes she felt as if she were a young girl again, alone and dancing the joy of her youth and herself before her admiring mirror, enamoured, excited by her own bright-eyed glances. It was as if she were dancing to music and *must* dance to it as a puppet dances. But the music kept changing and the dance changed with it. The mirror kept changing and in it she saw a host of shapes and forms, none of them lovely and soon all of them demons. Then faster and faster the music and the flash of the changing mirror, like the flash of a shuffled deck of cards, until finally she fell in a soft, breathless heap and dared not look any more.

In the little, fractioned world of fact she was still kneeling by the bunk with her eyes wide open and fixed on his. And she would not cry out or weep. He cleared his throat and spat in her face. She did not flinch away.

"Where is your husband?"

"I don't have a husband any more," she said.

"Tell me about him."

"No . . ."

He tightened his grip on her hair, knotting, twisting it between his fingers. And she began talking, at first halting and clumsy, searching for words, losing them, searching again, to body forth the ghostly presence of the man she had married and had now left. Then she found a wealth of words, and excess, and, as if gagging on their richness, she vomited hatred and scorn of the man and of all men save this one who was torturing her. Astounded, even as she was speaking, she knew that this moment and this shame was as near to the state of sensual ecstasy she had always dreamed of and hungered for. And then she felt tears in her eyes, wet on her cheeks, salty on her tongue.

266

She heard the words choke off and felt her body shaking with spasms of sobbing.

He let go of her and she knelt by the bunk feeling herself weeping, hearing herself sob, while her lips fumbled to shape a silent prayer of thanksgiving. For a while he must have left her there. For a little while she heard him being angry with someone else. She could hear their voices but not the words. Then it was very quiet again. Gently, from behind, he raised her to her feet.

"Take off your clothes."

She fumbled at the snaps and hooks of the costume she was still wearing. "What are you going to do?"

"What do you want me to do?" he said.

"Heal me," she said. "Oh, dear God, this time please let me get well."

"Look at me."

She turned to face him and raised her head to look into his eyes again, this time without pride or fear or fury, only with naked pleading.

"You hate yourself too much," he said.

"Help me."

"All I can do is help you begin."

He fumbled among the open suitcases and strewn rubbish until he found the scissors, then came back to her, holding them bright and clicking. She tried to move away, but he gripped her so tight she could not move, and *snip, snip, snip,* the scissors clicked brightly and great hunks of her hair fell away. She stopped struggling, feeling a great calm. Thinking: *Yes! Yes, this is what they do with collaborators. It is right. Now I can be clean again.*

Finished, he tossed the scissors aside and shoved her in front of a mirror. She looked into the eyes of a stranger, comically, grotesquely bald. She laughed out loud.

"Go back to your husband," he said. "Maybe he can love you now."

CARTWRIGHT

If only I hadn't of farted!

That's where my luck took a definite turn for the worse. The trouble started long before that and got to a kind of a peak when that nut threw all our money away. But, as the world knows, you can stand trouble as long as your luck holds out. When they take your good luck away from you, you might just as well send for the friendly undertaker and get yourself fitted for a pine box.

Farting was the worst part, though. Humiliating, to have it happen that way. I didn't figure they'd notice. I'd been holding it, fighting it for quite a while, ever since I hid in the shower. I guess I can hold a fart as good as any man alive in a social situation and I could have kept on too except I heard Red and the Bitch carrying on all that crazy talk and I thought to myself they would keep at it a while and even if they didn't notice me I would have to stay in the shower stall longer than I planned to. So I kind of relaxed. Might just as well relax and enjoy it, like they say. Naturally my stomach relaxed too and I could feel it building up. I thought to myself, *well, I guess I can cut one now and nobody will ever know the difference.* You know? I mean, it felt like it would be a bastard fart – a sneaky little fella with no pop. But I don't care how much experience you've had with all kinds of farts, you can always be wrong.

The long and the short of it was if I had had a bullhorn to amplify the sound, if I had blown it through a bugle, it couldn't have come out louder. And it was a long one too. Once you get started you can't stop – at least I can't – so I just stood there farting like a sousaphone and hoping for the best.

The next thing I knew Red jerked back the shower curtain and was looking right at me.

"Speak again sweet lips," he said. Or some such smart aleck remark like that.

I didn't have a whole lot of choice, so I tipped my hat and gave him a grin.

"Smile," I said. "You're on the Candid Camera."

BLAP! BLOOEY!

I barely had time to get the words out before my head was ringing and my legs felt like they was made out of two lengths of rope and I kind of eased down to the floor, banging my head against the faucet. By the time the ringing in my ears stopped and I could see straight again, straight enough to shoot him, he was gone. I figured that was his dumbest move. He should have stomped me while he could. I got my pistol out of my pocket and came out into the trailer after him.

The son of a bitch had done outfoxed me. Time I got there he had the shotgun in his hands and pointed right at me.

"I don't want to shoot you," I said. "I'm willing to let bygones be bygones."

"You're not real eager to get splattered all over the back of the trailer either."

"That shotgun ain't loaded."

"Are you willing to bet your life on it?"

"Get serious," I said.

He stepped back and lowered the muzzle of the shotgun.

"What if your pistol isn't loaded?"

"You want to find out?"

"I'll tell you what," he said. "You pull the trigger right now. If your pistol is loaded I'll be dead before I can get the barrel up."

"Don't try to trick me."

"I'm offering you a proposition. Are you game?"

"Keep talking."

"I propose to stand here and let you pull the trigger," he said. "Now, if your pistol is really loaded there will be a loud noise and considerable smoke and when the smoke clears there will be the late, great, Big Red Smalley, flat on his ass."

"I don't want to have to hurt you," I told him sincerely.

"But let us suppose that you pull the trigger and it goes *click*. That's all, just *click*. Maybe you get all excited and keep pulling the trigger and it keeps right on going *click, click, click* . . ."

"How would it get unloaded?"

"I don't know," he said. "It's pure speculation and we could sit around here and argue about it all night long."

"I'm losing my patience fast."

"I'm not going to argue with you," he said. "I'm just going to ask you one question. Have you checked to see if that pistol is loaded or not?"

"I loaded it myself."

I could see what he was up to. He was trying to get me to thinking about it. Maybe he thought I would be dumb enough to try and prove my point by taking out the magazine and showing him. Maybe he wanted me to cut my eyes away from him so he could jump me.

"All you've got to do is squeeze the trigger and find out," he said. "Let's suppose, just for the sake of argument, I'm right and you're wrong."

"Yeah," I said. "Then what?"

"Then I let you have both barrels and what's left of you will fit in a bucket."

"The shotgun ain't loaded."

"I say it is."

Right about then I noticed Miss Bitch for the first time. She wasn't paying any attention to us. She was kneeling down next to the bunk with her eyes closed and her hands clasped together and her lips moving, trying to pray I guess.

"Maybe we better just forget it," I said.

"It looks like a standoff," he said. "Well, Hookworm, no hard feelings . . ."

He shoved the shotgun away and stuck out his hand to shake hands with me. I thought the least I could do was shake hands with him. So I switched the pistol over and reached out to take his hand.

BLAP! BLOOEY!

Next thing I knew I was down on my knees again. He didn't give me a chance to get my head clear. He didn't give me a chance to fight back. He didn't even let me *say* anything. He just simply scooped me up and kicked open the back door of the trailer.

"Candid Camera, my ass!"

And I was way out there in the empty air thinking about how the ground would feel when I finally got there.

After that, a couple of good licks on the head that might have been fetched with a stick of lightwood and a ride through the air that should've broken my bones (*I thought I was lucky it didn't*), I was at a natural disadvantage. And naturally I fell for everything Miami said. Anybody could have made the same mistake. I figured that Miami needed me in the worst way for the big bugout. She couldn't do it all by herself and she damn sure couldn't do it if I was against her.

Maybe, it's true, I did let her flatter me and appeal to my Weakness but I couldn't help that, could I?

First thing I did was to sneak over to the truck and get her the snake powder like I promised. Then I went across the field to where the cages were to check them out. They were good and sturdy and in pretty good shape too, like somebody had been keeping them up in case High Pines should get prosperous again some day and they could put in a bunch of wild animals and be open for business. I found one where the hinges wasn't too rusty. I rigged up a chain and a padlock where I could slam the door and lock it in about two seconds flat. I practiced in a couple of times, laughing to myself thinking about the look on old Moses's face, and then I went back to the tent.

"You want a cup of coffee?"

"Wait a minute," I said, thinking maybe she had already put the powder in and was fixing to knock *me* out.

"You don't trust me, do you?"

She held up the packet of powder and I could see that it was still sealed up. Then she gave me a cup and poured herself one.

"How do I know you didn't slip something else in there?" I said.

"Here, I'll trade cups with you if it makes you feel better."

When she switched the cups and started right in drinking out of mine, I thought I was safe enough. We were sitting there drinking coffee when we heard the trailer door bang open and then slam to. It surprised me a little and I kind of jumped and spilled some of the coffee on me.

"Sit still," Miami said.

"I wasn't going anywhere."

"Shut up."

We waited, listening. Then we heard a sound in the dark. A kind of a soft, low sound like a hurt animal. Somebody groaning.

"It's the girl," Miami said. "Go get her while I fix the coffee for her."

"Okay."

I went out to see what was the matter. She was laying there in the dirt, without stitch one on and bald-headed to boot, just laying there and moaning. I found the black raincoat and tried to help her up to her feet and in it. She didn't try to fight me or anything. She was just dead weight. And I don't think she had a clue who I was or where she was.

"Clytie," she said. "Oh Clytie, I'm so glad you're here! I fell off the swing and hurt myself. I was going so high, but then I fell down . . ."

Miami got some water and a rag and tried to clean her face for her.

"You poor baby," Miami said.

I was afraid Miami was going to chicken out on me because she was feeling sorry for the girl.

"I'm so tired," she said.

"Red's done many a mean thing in his day," Miami said. "But damn if this don't take the cake! Shaving a woman's head . . ."

"It's all right," the girl said. "I'm going to be a nun anyway."

"Sure, baby, sure . . ."

"It's never too late, they say."

"Drink this. You'll feel better."

She shook her head. "Thanks just the same," she said, "but I'm in a hurry. I lost my husband somewhere and I can't find him."

"You better have some coffee first."

"All right," she said. "Just a quick cup."

I stood there wondering if she would taste the stuff and catch on. Her eyes looked kind of glassy and she looked strange. But, let's face it, any bald-headed woman with no makeup would look strange. She could have been crazy as hell or she could have been as sane as she was ever going to be.

All of sudden she stopped drinking and dropped the cup.

"I was going," she said. "I was leaving. Is it poison?"

Miami smiled at her. "It won't hurt you, baby. It's just a little snake medicine."

"Sweet Jesus!" the Bitch said, laughing out loud. "Snake medicine! That's the only thing I've never tried."

Then, still laughing to herself, she ran out of the tent.

"Go after her," Miami said.

"She ain't going nowhere."

Miami didn't know about the car. Everything was falling into the right place now. Just like I had planned the whole thing.

I just strolled across the field, not chasing her, like I had an hour and a half to get there. About halfway I almost tripped over the raincoat. I picked it up, thinking, she'd probably catch cold running around bareass in the night air.

She was in the car already, sitting behind the wheel of the blue bug. Just when I got there she closed her eyes and started to fall forward against the wheel. I grabbed her. Not wanting to take any chances, I was going to be sure she was out, so I lit a match right under her nose. She opened her eyes and blinked and damn if she didn't try to smile. She opened her mouth to smile and then got sick, puked all over the car and some of it on me too. But I didn't have time to worry about that. Because I heard the sound of the truck and looked and saw the lights coming across the field.

I dragged her into the cage as quick as I could. When I got her in there and got myself out, here came Miami and Moses running toward me.

"Where is she?"

"She must've crawled in that cage," I said. "Help me get her out."

Miami had a flashlight. She winked at me and then me and Moses went in the cage. He bent over the girl. I was just fixing

274

to knock him in the head when, *bang*! the door shut and *click* went the lock.

"Hey!" I said. "I'm still in here."

She turned the light in my face. I couldn't see a thing.

"That's the whole idea, Hookworm," she said. "You're all three in there together."

"Open that door, you bitch!"

"Say please."

I figured it was now or never, so I pulled out my trusty Army .45 pistol and pointed it right at her.

"Are you going to open that door or do I have to shoot you?"

"That gun isn't loaded," she said.

"Why does everyone keep saying that?"

She took the light out of my face. Then she held out her hand, open, with the light on it. I could see the shells in the palm of her hand, gleaming in the light. All I could do was whistle and sit down.

"Are you feeling all right?" she said.

"Just tell me one thing," I said. "When did you swipe my bullets?"

"This afternoon."

"Jee-ee-sus," I said. "It's getting where a man can't trust nobody."

"Live and learn," she said. Then to Moses: "I gave him the insides of two of your pills. In a few minutes, he'll be sleeping like a baby."

Then I remembered. I got up and grabbed hold of the bars and laughed right at her.

"Ha-ha-ha, bitch! The joke is on you this time. We switched cups, remember?"

"It's kind of a shame," she said. "You traded off a perfectly good cup of coffee of your own free will."

I didn't even have the energy to groan. I just sat down again on the cold ground, thinking *what's the use? What's the freaking use?*

JUDITH

Something has groaned in the night. I heard it groan and sigh like someone sleeping beside me. It is not I.

My body is groaning and it doesn't matter.

"Go to sleep," Clytie tells me "Time to go to sleep."

"Tell me a story," I say. "Tell me a story, please."

Once upon a time

Once upon a time there was this beautiful princess young & beautiful princess young & beautiful with red hair shining soft red hair silky & colour of flames & flames & her eyes & veils of sweet woodsmoke

Once upon a time one day she was spinning hay & turning it into gold so fine & thin you could make cloth out of it & sell it to the Emperor & then all would laugh to think he was walking around without no clothes on as in fairy tales again only now the joke's on them because he really does have a gold suit on only it's fine & pure and only pure eyes can see it though everyone laughs his laugh & the Emperor ashamed doth redly blush yet still is the Joke on everyone

Once upon a time one day as I say she was spinning hay & turning it into gold pure & fine when all of a sudden she pricked her finger on a magic needle which happened to have been as needles are wont hiding in haystack

Ouch she said ouch dear me & fell in a swoon & from swoon fell into sleep & from swoon & sleep into a dream where she drowned & in her dream she is asleep & waiting for a handsome prince to find her & find her he will & does & kisses her then she wakes up & he turns into a toad

276

It doesn't matter about the body that groans and sighs. It doesn't matter because, you see, it is not I. I am a princess asleep and dreaming. They can't keep me from sleeping by putting a pea under my mattress. Only . . .

only there isn't one prince in this bad world
only my body is a bad dream
Hold me, Clytie! Hold me! I am afraid.
I am afraid I am going to be sick.
Poor John, my poor prince of a husband. Here I am bald & bare, broke & full of snake medicine.
Where's my wedding ring?
Poor little car, little blue car. Little blue car, come blow your horn. Someone has hurt you too. Get well. Soon get well. And all manner of thing shall be well. Sky full of stars wheels. Sky full of wheeling stars. I am sick.
Hold, me, Clytie! Tell me a story, please.
Once upon a time
Once upon a time there was a bad little very bad girl who wanted to be a wicked witch & stepmother when she grew up
oh so wicked more wicked than Snow White's or Cinderella's to say mirror mirror on the wall who is the wickedest of all & all
but then someone wickeder broke the mirror to pieces
I did I broke the mirror I am the one when the mirror refused to answer I broke it
but the mirror did answer broken or not anyway saying there is no wickedness for you only folly only folly
no I said & I broke the mirror & hurt the mirror
then all the broken pieces flew away in the sky & we call them stars
hold me Clytie I am sore afraid
hush child it is only a bad dream that's all
why can't I wake up & why don't people ever wake up & instead go on dreaming bad dreams instead of happy ones

277

why did I break my mirror I broke it or I could tell you the answer
now in the mirror all broken many of me parts are dancing & each
& all are different
now I dance & dance but can't hear the music I'm dancing to
do stars make music
hush and listen
hold me Clytie
heal me God
I'm asleep & dreaming & can't wake up & I'm going to be sick
& must be sick so I can be well . . .

MIAMI

Poor old Hookworm. Curses, foiled again! Fighting sleep, speechless, he sat on the earth in the cage like a child in a sand-box.

"Miami?" Moses said.

"Listen," I said. "I'm sorry, but this is the way it has to be."

"I'm afraid the girl may catch a cold."

"I'll bring you some blankets before I go."

I turned to leave, then turned back and put the beam on the girl. She was asleep, wrapped up now in her raincoat. Then I went quickly to the trailer.

Everything was in a mess, but I didn't want much anyway, just a change of clothes. I found what I wanted to in the dark. I could have used the flashlight. I could hear him breathing on the bunk pretending to be asleep. And I knew and he knew that if he sat up and turned on the light and smiled at me, I would go to him. We would lie together and talk together and both of us would sleep. And everything would be all right again, at least until tomorrow.

I zipped up my little overnight bag and was ready to go.

278

"You're not going to leave me, are you?"

"Turn on the light. Look at me and ask me."

"Why? What difference would it make now?"

For a moment I stood there in the dark afraid to answer. I listened to him begin to breathe deeply again. I felt my heart pounding.

"I won't leave if you tell me you need me."

"Miami, I'm all finished. That's all there is. I'll never preach again."

I knew that he meant it and he was done. I knew that for him all the lights had gone out for good. And I pitied him for that. Which was maybe what he wanted. If he could get me to pity him enough, then I would stay anyway, no matter what.

"I don't feel sorry for you," I said. "You can stop if you want to, but it won't prove anything. It won't do any good."

"What the hell are you talking about?"

"The gospel. It's in the book," I said. "You used to preach the text – about the stones."

In the darkness he laughed softly. "You do remember things," he said, "Saint Luke, Nineteenth Chapter, Fortieth Verse: 'I tell you that, if these should hold their peace, the stones would immediately cry out.' You don't believe that, do you?"

"No," I said, "but you do and nothing can change that."

"Goodbye," he said. "Take care of yourself."

I tiptoed out and shut the door softly as if he had really been asleep, talking in his sleep the whole time. I got in the car and drove across the field to give Moses the blankets.

"I can still change my mind," I told him.

"We'll be all right."

"He needs me," I said.

"I wish you lots of luck wherever you go."

"God bless . . ."

I got in the car and drove very slowly across the field toward the road. There was still time, still time to turn back, to call it all a bad joke, to forget and forgive. But then, once I passed through the archway and I could feel the smooth highway under the tyres and the tyres were humming, I pressed the gas pedal down to the floorboard and watched the speedometer needle twitch and surge on the dial till it went above eighty. I was gone.

Where can a girl go to? A girl like me can always find a place. The signs on the road pointed to Tennessee. So why not Tennessee? I switched on the radio and listened to music.

No regrets.

When I end up in six feet of cemetery, in a firstclass, waterproof casket and all, I hope that's all they write on the stone at my feet – NO REGRETS.

It won't be much and it won't be true, not quite. But it will be enough and, true or false, a girl could do a whole lot worse.

MOSES

When she drove away the last time, Cartwright managed to open his eyes and to watch the lights disappearing. He leaned back his head and howled like a dog baying at the moon. He didn't seem to notice me when I put the blanket around his shoulders. But he found his battered straw hat and put it on his head and pulled the blanket around himself more tightly.

I spread one blanket on the ground, then lifted the sleeping girl and placed her on it. She was so light, a lithe, delicate lightboned creature. Strange that something so delicate and vulnerable could carry so much hunger, so much fury and torment. Her pulse was normal and steady. She would be all right in the morning, and, with time, her hair would grow back as richly as before. I placed my blanket on top of her.

Turning, I saw a flash, quick and red, a sudden flash of light in the trailer. Then came the sound and it was enough to jar Cartwright out of his doze and, stunned and fighting sleep, to his feet. The blanket fell away from his shoulders as he staggered weaving like a drunk, to seize the bars of the cage and stare into the darkness.

"The shotgun," he said softly.

Then he found an untapped source of energy somewhere within his drugged, numb, boneweary body. He shook the bars until they rang and the whole cage rattled.

"He kilt hisself! he's done gone and kilt hisself and nobody cares! He left us all locked in a cage and we'll never get out!"

"In the morning," I said. "We won't be here long."

He stopped shaking the bars and turned to me. There were tears streaming down his face. He looked his age, young, only an overgrown boy, with years and years ahead of him.

"What did he go and do that for?"

"God knows."

I picked up the blanket and put it around his shoulders again. He leaned against me, burying his head against my shoulder, still shaking with sobs.

"Take it easy," I told him, not out of hope or belief or faith, but out of duty which will have to be enough for me. "Everything's going to be all right."

HOWIE LOOMIS

I got good and drunk that night, as drunk as I've ever been I guess. Drank and got drunk until the room and then my whole house spun around me like a crazy kind of a carnival ride.

When I tried to stand up it wasn't so much that I fell as that the whole foundation tilted sideways and the floor came up to me.

Well, that's it, I thought to myself, lying there, sweating a cold sweat and still feeling everything turn and turn. In just a minute or two I'll have the stroke the doctor promised and I'll be gone. Or, if I'm not that lucky, I'll at least be struck dumb – paralyzed, probably brainless, speechless, helpless, a suffering carcass without even a name.

The damn doctor lied, of course. They don't know anything. I didn't have any stroke. I didn't even get sick to my stomach. I just fell asleep on the floor all night long. Woke up with nothing but stiffness of the joints and a hangover to show for it.

If that was all there was to it, it wouldn't be worth the telling. Just how an old man got drunk and then fell on his ass like you might expect.

While I slept I had a dream. I dreamed I was walking downtown to the store. All of a sudden I noticed everybody was looking at me and pointing and some of them were laughing and some were aghast and some were just mad, shaking their fists. I didn't even have to look. I could feel the air and the breeze. And, I'll tell the world I was plenty embarrassed and put out too.

I ran down the sidewalk as fast as I could go. (And I reckon that was something to see too!) Then I ducked in the store.

At first the store seemed empty, but then it was full. Not of people I'd see nowdays, but of all kinds of people, friends and enemies alike, I had mostly forgotten about. There they all were, walking around, evidently going about their business, just as naked as I was, and not much better looking either. Well, at least they weren't paying any special attention to me.

Then it came to me that they were all dead and maybe I was dead too. I didn't know for sure, but I thought the best thing to do would be to go back to my office and sit down at the desk and think about it.

Just as I was about to open the door, it opened anyway, and my wife came out and held out her hand. She had on some kind of white robe, and I remember she wasn't young and beautiful again or anything like that, but just the way she had been at the end when I couldn't even bear to look at her any more or to look at myself either I was so ashamed. Only now she was smiling and now I could look.

"Forgive me, Mary," I said.

"Don't be silly," she said. "I love you."

"Have you been waiting here long?"

"Not long," she said. "I worry about you though."

"I miss you," I said.

"Howie, I'm going to let you see something, just a peek, that's all, but it's all I can do for you. And you don't tell anybody, you hear?"

It wasn't the door of my office she was standing in front of any more. It was another door. And she opened it for just a second. Now, it's a strange thing, but in my dream I knew I could look and I would see something beautiful, like a beautiful landscape or maybe a beautiful distant city, I don't know. I only know it would have been more beautiful than anything I had ever even imagined. But I had to choose, you see. So instead I looked at her. The light of that place and the shade too was on her. She didn't change and yet she was changed. What I mean is the light wasn't magic and it didn't wipe away any lines or scars. They remained. Yet they were beautiful. Even the scars were beautiful. She was more beautiful than any bride. She looked at the place and smiled at it, and I looked at her and wept like a child, not for loss, but because the world was so large and so wonderful and we were both in it now and forever.

Then the dream was gone and I was back in myself again, a drunk old man asleep on the floor. A drunk old man who had slept like a baby all night long.

$\mathcal{V}$OICES OF THE $\mathcal{S}$OUTH

Fred Chappell, *The Gaudy Place*

Ellen Douglas, *The Rock Cried Out*

George Garrett, *Do, Lord, Remember Me*

Lee Smith, *The Last Day the Dogbushes Bloomed*

Elizabeth Spencer, *The Voice at the Back Door*

Peter Taylor, *The Widows of Thornton*